PORKY

PORKY

Deborah Moggach

JONATHAN CAPE
THIRTY BEDFORD SQUARE LONDON

First published 1983
Copyright © Deborah Moggach 1983
Jonathan Cape Ltd, 30 Bedford Square, London WC1

British Library Cataloguing in Publication Data

Moggach, Deborah
Porky.
I. Title
823'.914[F]   PR6063.044

ISBN 0-224-02948-7

Typeset by Oxford Verbatim Limited
Printed in Great Britain by
St Edmundsbury Press
Bury St Edmunds, Suffolk

Part One

Chapter One

At school they called me Porky, on account of the pigs. They
hadn't learnt to at primary school. When you're small you
just talk about yourself all the time; your little doings. You don't
have the interest in anyone else, do you, so you can't work out
how to hurt them.

But when I moved into the big school they were older and
they'd kept their eyes open. They'd driven past our place often
enough, with their Mums and Dads. Our bungalow, it's right
there on the A4. You probably know the road, it's the main one
running past Heathrow Airport. You might have seen our place,
in fact. It's the one with the pig field in front. I had no idea, then,
that it was different.

That's where we lived. Not far from the runway, us and the
pigs, and you might ask: was it noisy? If we'd had visitors they'd
have shouted that question, politely, over the roar. But we never
had any visitors. And because nobody did much talking at home,
nobody had to shout. The planes interfered with the telly, of
course, you couldn't hear the jingles, but then they always kept
the telly on loud, my Mum and Dad. Was that noisy? Yes.

Girls are meanest. It was the girls who stood in a huddle,

holding their noses. They didn't do it, you bet, where our teacher could see; they did it in the cloakroom. 'Now Wash Your Hands', it said on the toilet paper. I'd hear them scuffling outside. I could see their sandals under the door, waiting. I prayed for the bell to ring. But if it didn't, I had to go to the basins.

Then the chorus would start. 'Poo-ee', honking because they'd pinched in their nostrils. Maureen, the biggest, once bent down to inspect my shoes. For manure, she said. Sometimes they crooned a song, swaying, linking arms:

> 'Porky, Porky, no peace I find,
> Just that smelly old song
> Keeps Porky on my mind.'

It wouldn't have lasted so long if I hadn't blushed. They would have got bored with that Porky business. It was my blush that told them I minded. I have this fair complexion, pink and white. People liked it later; Arabs liked it all right. But then I hated the blush creeping up and my face swelling.

At school you see yourself for the first time. You're not really born until then. Gwen, who became my friend, she pinched a charcoal stick from the art room to draw eyelashes on our faces. She said to me ever so kindly, I remember the exact words, she said,

'Does wonders for little piggy eyes.'

It was a moment later that I realized she meant me. Her smudged, spider eyes gazed at my face.

That night I shut myself in the bathroom for a good look. They were. My eyelashes were so pale, you see. We just had a single light bulb and I turned my head this way and that . . . The light shone through them; my face got redder. I blushed for every reason, even when I was alone. I blushed at the fact I was blushing. Years later somebody called me shameless. They hadn't the first idea . . . Nobody had.

Anyway, the name stuck. I got to know the other girls, and the boys. They forgot about holding their noses; they lost the interest. But the name stayed. The teachers were the only ones who called me Heather – in fact, sometimes even the teachers let a 'Porky' slip out. I was a lump of a girl then, before I slimmed down. A big girl, with my pink face and my blonde hair; no wonder the piggy name stuck.

But they should never have sniffed the air like that. I was one of the cleanest people in the school. If I ponged of anything, it was talc. I used to bring the tin in with me. I'd go into the toilet and take off my socks and sprinkle my feet.

No, I was always scrubbing. My face felt starched from washing. Nobody knew, of course. I didn't tell anyone, not Gwen, not my Mum. How it was on the inside that I was dirty. I didn't tell anyone later, when I was older. Once or twice I nearly spoke. Just once or twice, sitting on some bar stool somewhere, thousands of miles away from here, I nearly did, just to see the expression on some stranger's face. As long as it was someone I'd never see again.

But I never told. I'm nineteen now. I don't know why I'm telling it tonight, except that I can't go out. I haven't gone out for a week. Nowadays I've got all the time in the world.

I'm sitting at the window; outside the sky is flushed. Swallows are sitting on the telegraph wires; each evening there's more of them, as if someone's stringing beads. Soon they'll be flying south, like I used to do. We used to take off in the evening and fly right over the sunset, right over the end of the horizon and never meet the night at all. We'd fly round into the next day. None of the passengers would see it because they were asleep, heads lolling, the portholes shut. But I did. Weird things happened inside me; I didn't have a regular period for a year.

It's easiest telling like this, to nobody. I couldn't tell it to a person. He's asleep. I can hear snores through the wall. I have all night . . . So I might be able to tell you, as long as I don't know who you are.

There were four of us, when my Mum was around. She wasn't, much. It was years later that I discovered why. At the time I thought all parents were like them. You think that when you're little . . . No, you don't even think. They're yours; you can't see any different. They're all you've got.

My Mum's name was Coral and she'd once been good-looking, before she wore herself out. Blonde, like me. She'd met my Dad in Ipswich long ago, when he was working on the fairground. It travelled all over the south of England. The Mercers, that's my Dad's family, in those days they owned four rides, 'Mercer' lit up in the electric lights. People called them travellers.

But when she got married my Mum wasn't having any of that, on account of the mud, and the moving from place to place. Even more, there was the lack of privacy. You'd hang up your washing, she'd say, and half the town would be counting your socks. (She wasn't the type to mention the other items.) I'd picture her, the pale bride. At night she never budged. She'd sit in the trailer, behind a nylon curtain, the lights flashing on and off against her cheek. At midnight they were switched off and there was no sound except the local girls squealing.

Years later, in the hen-house, my Dad told me it was because he'd been such a naughty boy. That's why she'd objected. I didn't try to believe him; I was just trying not to listen. Whatever the reason, they had some money saved and my Mum had her way, as she did in most things, and they moved into the bungalow where I was born.

My Dad said it broke him, settling down; he said he was a broken man. His eyes would grow moist at this point. He said you couldn't get a bloke like him to stay put for the rest of his natural days. He usually said this when Mum was telling him to get up and do something. He was a heavy smoker. He'd sit there in the haze, looking out of the window. We had a concrete yard. Beyond the railway carriage where the hens lived, there was this old caravan. It didn't have any wheels; it stood on blocks. The windows were rusted shut and the door was rusted open, hanging on one hinge. Nettles grew around it, and long, dead grass, like blonde hair. Indoors the haze hung, dimming the furniture, but outside the wind blew the pale grass flat. And every two minutes, overhead, came the roar of the planes.

So it was my Dad who stayed put, in home sweet home. He had the pigs, of course. They were in the field between our bungalow and the main road. Then there were his schemes. There was always some business project on the go. We had one other field, next to the pigs' field, adjoining the road. He'd painted this sign outside saying 'Long Term Car Park 50p a Day'. A lad he knew from West Drayton, the son of one of his mates, he was supposed to be there standing guard, but then it turned out he was still supposed to be at school, so the council took him away. Then Dad persuaded this old bloke Paddy to do it. But Pad was always complaining about his bad back, and the damp, he had the same problems as my Dad, so he'd pop off to warm himself at the café down the road, just beyond the roundabout. He warmed himself for days.

So it was left to my Dad. He'd keep watch at the front window, waiting for custom; on fine days he'd sit outside on the veranda, growing ruddier in the sun. That's why he stayed there, to watch for business. There wasn't a lot of it about. The airport authorities had an off-airport parking lot with a connecting bus service. The Excelsior Hotel had built another one, just down the road. And folk got fed up with being stuck in our mud. But there were sometimes four or five cars sitting there amongst the thistles. That meant money to collect, if he could catch them before they raced off.

Then he had his deals. He never spoke of them, he preferred to keep the mystery, but they meant driving along to the Two Magpies, or the haulage depot, or his mates in the airport taxi rank. This was a wire compound where they parked until the light flashed with their number. He knew a lot of cabbies. Years later, when I'd left home and I took taxis for granted, I chatted with a cabbie called, would you believe it, Bernie, and he said that down at the airport were the hottest poker games around. He said they'd sit in each other's cabs; their numbers would flash up on the board but they played on like the blind. They gambled away their cabs and had to start from scratch, hiring another one from the big boys and working up from the bottom again. I don't know what my Dad gambled away. All I know is that we never had any money coming in, apart from what my Mum earned.

Dad's other business was haulage. He had a truck that he used to transport the pigs; also a lorry. But we didn't have a phone and usually one or the other was broken, its pistons or its big end gone, something impossible like that. He'd lie underneath, fiddling and cursing. But sometimes, just sometimes, he had to make a delivery. And then he would be gone, to Nottingham or to Hull. When I was young I didn't want him to leave. But when I was older, those were the best days.

Sooner or later I'll have to describe him. But I'd rather wait. First I'll tell you what my Mum did. There was no shortage of jobs round our way, what with the airport, and all the hotels coming up. You must know our area. Not so many people live there but the whole world seems to be passing through. As fast as they can, too, in order to reach somewhere else. Nobody stopped longer than a night at one of the hotels, and that's if they had a flight to catch. What would they stop for? Whoever stood guard at our car park, they were buffeted by the passing traffic. Old Pad couldn't keep his hat on. Apart from him, you'd be lucky to see another human being walking along the verge. They all whizzed by in cars. It was this one great transit area, catering for people who were going somewhere else . . . With us in the middle.

There weren't many fields left, they'd mostly been developed. The few vacant patches, they had signs amongst the bushes saying 'Flyways Hotel: Opening Soon'. They were all being built for the airport trade. The airport was right opposite our gate, on the other side of the road. Through the wire fence you could see the prefabs where they kept the ambulances, and the animal hostel, and what I'd been told was where they put the Pakis. Day and night, the odour of kerosene hung in the air. It was always in my nostrils; it was the smell of my childhood. I could never get rid of the memories, even though I travelled to airports all round the world.

You'd think the old associations would fade, once I'd smelt it everywhere. But one whiff and I was back to the beginning again. It didn't work . . . Take it from me: nothing does.

There were plenty of jobs at the airport, on the catering side and in the toilets. When I was little I never knew what my Mum did, I just saw what she brought home. Slabs of soap, and Danish pastries. Sometimes every item of our tea was wrapped in Cling Film.

On occasion she gave something to me. She wasn't used to showing affection, so it meant a lot. I kept a shower cap for ages. That must have been when she was working at the Post House Hotel. It's a huge building like a barracks, spotlit at night, rising out of the vacant land by the flyover. You could see it from our bungalow. I never knew how anyone got into the hotel, it was marooned amongst the slip roads and the elevated section of the motorway. Somehow my Mum did, catching the early-morning bus through the grey dawn. I cherished that shower cap. It was made of the thinnest, crinkly plastic. It was made for overnight visitors but I made it last for months, until it was all torn around its frail elastic band.

It wasn't just for the money that my Mum worked long hours. It was because she didn't want to come home. It was only later that I realized this, with a thud. As I said, you take everything as normal when you're a kid. What my Mum and Dad were like together, for a start. What they were like with me and Teddy, that's my little brother. How we never seemed to eat the same food at the same time, sitting around the table like a family.

Gwen's family did. Soon after I'd started at the big school, I went home with her. There was her Mum, making clucking noises because Gwen's hem was coming down; but fond cluckings, I could tell. She called me by my name, saying how much we've all heard about you, Heather. 'We' kept cropping up in the conversation, quite naturally. In Gwen's too. I felt included but excluded, if you see what I mean. They had a lovely lounge; it had a big electric fire with the coals radiant as a mountain range, you could dream yourself away into that fire. And little lamps, and a copy of the *Radio Times*. I mean, at home nobody thought about deciding what they snoozed in front of. And then her Dad came home, and he was ever so nice to me but cross with Gwen because she hadn't done last night's homework. He minded, you see. He said he was angry because she wasn't doing herself justice. Oh yes, they sometimes shouted at me, my parents, but never for anything like that.

When I got home I shut myself in the bathroom. The lock didn't work; you had to wedge yourself against the door. When I cried nobody could hear because the wind was up and the loose guttering was banging against the wall. I cried about Gwen. Not just Gwen but the other people in my class too. Their homes must be like hers. I realized it then.

And I cried because I'd made up my mind to tell Gwen about me and my Dad. She was the only person I'd ever known who I thought I might be able to tell. I was twelve years old; I longed to speak to someone.

But I couldn't tell her, after this. And if I couldn't tell Gwen, there was nobody. I thought I'd been lonely before, but I'd never felt really lonely until that moment.

I tried to feel the same towards Gwen but I never did, though we stayed best friends for years.

Chapter Two

I must tell you about him now. I can tell you how he smelt. He smelt of old cigarettes and warm skin. He smelt of wool, with a sharp, sour whiff about it. He wasn't really a dirty man, despite the mud around his trouser legs. He washed every day – not that I saw him, because he kept the bathroom door shut. I never saw him or my Mum bare, they were both modest about that. When he'd been sitting out the front, watching his car park, then, when he took me on his knee, his skin smelt baked and biscuity. His face was reddish-brown but it stopped at his neck. Below that, when he opened a button of his shirt, his skin was white and quite smooth. He was a big, fleshy man. I thought he was really handsome, but you'd say he'd gone a bit soft. His hair was brown but his moustache had all these colours mixed in it, I used to point them out to him and count the red ones. He said I was the only person who'd noticed; he hadn't, for a start.

Let me get one thing straight, though you might not believe me. He was an innocent kind of man. In the paper, he never paused at the busty brunettes, he turned straight to the cartoons. My Mum didn't really understand us children, but he did. He said he was just a kid at heart. He liked the sort of games we did, though I could never quite trust him. He would suddenly get impatient, or the romps would get too boisterous. He liked tickling us breathless; he liked hiding our toys.

Just an edge of me used to feel wary. He could get violent, you see. It hardly ever happened with us, though; he was much nicer with us. It happened with my Mum. Our bungalow had thin walls. One night I remember lying curled, all clenched, the pillow pressed on my head so I wouldn't hear the words being shouted in their bedroom. '*Bitch, bitch!*' The morning after that, my Mum went to stay with her friend Oonagh in West Drayton, a couple of miles away, and didn't come back until the Monday, when she returned from work as if nothing had happened. He'd fed us sweets all weekend.

When I was little I adored him, even though he sometimes let me down. I always forgave him. You do, when you're small; you have to. For instance, there was my Kanga house. I didn't have any dolls, I don't think I wanted any, but I had a grey knitted kangaroo. I held Kanga wherever I went and I told her everything. In her pouch she had a small Roo made of tighter knitting. Dad had promised me he'd make them a house. He was the one who suggested it; there were lots of planks around. When I reminded him he kept saying he'd do it tomorrow, he had a lot on his plate at present.

That autumn, I must have been eight, they were building a petrol station at the end of our drive, right beside the main road. I used to watch the workmen for hours; they were my friends. One evening, when I'd given up asking him in case he lost his temper, he came into the kitchen looking ever so pleased, with some plastic panelling under his arm. It was fancy, hinged panelling, punched with holes. I recognized it.

'But Dad, did you get that from the garage?'

He stopped in his tracks. 'Me?' His eyes wide. 'Little me? Oh no.' Then he winked. 'It came by special delivery.'

I knew he'd pinched it after the workmen had gone home. I minded a lot, of course, but what I minded more was that he'd lied to me.

16

After a week or so he did build a sort of house, a sort of lean-to. I made sure that I was popping Kanga in and out of its gap whenever he was around. But from then on I didn't talk to the workmen in case they became too friendly and dropped in for a cup of tea and saw it. They thought I was sulking. Soon they even stopped calling out, 'Give us a smile, ducks' or 'It might never happen'. It took all winter before the petrol station was built and they left.

Something else I remember. When he had a short job on, he would take me with him. He loved me looking nice, to show me off to his mates, so I'd wear my best dress. I'd sit up in the cab, lording it over the dual carriageway. By the time I was nine he'd let me steer, if he was in the mood, and I'd sit pressed next to him, the gear-stick digging into my bottom. He'd laugh, urging me on. Actually I steered very carefully, but tense, because just when I wasn't expecting it he'd put his foot down and we'd shoot forward, too fast.

Anyway, he often made promises. Like at the end of the delivery he'd take me to the Excelsior Hotel Coffee Shop   that was the newest place – where he'd buy me hot chocolate with sprinkled foam on the top. All the customers could see me in my tartan frock. But before we got there he was detained at the Spread Eagle. I sat in the cab. I knew I was in for a wait when he came out.

'Won't be long, Podge.' He gave me a bag of crisps, pinching my cheek.

I can't remember if this episode happened once or several times blurred together. I watched it growing darker and more cars pulling up until the car park was crammed. The street lights flickered on, one by one, red fading to orange. It was so cold that I could easily stay awake. There was a sign over the door, lit up, saying, 'Tonight: Shaun and the Sounds'. The Spread Eagle was a big place built in a bygone style with pointy roofs and attics. When it was nearly dark the neon light was switched on; it was a thin blue line zig-zagging up and down the eaves. Later, when my eyes started closing, the lines danced and it was a palace out there, far off, and if I reached it something beautiful would happen.

17

When I heard the door handle turning I woke up quickly and pretended I hadn't been asleep. It took him some time to open the door. He had some of his friends with him; they were all very affectionate, their faces crowding in, with fruity breath and cold air. I wanted him to be proud of me so I laughed at their jokes. I never had my chocolate drink. Last thing I remember was falling asleep against his shoulder, lights swinging as we swerved round the roundabout, and his hand rubbing my thighs to warm me up.

Next day he was full of remorse. In fact, over the next few years, when things became more confusing, his remorse was one of the worst aspects because I didn't know how to make it better. I tried to think up excuses for him but that made him angry. Sometimes he cried, his big body shuddering, and that was the most terrifying thing of all.

That was when I was older, when I didn't want to sit in his cab. In fact, when I had to find any reason not to go.

I'd always been closer to him than to my Mum. As I said, she wasn't one for showing affection. I never knew how much she felt, deep down – I wondered about it a lot but I don't think I wanted to come up with an answer. She never hugged me, but then I never saw her hug my Dad either; she wasn't the type. The way I remember her best is from the back, walking down our drive to catch the bus. She looked sadder from the back. I wasn't nervous of her then. The cars would be speeding past, there was always the hum of traffic where we lived. She would be picking her way around the potholes, wearing her headscarf with the polka dots and her ageless turquoise coat with its fitted waist. Then her thin beige legs with the flat shoes. She always carried her plaid shopping bag, with a change of shoes and her purse in it. She'd never been in an aeroplane and yet there they were, slicing up into the sky in front of her, trailing smoke. Watching her go, I felt I should be running down the drive to tell her something that she'd been waiting to hear.

She made it plain, without saying it in so many words, that she was disappointed. For instance, she never went near the pigs. The

18

usual number was three sows, and piglets when they had them. It was a small field – we didn't have much land – its tussocks roughed up by the pigs' rooting, and with pitted mud around the troughs. There was a container crate where they went when it rained. It didn't look much, but Dad's sows meant a lot to him. The only contact she had was to empty the peelings into an orange plastic bucket which she wouldn't allow in the kitchen – she had to carry the damp handfuls right out to the back porch. She set herself these tasks, you see.

She must have loved him once. I tried to believe that I was the result of passion – that tenderness had made me – though it was hard to credit it later. He must have been a fine figure in his younger days, and her so shy, and petite as a deer. She must have gazed at his balancing act on the dodgems and known, with a pang, that he wouldn't be there next week. Our bungalow showed some signs of their early married bliss: curtains she'd rigged up below the kitchen sink, matching the window ones, and cones of plastic flowers on the wall. Above their bed hung a framed photo of a woodland glade with sunlight slanting through the branches. Those trees must have blessed them once. It was made of wood, our bungalow, and stained by the rain, but two wire baskets hung outside the front veranda. I'm sure I remember, when I was a toddler, blooms trailing down from them. I saw them. Later the veranda was just the place where things were dumped – mostly Dad's empties, the bottles cobwebbed together.

She'd expected something better from life, no doubt about that. I felt included in the general dissatisfaction, I suppose because I was big and clumsy, like my Dad, and content with our lot – I mean you are when you're a child, aren't you? She wasn't. She gave up with the house; she tidied it, with sighs, but there weren't the little touches. But she still put her hair in rollers. They weren't for us, her faded blonde curls, but I'm sure they weren't for some fancy man at work either; that wasn't her temperament. They were for something that nobody could supply.

They had their rows, her and Dad, but most of the time they just didn't talk, except for where did you leave this or that, or when are you going to do something about the lounge ceiling (our roof was always leaking). That was parents, I thought. It was only later that I realized what an outsider would see, after one glance: that they didn't get on. I don't suppose they ever admitted that they weren't happy; neither of them thought in those words. If they'd admitted it they would have to start making decisions and neither of them was used to that. Anything was better than a choice.

And, really, it's remarkable how seldom two people meet each other, even when they're living under the same roof. Either she was out at work, or she was home and he was off on some job. She didn't drive; she preferred the bus and she knew the timetable by heart. She'd be off to the supermarket in West Drayton; or she'd be in the kitchen and he'd be fiddling about outside. Days at a time she'd be out each evening on the late shift; and then he had his deals to negotiate down at the Two Magpies or the Spread Eagle.

Then, when they were together, there was the telly. They could both watch it for hours; they looked quite content then. They even made the odd remark; they both knew the programmes so well that these remarks sounded quite intimate, for them. And their cigarettes made them look companionable; my Mum was a surprisingly careless smoker, she was always leaving them lying around, smouldering in ashtrays, something my Dad never did even though she considered him such a slob. Although she smoked Embassy and he smoked Weights they were always running out – they never bought more than one packet at a time – so, eyes on the screen, they'd fumble around for each other's and he'd light hers. A man looks tender doing that, doesn't he? Although I knew it was bad for their health it made me happy, seeing them at that moment.

What happened in their bedroom is something I still don't want to know. He tried to tell me several times, later, but I could make my mind go blank then – a knack I'd learnt in the same way that people chant '*om, om*' with their guru. I locked a muscle in my brain. He said she was cold . . . his voice thickening. But I knew, when I was little, that through the wall I'd heard noises as if she were in pain, even though something, thank goodness, stopped me rushing in to save her. At school the girls read *Photo-Love* and talked about animal charm. That's what my Dad must have had once, when he was younger. He must have had it for my Mum.

But as I said, she wasn't too keen on the bodily functions. I remember being sick; it was Dad who knelt beside me supporting my clammy brow. She was always going on about the way he ate, though I didn't see anything wrong with it myself. He irked her, the way he sprawled in the armchair, his legs spattered with mud, such a big man in our cramped lounge. When he came out of the toilet, in she'd go and we'd hear the puff-puff of the air freshener.

I don't remember her playing with me. I don't think she found children interesting. When I was helping her like a little housewife, that's when she seemed most at ease. Sometimes she talked to me then, when she was washing up and I was drying, the sun through the window shining on the brushes in their Nescafé jar. She talked about her childhood in Ipswich. Her father, my Grandad who I never knew, he'd worked on the trawlers. One day he'd sailed off and never come home; he'd disembarked in Oslo and started another family, all over again. She would pause, her arms in the suds, and gaze out at the sky with the gulls blown about in the wind and the planes taking off. She used to dress up in her hat and coat, she said, and walk to the end of the pier to wait.

I always felt awkward; a conversation was what I wanted, so much, yet when it actually happened I didn't know how to answer . . . No wonder she was disappointed with me. In fact I don't know if she expected me to answer; she was remembering out loud. The only way I could please her was by putting the crockery away without fumbling it. She wouldn't say anything, of course, but I could feel her silent approval. I did long to please her. My Dad was so hamfisted; he was always breaking things. Then he'd say 'Fuck me', which made it worse.

She didn't exactly neglect me; she simply wasn't there. Before I was old enough for school it was mainly my Dad who looked after me. We went our separate ways but we always knew what the other one was doing. Thinking back to that time is difficult, but I try to picture us as companionable. We were; I'm sure we were.

We both liked messing about outside. I'd drag a square of carpet through the dust. On it lay Kanga, and Prod, my rubber duck, and an ambulance. I'd just drag them around; I wasn't an adventurous child. No wonder my Mum thought me dull. I'd sit them on one of Dad's piles of sand, surveying their domain. Roo would be out of his pouch, ready for action. Then what? Nobody ever came to play with me; this was long before Teddy my brother was born. The only things I wanted to make were homes. I'd put a White's Lemonade crate under the apple tree and sit them on that.

But the best place was the caravan. Our yard was good to grow up in because there were so many places where nobody went – my Dad rarely, my Mum never. The cats dozed in the caravan but they were wild creatures and leapt out when I arrived. Inside, things were stored which Dad had forgotten about – paint pots, and sticky bottles of pig linctus. All our outbuildings were full of junk. Mum had given up complaining about them.

I called the caravan the Rosy Arms; I suppose it must have been a pub because I collected Dad's empties from round the front and laid them out on the caravan floor. I sat in there for hours; the name Rosy Arms comforted me. I sat humming to Roo. When Dad's whistling approached I stopped humming and pretended I was clearing my throat. I was embarrassed, you see; but in those days I didn't dread his step.

There were other places, surrounded by nettles and that long, pale grass. There was a chilly concrete building full of farm machinery that was probably left by the people before us. Beside it was the railway carriage where I collected the eggs. There was a shed, with our dog tied up and stacks of dusty flowerpots that perhaps my Mum had once used. There was an old car, a Ford Anglia. Years later, Teddy would sit in it all afternoon, heaving round its wheel and zooming off towards horizons only he knew about. Its seats were broken, with the wires sticking through.

Then there were more daring places to explore, farther away from our bungalow. Down by the road, before the petrol station was built, there was a tangled, brambly plot. In the evenings rabbits came out, nibbling unconcerned as the cars passed by.

Little did they know the fate in store. The sunlight lit their fur, like haloes . . . You see, I do remember it as sunny.

Outside, the sun has sunk. I'm trying to tell you exactly what it was like. It's not just for you that I'm trying to fix these memories, it's for myself. Just now, talking about the potholes in our drive, I suddenly remembered squatting there beside the puddles. There's this oily film on puddles like that, isn't there? Aren't I right? I was there, I know I was, dangling string into the sheeny violet . . . Mauve swirls . . . I shifted them with my string. My sandals were canvas, and scuffed paler round the front. And the edges of the drive were muddy . . . Ribbed mud, where my Dad had steered around the holes.

I'm getting it back; I thought I'd never be able to. Can you picture it now, with me telling you? Last week, when the doctor saw what had happened, he suggested I visit a colleague of his. A psychiatrist, he meant. No fear, I said.

Perhaps that's why I decided to tell you, because it's easier. I couldn't tell a real person what I might be able to tell you. And it's working . . . It's coming back to me. This little girl . . . I can recognize her now as somebody who once was me. You've helped me, you know.

I'll continue the conducted tour. Out front was the pigs, and the road, and the brambly garage site. Up beside our drive ran another road which led past our bungalow to a brick depot out the back, behind our yard. This didn't belong to us. I didn't know who it belonged to, I hardly ever saw a human being there, though each morning cars drove up to it and at lunchtime a hooter sounded. Like most of the buildings down our way, it was a block put down in a field, just like that, and fenced in with ornamental shrubs. Years later it was bought by Avis Self-Drive and then it was Cortinas driving in and out, shiny saloons with UK visitors inside, wide-eyed from the airport. They stared at our yard.

Behind the depot stretched a large, flat cabbage field. I never went there – it was too big. In winter the smell of rotting vegetation hung over us, with the kerosene. The few fields around us, they all belonged to the market garden down the road. Down there were rows of greenhouses, and along the road stood a sign saying 'Chrysanths!', then the next saying 'Bedding Plants!', then the next, 'Buy Now!' . . . So people had time to slow down.

Cars, cars, whizzing to and fro. Cars out the front; and way across the field, at the back, misty-far, the elevated motorway. But you don't notice that when you're little, do you? You just sit there in your nest of grass with nothing larger on your mind. I was like that too, then . . . I'm remembering it. I'm sure I was just like you.

My Dad made the meals, before I was old enough to take over the cooking. He fried sausages in a haze of fat. When my Mum came back she tut-tutted at the mess, but what could she do? There was no one else to look after me.

I think of her a lot now. I try to work things out, how we might have been if events had been different. She was inhibited, but she wasn't deep-down cold. I don't think most inhibited people are. It just takes more skill to reach them, and when I was young I didn't know how. I was too little to be a companion and that was what she needed – companionship. She must have been lonely, with my Dad. And stuck in that place, with the airport lit like a city at night, but not for her, and the black fields behind with their far string of lights. Nobody except us lived along that stretch of road; they only worked there.

We would have got on better when I was older, I'm sure we would. I think she was looking forward to that. We could have discussed what clothes suited me, what matched my eyes and so on, like mothers and daughters do. I could have asked her about my periods. She'd never mentioned this but I'd seen her sidling through the kitchen with a newspaper parcel in her hand. Once, in my innocence I asked her if it was fish and chips and she'd been furious; I realize now that she was just terribly embarrassed. But later, when I wasn't a stupid kid asking stupid questions, and old enough to have female problems myself, then I'm sure we could have become quite comfortable together.

But the bleeding began early, when I was twelve. By that time

24

I'd made a habit of going down to the toilet at the petrol station. I sat there in the concrete cubicle, my knickers round my ankles and my face swollen hot. I didn't know what to do. Now it had happened, she was the last person in the world I could tell. The words thumped in my skull: I was bleeding because of what my Dad was doing with me.

Perhaps it was true – that I started early because of him. I never knew. But that's what I believed. Outside a car hooted for petrol, from the other side of the world.

So I kept it a secret for months, more furtive even than my Mum. Just when I should have been getting closer to her – and when, I'm sure, she was feeling more interested in me – I was prevented. It must seem ironic to you . . . But there was no such neat word for how I felt.

And it was all because of me. I didn't blame him. It was my fault; I was the wicked one.

Chapter Three

I t all started when Teddy was born. I was ten. I don't remember my Mum being pregnant; I don't think she liked to remember it either. She wasn't keen on babies. I'd nearly killed her, she said, being born. The complications, she said, hinting and sighing, with dark remarks and exhausted, knowing looks. But though she went on about them she never actually told me what these complications were, she was secretive about that, so I could only guess. I imagined I'd pulled out her stomach with me; that accounted for her small appetite. Or that she was all tangled inside, like a mixed bag of knitting. Shirl, our sow, once dropped her womb, said Dad. I imagined Mum's pulled out by me, by great big me, and her having to tuck it back inside with tears streaming down her face.

She had a pile of *Woman's Realms* in the lounge; she read magazines avidly. Inside were dreamy romances and Dear Doctor letters about athlete's foot. When nobody was about I'd pull out the magazines and have a search. I found an article about having a baby, and at the end there was a paragraph about stitches, and how soon before you could resume marital relations. I thought this meant meeting your uncles and aunts. But we never did that anyway; perhaps the pain of having me had put an end to these weekend visits. I looked, but I couldn't find anything called Complications.

So she'd vowed never to have any more babies. But along came Teddy. She was away a long time. For a month before he was born she had to lie flat on her back, at Ashford General Hospital, suffering from something I couldn't pronounce.

And then she was kept in for some time after he was born. It was probably only a week or two but it seemed an age, because I felt responsible. I was the big lump of a baby who'd done the damage.

It was a cool, blustery spring and the hens were laying again. Mum's, though, was not as easy as an egg. It was the school holidays. Behind our sheds the hawthorns were sprouting green tufts. My Dad called them bread and cheese and said he ate them when he was a boy. He said he nibbled the hedges like a pony. I didn't know whether to believe him or not. I nibbled them but they tasted bitter; when his head was turned I spat them out.

Our home felt different, without Mum. It changes, doesn't it, when you know the person won't be back. Time slowed down, like a watch someone had forgotten to wind. There was nothing to prepare for, no step at the back door. I always kept my bedroom neat, I loved my little room, and I tried to keep the kitchen and lounge tidy, but I wasn't much good at that. Without Mum to shop, we ate pilchards and jam tarts. Dad liked the yellow tarts best, he called them 'dirty boys' ears'. The air felt empty and waiting. She must have felt the same over in Ashford, the other side of the airport. I can't tell you how much I was longing for a baby brother or sister.

One day Dawn farrowed. Dad had been on edge for some time. Dawn was a sow he'd bought in January, when the prices were cheap. Actually he hadn't bought her; he had a mate in Slough and he'd swopped her for a generator. Ever since then he'd been uneasy about her temperament. She was a Large White, like our other sows Shirl and Celeste, but he'd raised the other two from birth and they were old friends of his.

Dawn lay in the container. We stood at the entrance. He was silent; he was always stumped for words when he saw new-born piglets. Then he counted them: nine, pink and struggling, pushing for her teats as she lay like a slab on the muddy straw. Her small, sunk eye watched us.

He didn't give them names because they would be sold as weaners. He went off to the pub at lunchtime, his truck bouncing cheerfully down the track. Later he told me that Archie, the landlord, had poured him a pint on the house because he'd looked so chuffed when he came in. When Archie heard it wasn't my Mum, but Dawn, who'd given birth he laughed so much that he gave Dad another drink. Dad brought me back a *Bunty* in celebration.

Next day it was pouring with rain. I was lying on the settee reading the best stories in *Bunty* for the third time. He said he was just checking Dawn and then he was off. He was meeting someone who might be putting something his way, he said, and he'd bring me back a Tizer.

He was outside for a long time. I don't know how long, because our electric clock had been stopped for years. I only know that when I heard the truck door slam, and the gravel scrunch as he reversed and drove off, I was surprised that he'd been there all the time.

It was still raining when I heard him come home. Outside in the yard, Rinty barked. I waited. The rain drummed on our roof. This being made of corrugated iron, I couldn't hear many noises except the planes. I was lying on the settee watching the afternoon movie. I kept the sound off; I just liked the friendly picture. With my Biro I was inking in the ps, ds and os in my comic.

The back door slammed; the windows rattled. He came straight in, boots and all, dripping with water. He flopped into the chair.

I jumped up. 'Give me your coat, Dad. You'll catch your death.' I'd heard grown-ups saying that.

He leaned forward, like a rag man. It was difficult, getting the coat off his shoulders. I was used to this, but usually he thanked me over and over again while I was tackling it. I didn't know how to start on his boots; they were plastered with mud, so I left them.

He said something, but a plane was roaring overhead.

'Pardon?' I asked.

'Six.'

'Six?'

He shook his head in despair. Drops flew.

'Couldn't trust her,' he said in a slurry voice. 'The stupid . . . the stupid . . .'

'What's happened?' It wasn't Mum, I realized. 'Shall I do your head?'

He looked up at me then, under his sopping hair. His face was wet. He said, 'You take care of your Dad, don't you?'

'Oh yes.' I went to hang up his coat and fetch a towel.

'Here.' He patted his knee.

I sat on his knee, as I always did. I didn't mind it being damp. Something had happened but I didn't want to ask him until he was ready, in case his mood changed. I rubbed his hair. I loved him letting me care for him. My hands felt clever and adult; I felt as stern as my games teacher. I rubbed briskly to and fro.

Then his voice came muffled under the towel. 'She went and laid on them, that's what.'

'Dawn?'

The towel moved as he nodded. I waited, but he went on nodding.

'They're squashed?' I asked at last.

He was still nodding. 'Know something? . . . There's nobody dries me so well as you do.'

I went on rubbing, pleased. I rubbed round his neck, then his ears. Then I was rubbing his face and the bump of his nose. I minded about Dawn, but not as much as I minded about him.

He raised his head, his hair sticking up. 'Heth,' he said, 'know what you're looking at?'

'What?' I asked, confused.

'Want me to tell you?'

'Yes.'

'You're looking at a disappointed man.'

He looked frighteningly sober. 'Don't say that, Dad.' I flung my arms round his neck. The towel was wedged, a thick sausage, between us. I didn't want to see his face.

'A disappointed man . . . And I'm not just talking about the pigs.'

Pressed against him, I could feel his jaw moving as he spoke. His skin was rough and damp. I whispered, 'What did you do with them?'

'Buried 'em.'

I clung tighter. I was so grateful that he'd stopped me seeing the piglets. But how could he be disappointed, with Mum's baby on the way? I moved my face and pressed against the warm rubbery rim of his ear. I wanted to close off those words he'd been saying; I wanted to press the breath out of him so he couldn't say he was a disappointed man. It must be me who'd disappointed him.

His jaw moved. 'Squashed 'em flat . . . her wee ones.'

He squeezed me tighter. I could hardly breathe. I gripped him hard.

'How could she do that?' His voice hummed against my cheek. '. . . Her own wee babes.'

'She must be mental.'

I'd just learnt that word. I felt his body shudder. He was laughing. Why? But I was so pleased . . . I relaxed. Then he stopped. He said, 'Where would I be without my Heth?' He paused. 'Jesus above, what would I do without my little girl?'

I couldn't think of a reply.

'Give us a kiss,' he said. 'A kiss for your Dad.'

I removed my face from his ear and kissed his cheek, as I always did. Then I drew away but he pulled me back. He kissed my lips. His moustache tickled. Then, with his lips he opened mine. His tongue slid into my mouth, warm and wet. Inside it moved around as if it was searching for something, deeper and deeper. Despite the smell of his breath, his saliva was as tasteless as my own. It felt uncomfortable. His mouth was bigger than mine; he was going to swallow my face. Not moving, I kept my arms gripped round him.

He must be so upset. He'd pulled out the towel and thrown it on

30

the floor. I couldn't breathe . . . He was breathless too; I could feel his chest pumping in and out, against me. His mouth stayed glued to mine, his nose digging into my cheek. His hands rubbed up and down my front.

Just when I was going to suffocate, he let me go. I stayed on his knee; I didn't know whether I was supposed to get up, or what. His moods made me nervous. There was a silence, except for his breathing. I heard the rain, still drumming on the roof. Then he shifted a bit, and I jumped up. He was fumbling for something in his trouser pocket. He took out his handkerchief and wiped my face, ever so gently, as I stood beside him. He wiped round my mouth.

'Don't want our lipstick smudged,' he said in a shaky voice. 'That would never do.'

'I don't wear any lipstick.'

Silence, then he said loudly, 'I know you don't!' There was a pause, then he said, 'Don't listen to me . . . Didn't mean to shout.'

His breath made a wheezing sound as he sat there, without moving. Then he said, 'Do us a favour and fetch me fags.'

I'd hung up his coat on the hook behind the door. I fetched the packet. He took a cigarette and tried to light the match. He must still be cold because his hand was wobbling.

'I'll do it,' I said. I struck the match and lit it. I always felt special, doing that.

'You'll catch a chill,' I said. 'Just look at you.'

I went into the kitchen. My ribcage ached from the squeezing, so I breathed several times, deeply. As the kettle heated up I refolded the tea-towels and put them in the drawer. I must keep the kitchen neater. I mustn't disappoint him . . . I must keep the house as tidy as Mum did. While the tea was brewing I collected the foil cases from yesterday's jam tarts and put them in the bag for blind children. Next term Mrs Mason, my teacher, would be so pleased with me; I'd collected a whole stack of meat pie containers too.

He hadn't turned the sound up. When I came in with the teapot, there he sat, just staring. Do you know, this frightened me more than anything else? Dad always turned the sound up. But there was John Wayne, mouthing at us.

I pulled up the little table and set the tray down carefully, so as not to slop the tea. I couldn't bear him being so upset.

Pouring the tea, I tried to comfort him. 'Dad, I'm so sorry about the pigs.'

He stared at me. 'The what?'

'Sorry, I meant the piglets.'

'The *pigs*?' he shouted.

I shrank back. There was a dead silence as we stared at each other.

Then his face seemed to collapse. He jerked forward, stretching out his arms. The mugs clanked as the table rocked. 'Oh Heather, Heather, I'm sorry.' His voice was all choked up. 'I didn't mean it, honest I didn't . . . Come and forgive me.'

But I had the teapot in my hand and I tried to pretend his mug needed topping up. It alarmed me, the way he called me Heather. He never did, usually. I took my mug over to the settee.

'Didn't want to frighten you,' he mumbled. 'Didn't mean it.'

'Don't worry,' I reassured him. I tried to sip my tea, all calm, but it was too hot and burnt my lip. 'It must've been horrid, burying them.'

'Just meant to be affectionate . . . didn't mean no harm.' He lifted his head and looked at me. To my horror, his eyes were wet. 'Won't do that to you again . . . Honest I won't . . .'

'Dad, you only shouted. I don't mind, really I don't.'

'Let's you and me forget it . . . Nothing happened . . . OK?'

'OK,' I said, to make him happy. I still didn't understand. Anything, though, to change that expression on his face.

When we'd finished I took the tray into the kitchen. He stayed in the armchair in a thickening cloud of smoke. Why didn't I go over and comfort him? I wanted to get out of the house, but for some reason I didn't want him to hear. I crept out of the back porch.

Outside the rain had stopped. It was damp and absolutely still, as if the world held its breath. I stood there for a moment; behind me, where the broken gutter hung, came a plunk, plunk, as the drops hit the concrete. I walked across to the gate. Shirl and Celeste were out, slurping around in the mud. They pulled out their legs with a sucking sound, like jellies. I walked over to Dawn's container.

She lay there, just as before. Her eye gazed up at me; a fly settled on her face and she flicked her ear. The three piglets were asleep, flopped across each other. They slept as lightly as puppies, twitching with their dreams. Hadn't they noticed that the straw was smeared with blood?

I didn't stay long. When I went back I found Dad asleep too. I paused behind the armchair; his hair was dry now, his head slumped sideways. I'd never felt so alone. But then I couldn't think who I wanted to talk to either, which made it worse.

Blue Peter was on. It was the children's programmes I'd been waiting for earlier that afternoon. They were showing the finals of the cat championship, and they had these children there, looking ever so grave, holding their pets. Valerie, who was my favourite, walked from one child to another, bending down, smiling, and asking them questions. I'd wanted to enter one of our cats but I'd never been able to catch them, they were that savage.

I stood for a while. The winner was a girl my age, wearing plaits. Eyes lowered, she answered a question to the accompaniment of Dad's snores. I wanted to see the rest of *Blue Peter*, and then the cartoon, but how could I turn up the sound when Dad was asleep? The one thing I didn't want, for some reason, was for him to wake up. Then I remembered about the Tizer. I went over and felt inside his coat pockets, inside and out, but I couldn't find a bottle. So I went into my bedroom.

Later that evening it was Visiting Hours. I wanted to see my Mum badly. But when we got there I felt shy. There she lay as usual, propped up against the pillows, her face sallow in the strip light. She looked like an unknown person, with her neat features and her thin lips. She'd curled her hair and it looked like a wig around her face; below it were the knobs of her collar bone that I wasn't used to seeing. My Dad sat looking cowed and oversized, as if he shouldn't be there, with his hands hanging down. He'd stopped bringing her grapes and things, she'd been there so long. He told her about the piglets, in a flat voice, but that lasted about a minute. There was a long silence. I felt the breathing bulk of him beside me, as if for the first time. I glanced at his clumsy, dangling hands . . . He was probably dying for a smoke. In official places he looked hunched and awkward; he shifted in his seat when a nurse passed by.

The silence continued. I fiddled with the pin on my C & A kilt. Dad half rose when a trolley rattled past. With any luck it was their evening meal beginning. What could we talk about? None of us understood the technical things that were being done to Mum. I watched the bedclothes bulging with her tummy.

It was hot. Hospitals always are. Dad took out his handkerchief and rubbed his forehead, then round his mouth. In the light I saw how grimy the hanky was. Then I remembered it rubbing my lips; I remembered his wet mouth, and his tongue squashing mine.

Mum turned her head to me. 'Lost your tongue?'

That word started the blush. I felt the blush rising, hot and humiliating. They must both be seeing it, surely. All the people must be seeing it . . .

But nobody seemed to notice. Or if they did, they weren't letting on.

Nothing much had happened that afternoon, had it? Nothing that dramatic; not the sort of shock-horror stories you read in the Sunday papers. Our little scene wouldn't have made the headlines.

And it hadn't really disturbed me, him kissing me like that. After all, grown-ups did incomprehensible things all the time, like puffing horrible cigarette smoke in and out. They spread mustard on their food – how could they? – and got emotional about dull things while not minding the important ones, like me never having proper, long socks for school. No, that part wasn't so disturbing

. . . I'd always loved him hugging me. What terrified me was how he behaved afterwards. What had I done, that he'd shouted like that, with tears in his eyes? If I didn't know, how could I stop it happening again? Wasn't it my fault?

All I felt, that afternoon, was that I'd stopped knowing him quite so well.

Chapter Four

Nothing much happened the rest of the time Mum was in hospital. At least, nothing much that an outsider would notice. It was cool and showery; I spent most of the time in my bedroom. The day after the one I've described my Dad went into West Drayton and he came back with a bumper colouring and puzzle book, the best I'd ever seen. It had its own Cellophane bag of crayons too. They were too blunt for the join-the-numbers so I used my pencil for those pages. *Hours of Fun*, it was called; and I did spend hours lying on my bed, Kanga within reach. It was too young for me; I was ten after all, I could do all the puzzles easily. He often misjudged my age. But I liked that; it made me feel secure, it made me feel in control of things. And I didn't have to ask my Dad about any of the brainteasers. Before, I'd enjoyed plonking myself on the settee beside him. We'd ponder together, him gnawing my pencil until it was damp and frayed. But now I preferred my room, with its glass animals all attentive on the shelf and the door closed.

Nobody came into my room, you see. It might have been out of shyness – after all, I never went into their bedroom either. We were a modest family, I've told you that. On the other hand, perhaps they just weren't bothered to visit my arrangements. My Mum and Dad always said goodnight in the lounge – they were usually in position by then, in front of the telly; often it was late because I didn't really have a bedtime.

It meant everything to me, my bedroom. It was small and narrow, but that made it safer. My Dad had put up a shelf; then there was the bed, of course, and my furry lion called Leo, with a zipped tummy with my nightie inside. I'd sorted my toys into different cardboard boxes which I'd covered with Christmas wrapping paper. I had several books; my favourite at that time was *Gaye is a Ballerina*, though I already knew I was too big to become a ballet dancer like Gaye. At night I closed the curtains. They were too short; from my bed I could see the black night beneath them. But I kept my eyes away from that before I went to sleep, and gripped Kanga instead.

No, nothing could have looked much different. Dad behaved quite normally. A gale had blown down some corrugated iron; that was how the pigs' field was fenced. My window looked out that side. I watched Dad stomping through the mud, wedging the gaps with planks and bits of rusty machinery. Around our place, things were always collapsing, or just about to. You couldn't trust the floors not to give under your weight. He would have been pleased if I was out there helping him. But I stayed indoors, setting out the fences of my model farm. I only had six bits but they all slotted together and stood upright. I had two cows, a lamb and a carthorse with a harness on. It was satisfying, fencing them in. Outside it looked grey and treacherous.

I did go and look for the piglets' grave. I found a patch of lumpy clay, behind the caravan. This was a shame as the caravan was my special place. And I was anxious in case Rinty dug them up. But he was usually chained in the shed, or outside in the yard; he didn't run loose like a pet. I went and sat in the caravan for a bit; I think it was still the Rosy Arms, that spring. It started raining again, pattering on the roof. I watched Dad come home. He stood at the porch, his jacket hunched round his head, banging first one boot and then the other to knock the mud off. Then he went inside.

I remained sitting on the pile of sacks. I wanted my Mum to be home. I didn't know why, but things had changed. In a word: I felt cautious. For instance, I didn't want to go back indoors now, all wet, because then he might try to dry me. I wanted him to hug me, but I was frightened that he'd get upset. Over the next months I learned never to come in looking wet or shivery. I stopped saying I was cold, because then he might jump to his feet, all affectionate. I learned how to be clever and get myself indoors when he wasn't there. Or else, whatever the weather, to come in all *insouciante* – a word I heard years later, and whose meaning was then horribly familiar.

I stayed in the Rosy Arms some time, hoping the rain would stop. I was anxious about him coming out and finding me doing nothing. That would make us both uneasy. On the other hand, I couldn't think of anything I wanted to do. This was the sort of thing that happened – or didn't happen. As I said, it was nothing dramatic.

What happened next may not seem dramatic either. It was a couple of days later and I'd gone along the main road to see my friend. I didn't know her name; she was a grown-up. We often had a chat together; she was always kind to me. She sat at a lay-by not far from our gate, selling flowers. She had beautiful flowers, in buckets, and she sold them to the passing motorists. The blooms came from the market garden farther down the road. I suppose people bought the flowers on their way to the airport to greet their nearest and dearest. Then there were the businessmen flying home; perhaps they bought a bouquet for their wives as a peace offering. She was always well buttoned-up, because of the wind and the traffic, and she had a tiny dog, which was her pride and joy; he had a jewelled collar and I used to play with him.

Anyway, that day I'd told my Dad I was going for a walk. I must have been away about an hour. My friend chatted, as usual, about her boys and how well they were doing. They were both grown-up now. She said she lived for them and for her little Shoo-Shoo or something, I could never understand her dog's name. In the end I wandered back home. There were bangings from the shed, where my Dad must be busy. I went indoors.

I stopped at my bedroom door. I'd left it closed, and now it was open. Inside, there was a stale smell. I knew exactly how I'd left it. Now I saw that the eiderdown had been sat on: the sateen had sunk in the middle. My *Girl* annual, which I'd left shut on my pillow, now lay open. And on the floor was a saucer with two cigarette stubs in it.

I don't know how long I stood there. Outside, the hens were clucking. I'd always felt reassured by the hens; they seemed like aunties, comfortable and gossipy. But today they didn't sound like that; they knew what had happened, they were clucking amongst themselves, they were keeping it from me. I kept looking at the stubs. He must have sat there a long time, to smoke two.

Teddy was born in the middle of the night. Next day we went to see him. I couldn't believe he belonged to us, with his red face and his froggy legs jerking. He didn't have a name yet. I didn't dare touch him.

Dad laughed at me, but then I could see him hardly daring either. He sat there, pushing his hand through his hair over and over again; he was as silent as when he saw the piglets. Then he said, 'Well I'll be buggered.' Dad's fingers were so big, and stiff from working outdoors. He'd cleaned his nails specially but the cracks in his skin were always black, he couldn't do anything about them. He leaned over and, very carefully, pulled down Teddy's nightie so his mauve feet were covered. Mum was telling us about the trials she'd been through, the agonies, but I couldn't take my eyes off the baby. Just then he sneezed – a tiny, wet, human noise, and I knew that I would love him always.

They were both ever so pleased, of course, that he was a boy. My Dad was so proud he behaved as if it was him who'd given birth, not Mum. It was Tuesday, the day we did the bins at the Skyscape Hotel. We drove round the rear as usual, the empty bins banging in the back of the truck. One of the waiters was out there having a smoke. You know what the Spanish are like about

39

babies. He put his arms around my Dad and kissed him on both cheeks.

'A son!' he shouted. 'You dirty sod!'

Then the maintenance man came out. His name was Frank, like my Dad.

'I have to say it, Frank,' repeated Dad. 'I'm over the moon.'

Frank wiped his hand on his overalls and pumped my Dad's arm up and down.

'Over the moon,' my Dad said again.

Then the waiter fetched a bottle of green stuff and four little glasses. I tasted it, and they laughed when I winced. Dad offered round the fags. There was a festive mood in the yard, which smelt of everybody else's rotting dinners. Then a man in a black suit came out and shouted something Spanish at the waiter. By now Dad and Frank looked as if they were jointly responsible for Teddy's birth. They heaved the pig bins into the truck.

There was a festive mood at home too. Dad went out to the pub that night, and when he returned I heard shouts in the yard and Rinty's hysterical barks. We hardly ever had people in. I was in bed.

When I heard them I got up and put on my dressing gown. I knew all the men. Dad carried in a crate of bottles which rattled when he banged against the table. They sat around being very friendly with me. Archie, from the pub, kept talking about the gooseberry bush and winking at the others. Of course, I knew perfectly well that babies came out of people's bottoms because I'd seen the kittens being born. Dad must know that I knew, too, but he kept making jokes about the stork and how the stork had a job of it, what with the aeroplanes. Then they all had a laugh about flight arrivals and – because Teddy was overdue – about flight delays.

It was then that it hit me. I can remember every detail, even now, nine years later. I was sitting on the floor between Dad's feet; he liked me sitting there. There were his boots, one on each side, and the carpet. Glasses stood on the carpet, and an empty Cellophane square from a packet of cigarettes. Our single lampshade

40

hung from the ceiling, casting a dim yellow light; ahead of me the telly was a grey blank. I concentrated on the carpet. My cheeks and my scalp were prickling hot.

You see, I knew how babies came out, but I also knew how they got in. With saliva. Nobody had told me in so many words, but I knew about a seed being passed from the man to the woman, once they were married, and I'd worked out how it happened. It could only happen during the long, uncomfortable kissing at the end of TV films. They had to keep glued like that to give it time.

My Dad and I had done that. It had lasted too long, hadn't it, and all the time his big wet tongue had been pushing the seed in.

I kept my eyes on the carpet. It was dark red, and dirty, with a swirly black pattern like smouldering fireworks. The laughter echoed miles above me, from a canyon. Why hadn't I realized this before? Had I been deliberately putting it out of my mind? I sat with my knees hunched up, pressing my face into my dressing gown. I'd never seen my Mum and Dad kissing but then I knew they did that in their bedroom. After all, my Mum had made those stifled noises, as if she couldn't breathe.

'Look at her, then,' said a voice. 'Popped off.'

'Don't she look peaceful?'

'Should be tucked up safe and sound.'

'Shouldn't we all?'

I sat very still. I didn't want them to leave.

Dad's boots moved. 'Upsy-daisy, Podge,' said his voice. 'Action stations.'

I made myself go limp as he lifted me up and carried me into my room. He didn't attempt to undo my dressing-gown buttons, thank goodness. I kept my eyes squeezed shut. He couldn't manage the sheets so he laid me on them and put the eiderdown on top. He sat down heavily for a moment, catching his breath; then he climbed to his feet and I heard him tiptoe out and shut the door.

Next morning he slept until midday. I'd already let the hens out. I could tell the time by the animals' noises – noon: the hens standing around the back porch making enquiring sounds in their throats; Rinty stirring in the shed and rattling his chain. I was usually right, because then the hooter sounded in the depot.

I stood in the lounge. I'd drawn the curtains and opened the windows. I looked at the bottles, and the saucers full of ash. How could my baby brother survive in a house like ours? My Mum had been given a plant once, when she'd left a job. It was a big glossy one. She'd watered it all right but the leaves went mottled, then crinkled brown, as I knew they would. It died, still wrapped in its ribbon. It was too new for the place we lived. Wouldn't the same thing happen to our baby?

I was worried about myself too. I cleared up the lounge and emptied the ashtrays. I tried to concentrate on what I was doing. In the kitchen I stopped and felt my tummy. It was the usual firm bulge. I knew I'd get fatter, of course, but surely you had to be grown-up, and married, and wearing a bra, to start a baby?

I couldn't think who to ask. Not Dad, for a start, and certainly not Mum. I wouldn't be seeing my two friends at primary school, Nancy and Debbie, until next term, and anyway I had a feeling they didn't even know as much as I did. I needed an adult. The ones I knew were mostly men, Dad's mates, which ruled them out. Oonagh, who'd minded me when I was little, was also no good because she was my Mum's friend; they talked together in a hushed, significant way. I'd chatted to some of the ladies who picked the cabbages in the field behind us, but they weren't around now because it was spring.

I decided to ask my friend with the flowers. She was kind and I felt, because she was always going on about her boys and her cruel kidneys, that she wouldn't be too nosey about why I wanted to know.

I went down the drive and out along the road. Cars roared past. I'd brought along Kanga for security. Her neck was getting thin and her grey head nodded as we walked. If only I could ask her; after all, she was a mum. Roo's head poked out, with his dear glassy eyes. They both looked wise but I knew by then that I could no longer ask them questions.

The lady wasn't there. Beside the lay-by was the bald patch of earth where she usually put her chair. Some days she didn't turn up. She'd told me she was a happy-go-lucky soul, despite her complaints, and life wasn't going to get her down. She must be off somewhere, gadding about.

I walked slowly home, Kanga's head lolling. I went into our garage, where my old pram was stored. Dad had removed the heap of plastic sacks and newspapers, in preparation. I looked inside it, for the first time in years. There was the rubber mattress where I had lain, once; there was the tear in the lining where I had liked inserting my forefinger, wriggling it to and fro. How snug I must have been, tucked up, with nothing on my mind. I shivered; the garage, being concrete, was always chilly. It was full of junk; there had never been room for our truck. I wanted to pull out the pram and wash it for my new-born brother, but I couldn't move all the stuff without Dad.

Mum had given him a list for Woolies. We drove there that afternoon. I followed Dad down the aisles. He kept pausing with his piece of paper and rubbing his nose. I usually loved shopping with him, and today should have been the best day of all. Soon he gave up and I took over the list, collecting the terry nappies and the bags of cotton wool. I felt light-headed and queasy, both at the same time; I couldn't catch up with what we were doing. How soon before I had a baby too? I found a packet of bootees: cream knitted ones. 'Birth – 6 months', said the label. It was six whole days since that thing had happened in the armchair. He hadn't said a word about it; all I knew was that later he'd sat in my bedroom.

Today, since he'd woken up he'd been more silent than ever, and his eyes were rimmed pink. I dreaded him saying something, of course; I felt sick at the possibility. But there we were, choosing baby clothes together. I should be thinking about my baby brother, not myself. Was Dad ever going to tell me the truth? I must be too young to have a baby, with my flat chest. I would have to ask a stranger.

I inspected the check-out lady . . . Someone like her, who I might not see again. But I couldn't just blurt it out while she pinged the till, could I? And with him there.

On the way back he put his hand on my knee.

'Sorry, Podge. Not quite myself today.'

Silently I pleaded with him not to explain why, and it worked. He didn't.

Mum's bandages made it all more confusing. I'd noticed them, of course, but I pretended not to see. I thought I knew how babies were born, but there she was, trussed up half-way to her collar bone. She'd buttoned up her nightie but you could see gaps when she moved. There was woolly bandage in there, wrapped round and round and fastened with safety pins. I made sure on my second visit. Was this part of the Complications? I must have got it wrong, this baby business. I'd thought you had to have bosoms, but now she'd bandaged hers flat. They looked as flat as mine. So did that mean I could have one too?

That visit I had to go to the toilet. I was just washing my hands when a nurse came through the door. She stood beside me, filling a vase with water. If she hadn't smiled at me, and if we weren't alone, I would never have dared.

I just turned to her, calm as calm, and asked, 'Do you know why my Mum's wearing bandages?'

'What – here?' She indicated her chest. I nodded. My courage was draining away now.

'It's Mrs Mercer, isn't it?' she said.

I nodded again.

'They're to help stop lactation. You see, she doesn't want to feed baby herself. Some of our mums don't.' She paused, smiling kindly. 'That answered it?'

I nodded, of course. She went away. I stood there, rigid. There was a roaring in my ears.

Acting as if nothing had happened, I made my way back to her bedside. Dad was standing, jiggling the baby. Mewling hiccups came from the bundle. No wonder the little thing was crying.

I said quickly, 'Can we take him home now?'

Dad stopped. 'Eh?'

'Can we bring him home?'

Dad burst out laughing. Even my Mum smiled. There were some other babies crying, I could hear them now. They must be the other ones who weren't going to be fed.

'I'll feed him.' I looked desperately from Mum to Dad. 'I promise.'

'You're an odd little thing.' My Dad smiled. 'Aren't you just?'

'He's staying here with me,' said Mum. 'It's the rules.'

'Go on, give him a cuddle.' Dad passed him to me. The bundle felt so light – I knew it would, he must be getting thinner by the minute. I touched his mouth with my little finger. He opened his mouth and my finger slid in.

'That washed?' demanded Mum.

'In the toilets.' His gums gripped me. He was sucking so hard I had to stop it showing on my face. I felt a sharp ridge where his teeth would be, if he lived to grow any.

'Greedy little bugger, isn't he?' said Dad, with a stupid grin.

Back home, I helped with the preparations because Dad was so excited. We tucked sheets and blankets into the pram. In my alarm, I'd forgotten about my own baby. My brother had been called Edward; Teddy for short. Why did they bother to think up a name?

Because Dad seemed so expectant and cheerful, I didn't feel as cautious in his company as I had done recently, which I suppose was one good aspect. He patted my bottom in his breezy way, like the old Dad did, and promised that they'd be home in a couple of days, so little Podge mustn't look so worried. By now I'd seen Teddy suck at a small hospital bottle, but I knew that would stop when he came home and then it was up to me. He would be my responsibility; would I be feeding him in secret?

One night, when Rinty was howling outside, I went to sleep and dreamed that all our sheds were crammed with babies. There were rows of them in the caravan too, lying bare in the straw, like piglets. The caravan had grown as big as a warehouse. They were all crying, they wouldn't stop, and I was trying to feed them from the bucket, trying to cram in the food with my fingers, but why would they be eating apple peelings and why wouldn't they stop crying? I knew it was hopeless, and I knew that my own baby, and Nancy's and Debbie's, were amongst the others but I couldn't find out which ones they were.

Teddy and Mum came home at last. Dad had bought some tulips from the lady at the lay-by, and put them in a vase on the telly, all by himself.

'For our boy,' he said, wiping his wet hands on his trousers. Then he saw my expression and pulled a mournful face. 'Give us a hug.' He had been celebrating again. 'Dad loves you too . . .'

He pressed me against him. We stayed like that. For a moment everything fell from me, all my worries, and I thought: Dad will make it all right. I clutched him round his chest and smelt the warm wool. I'd been so silly; this was how we should be, me pressed against his belt buckle and him stroking my hair. How could I have felt unsafe? He was here, he was mine, I loved him.

He took away his arms and I stayed there, clinging. 'Look, no hands!' he cried to the furniture. Then he enfolded me again. At that moment I felt exactly right: I felt exactly ten years old. He lifted me up in the air.

'Phew!' he said, and put me down.

Soon they'd be home, and then, perhaps, everything would stay being all right. We'd be a proper family at last.

I was feeding Teddy when the lady arrived. I heard the car stop outside, and Rinty barking. Teddy was gulping down his milk, his eyes fixed on me. Mum was in the bathroom, pulling out her curlers; the door was shut but I could feel the curlers fall one by one into the sink. I carried Teddy to the back porch.

'Who's the little mum, then?' she said, smiling. 'Taking lessons already?'

She was the health visitor. We'd been expecting her, but she was early. There was a pleasant look on her face as she glanced around the lounge. I hoped she was noticing Dad's tulips.

'My Mum'll be out in a minute,' I said.

'May I sit down? – No, no, you've got little Edward.' She removed a plate from the settee and sat down, her handbag in her lap. She had a bigger case, too, which she put on the floor.

'Do you want to look at him?' Holding Teddy carefully, I passed him to her. 'I haven't burped him yet.'

She held him against her shoulder and rubbed his back. 'We're a bonny big boy, aren't we?'

'Is he?'

'Don't you think so?'

'I don't know.'

'We put on lots of lovely ounces in hospital. Didn't we, Eddie?'

Teddy burped, and we both laughed. I stopped laughing, to hear if anyone was coming, and then I said quickly, 'Do some mothers not want to feed their babies?'

'They prefer not to.'

'Why not?'

'They choose not to, dear – especially if they want to get back to work, which I understand your mother does.'

'But what happens to their babies?'

I heard the handle turn on the bathroom door.

'Oh, this powdered stuff's marvellous now. Dear me, don't look so worried.'

Mum came in then, her hair stiffly curled. While she was telling the lady how her complications were getting on, and while the lady took out a metal thing and weighed Teddy, I had a think.

I'd got it confused, I was realizing that. This lady just made it official. After all, these past three days, since they'd been home, my Mum was often mixing Teddy's bottle herself. She'd fed him, sitting on the kitchen chair and looking quite normal. Comfortable was not a word you'd use to describe my Mum; she wasn't a cosy person. But she didn't look as if she was forced to do it, or that she'd suddenly stop tomorrow.

It was all my fault. I'd mistrusted my Mum. I shouldn't do that, it was wicked. Just because she wasn't interested in me, that didn't mean she was going to lose interest in Teddy and let him shrivel up.

I did another stupid thing. While they were away in Mum's bedroom, putting Teddy in his crib, I hurried over to Dad's tulips. This lady, she'd made me see them for the first time; he'd stuck them in all lopsided, still with the rubber band around the stalks. But their petals were already curling back like pink tongues; when I moved them the petals fell off, all of them, silently, and lay on the top of the TV. Green rods were left, with knobs on. Blushing with shame, I picked up the vase, with its bendy stalks, and hid it behind the chair.

I brushed away the petals just in time. They came back into the lounge; Mum was still telling the lady about her aches and pains and I slipped out of the front veranda. When the lady was opening her car door, and Mum had gone back inside, I was sauntering round to the yard quite casually.

'Goodbye, Heather.' She stopped, her hand on the handle. She was dark and hairy; there was a blotch on her cheek with a tuft growing from it. I trusted her.

'How old are people before they can have babies?'

She raised her thick eyebrows and smiled. 'Someone's in a hurry, aren't they? There's plenty of time for that, I can promise you, dear.'

'But how soon?'

She paused, half-frowning. My face was burning; but she was my only chance.

'You love your little brother, don't you?'

'Yes.'

'Yes, I could see that. But they don't stay babies for ever. It's easy when they're tiny . . . like dolls. My dear, I've seen it so very often.'

'What have you seen?'

She had put down her case. She shrugged, her eyebrows raised. 'You see, Heather, it's so easy to have a baby.'

'Is it?' My heart stopped.

'It's such an easy way out.' She gestured around our yard. 'But that needn't be the only escape.'

I didn't understand this; I waited.

48

'But times have changed,' she went on. 'Thank goodness.'

'What's happened?'

'It's different nowadays, for girls . . . Heather, dear, I hope you'll find that out . . . I'm talking about opportunities – do you understand? Opportunities for, well, expanding your life . . .'

'But when can you start one?' I went on, desperately. 'When you're little? When you're, say . . . well . . . ten or eleven?'

She stared. '*Ten?*' She was frowning now. 'Someone's been telling you stories?' She glanced at the porch. 'Your parents?'

'No!'

'I know your father enjoys a joke.'

'No! Don't tell Dad!'

'My dear . . .' She put a hand on my arm. 'Nobody can possibly have a baby when they're ten. Or, indeed, eleven.'

'But what if you love someone?'

'Love?'

'If you really love them? What then?'

'Heather, you can't.'

'You can't love them? Can't you?'

'You can't have a baby.' She smiled. 'Understood?'

I nodded. I was afraid she was going to look at her watch, and she did.

When she'd driven away I went into the caravan. I wanted Kanga but I didn't dare fetch her from my room.

I met other people later, when there was much more to tell. Scores of them. Some, I'm sure, were the understanding type . . . You never know, they might have been able to help. But I never dared talk to them like I talked to that lady.

Chapter Five

By June Mum was back at work in Terminal Two. That's at the airport. I was back at school. So clattery-bright, my school, after those weeks at home. Every term-time I was startled by the voices and the laughter.

Teddy was sent to Oonagh's in West Drayton. I went to school on the bus; Dad picked me up at 3.30 and then we collected Teddy and came home. School had just been playing; I felt I was starting my proper job when I was home with Teddy, changing his nappy and then wrapping him up for his walk. I tied his bootees and swaddled him up in his shawl. The afternoons were long and sunny; looking back on it, he was lucky not to suffocate. I liked him close to me, so I didn't want the pram. I held him tightly in my arms; we'd walk over to the railway carriage and I'd show him the eggs. I talked to Teddy all the time; I'd never known I had so much to say. He kept his passionate blue eyes fixed on my face.

I showed him the piglets, galloping round the field with their stiff legs and their flapping ears. He knew my secret names for them, of course. In his bonnet he looked like a piglet himself. I just stood with him, for hours, watching his teeny fingers fiddling with his shawl. I felt weak from loving him.

Dad loved him too, though I got nervous when he whooped the bundle up in the air. I thought he'd toss Teddy up like a beach ball. Dad laughed at me then, and Teddy made chortling noises too. But when Teddy cried I had to spring into action, because Dad panicked.

'Shut up!' he'd shout. 'Shut up bawling!'

I remembered Mum's bruises. Dad had such a quick temper; I could never trust him that way . . . Not quite.

That summer was my last as a little girl. For one thing, I was eleven; in the autumn I'd be moving up into the new school, West Drayton Secondary. Nancy was going to another school and Debbie was going to Canada, so I'd have to make new friends. The big school filled me with terror and pride.

But there was another reason too. The day things changed, it was hot and sunny. Half-term, it must have been, because I was home. I was in the caravan when I saw a car drive into the yard. Two men climbed out. They wore suits. Hardly anyone visited us, specially not in a suit. The two men talked to each other for a moment, then they glanced around the yard.

I ducked below the window. When I raised my head they must have gone round the front, to ring on the bell nobody used. After a while they reappeared and knocked on the back porch. They moved away and looked our bungalow up and down. The way they did this, I suddenly saw it clearly: the green wood, stained under the windows; the rusting, corrugated-iron roof. One man rubbed on the window; then he wiped his fingers on his hanky and smiled at the other one. When he did that, I knew I wasn't going to let them see me.

Then Dad came up. He must have been down at our car park field. They talked for a moment, then Dad went inside and came out again with his jacket. As he put it on he bellowed,

'Heth!'

I climbed down from the caravan.

'Where's your manners? There's two good friends of mine here.'

I had to shake their hands.

'Say hello to . . . er – '

'Mike,' said one.

'Tony,' said the other.

'Just popping off,' said Dad. 'What'll it be?'

'Pepsi?' I asked.

He gave a thumbs-up sign and climbed into the car.

It was hours before he came back. Out in the depot the tea-time hooter was sounding when I heard the car returning. They must have enjoyed themselves because they were laughing and joking outside. I slipped out of the front veranda and sat down on the grass. I leaned against the wooden frame and watched the car bouncing away along the ruts. It turned left, into the traffic.

I didn't know, then, how I'd look back to that afternoon; how I'd try to remember it as it was, before everything happened. An ant was walking up my leg; it struggled over the pale hairs. I've got hairs, I realized; that was the first time I'd noticed them.

'Heth?'

The inner door opened, then the veranda door. His trousers stood in front of me. His hands were behind his back.

'Go on,' he said. 'Guess.'

I squinted up but the sun was in my eyes, so I couldn't tell from his expression.

'Left,' I said.

He usually cheated and changed hands, but today he didn't. He held out his palm; in it lay a scrunched-up paper napkin. He lowered himself down beside me and opened the napkin, carefully, on the grass.

'Whoops,' he said. The little cheese biscuits were all broken. 'Must've sat on them.'

'I don't mind,' I said truthfully. I picked up the bits and ate them.

'Had them in these bowls,' he said. 'Them and olives, but I know you don't like the olives . . . Ever so smart, it was. Know the Global?'

I nodded.

'In there. Got this Eurolounge . . . Velvet seating and all, with dinky little whatsits on them. Tassels. You'd have loved it, Heth. I told them . . . I said, my little girl would love this.'

'What were those men?'

'Who?'

'Those two men you went with.'

He smiled and closed his eyes. He was leaning against the veranda.

'Know something, Podge?'

'What?'

'Promise you won't tell?'

'Cross my heart.'

He paused, still smiling. 'We're sitting on a gold mine, that's what.'

'What?'

Eyes closed, he put a finger to his lips. 'Sssh.'

'A gold mine?'

'I knew it . . . Didn't have to tell me. Didn't have to tell old Frank. Not that they did, in so many words . . . Oh no, not them . . . Devious buggers.' He looked at me with one eye, and tapped the side of his nose. 'Mum's the word, eh?'

I stared at him, but his eyes had closed again. Then his head slid sideways and he started snoring.

I sat there for a moment, too panic-stricken to move. Down beyond the pigs, a car bumped slowly out of our field and drove off. Bye-bye, 50p. I looked at my Dad's poor, frayed cuffs. I thought of my Mum, working herself to the bone, she said, to make ends meet. Where's the money to come from? she said.

The problem was to find out where the gold was hidden. Why hadn't Dad told me about this before? He couldn't know where it was, or he would have dug it up by now. How could he sit there, when those men would surely be coming back? They knew. They would find it first, unless I hurried.

I found a trowel in the veranda and went round the back. Our yard was cracked, but none of the gaps were big enough to insert my trowel. Anyway, where would I go from there? Even with a spade, I couldn't lever up our yard, I didn't have the strength. Around our bungalow the earth was hard and dusty, all scratched by the hens. They gathered behind me, to watch. I stabbed at the ground; it hadn't rained for weeks, it was like iron. The handle was wobbly because a screw was missing. I jabbed and stabbed: why was nothing ever mended in our house? If only I could dig properly, Dad could buy himself a new trowel, a new anything. He could build himself a pub in the yard instead of leaving us alone.

The possibilities made me dizzy. I didn't really want anything for myself, nothing big, but that afternoon – probably because for the first time I could do something to remedy it – that afternoon I realized how money might make my parents happier. The words sprang up: we are poor. It wasn't my Mum going on about it, but me realizing it for myself.

I made no progress. The ground was just chipped, here and there. I was useless. I didn't like to try the grass out the front because Dad was there.

I went indoors. Thinking back now, I'm not sure I knew what I was seeking. Gold coins? I was too old to believe in hidden treasure. But I was still young enough to believe in miracles: that something could be found that would make my parents happier . . . That I could do it if I tried.

Everywhere the floor creaked. I knew there were holes under the carpet because we'd all learned how to avoid them – a stride was necessary, for instance, outside the bathroom door, and there was a subsiding area of carpet behind the telly. When my Mum went on about them, Dad said he only had one pair of hands.

I started in the kitchen because the lino was loose. Lifting it, I saw the floorboards all broken. Dusty gaps showed what must have been earth but it looked even less promising than outside. I felt foolish, kneeling there with my trowel.

Just then I heard a car outside. Mum was back from work; Oonagh's husband had given her a lift. By the time she'd come indoors I'd put back the lino and also hidden, in the fridge, Dad's plate of Spam and tomatoes that I'd made for his lunch, and that he hadn't seen. I hid the trowel in the cupboard. Her footstep made me feel infantile. I jerked shut the cupboard door, which was warped.

It was late that night when the shouting started. I was in bed but I woke up at the noise. I couldn't hear the TV, which alarmed me; Mum must have switched it off. I knew then that it must be bad, so I went under the blankets and put Kanga's arm in my mouth.

'Keep your voice down!' shouted my Dad.

'Let her hear. Let her know what sort of a man she has for a father.'

My bedclothes muffled the voices but they were all too recognizable. My teeth dug into Kanga.

'What a spineless nobody he is . . . What a good-for-nothing slob.'

'Say that again, Coral. I'm waiting . . . Go on.'

'No need, is there?'

'Oh yes?'

'We both know it, don't we?'

'Look – '

'I'm wondering what they were saying, when they dumped you here . . . When they'd opened their door and let you roll out – '

'I told you, we got along fine. Real matey, we were – '

'Don't tell me! Can't I imagine it? I don't want to, mind you, but – '

'We're not selling this place!'

I stiffened.

'Don't care what they offer,' he said. 'Don't give a monkey's fart.'

From a long way off I heard her laugh. '*You* don't care! That's a fine one . . . No, I'm sure you don't. You don't have to earn it, do you?'

Selling? Selling our home? I lay rigid. She was just finishing saying something. '. . . Sitting on your fat backside all day . . .'

'I'm not budging. I like it, the kid likes it – '

'And what about me? Thought about that? I know you don't

like to bother about *my* feelings, too much of an effort, isn't it? I don't suppose you remember our plans.'

'What?'

'When we bought this place. Our plans. Building up the business, getting out. Getting *on*. Somewhere else, somewhere better. This land is worth a fortune now – all this development land . . . Dear God, I hate this place. I should've listened to my Mum.'

'Here we go!'

'When she told me what it'd be like. What I could expect, with a slob like you. Damn all, as it turns out.'

'You're a bitch.'

'You're a fool. You're such a *fool*.'

'Cold bitch, too. When was the last time –'

'Such a *fool*.'

'Go on, say it again.'

'A big, stupid, drunken –'

A thud. I bit Kanga, hard.

'Don't you come near me.' Her voice was flat. 'Stay away.'

'Nobody talks to me like that.'

'I've had enough. See?'

'Not good enough for you, am I? Hoity-toity?'

'You hit me again, and I'll, I'll . . .'

A chair scraped. I didn't hear any more because I pressed my hands against my ears. You probably think I was a coward. But nothing could have pulled me out from those blankets.

A few moments later I loosened my hands, just a little. Teddy was starting to whine; otherwise there was silence. I pushed back the bedclothes and ran into the lounge.

My Dad was sitting there, smoking.

'Where's Mum?'

'Your Mum? Just popped out.'

'Has she died?'

He gaped at me.

'Has she?' I asked.

'Come here, ducks.' He patted the settee beside him. ''Course she hasn't. Heard a bit of a ding-dong, eh?'

I nodded.

'She'll be back,' he said.

'Has she gone to Oonagh's?'

He nodded.

'But it's miles.'

'Only a mile, that way.' He jerked his head towards the back door.

'Across the field?'

He nodded.

'Couldn't we fetch her back?'

'No sense in it. Till she's cooled off.'

'What about Teddy? And us?'

He leaned forward, rubbing his face in his hands. 'No problem, princess.' He held out one hand; I took it. 'We'll manage.'

He looked so large and helpless. I didn't know what to do. Teddy was crying louder now, so I went into their bedroom. It was only these last few weeks, to see Teddy, that I'd been into their room. Their cupboard door was open; so were two drawers. Her hairbrush was gone. I picked up Teddy and took him into the kitchen, to mix his bottle.

By the time I'd put Teddy down again Dad was asleep, toppled sideways on the settee. I couldn't think what to do with him. I bolted the front and the back door; then I thought: what if she comes back? So I unbolted them and went to bed. As I lay there, gripping Kanga, I remembered I'd been digging for gold. It seemed like a week ago.

I dreamed I was falling through the floor. There was just space below, endless space . . . black and echoing. There was nothing for me to grab on to. They'd all been packed away, the floorboards, they'd been sent away . . . Nothing left, no house, nothing . . . Somebody was crying for me, miles above, but I couldn't hear what they were trying to tell me . . .

It was Teddy crying, through the wall. I heard him now. Mum will see to him, I thought . . . Then I sat up suddenly, awake.

In the lounge, the light was still on. The room was empty; Dad must have gone to bed. I stood outside their bedroom door. Teddy was still crying in there, but I couldn't hear any noise from my Dad. Beside the handle, I hesitated. Teddy's crying grew more purposeful. What happened if Dad woke up, like a wild man, and started shaking him?

The door creaked as I opened it. No wonder he was crying; it was pitch dark in there. Mum always left on the bedside lamp. The light from the lounge fell across the bed. Dad's head lay on the pillow; he was still asleep.

Teddy had kicked off his bedclothes. I unclipped the bars of the cot; they rattled down. Behind me, Dad grunted.

'What's that?' he mumbled.

'Only me,' I whispered.

I leaned over and picked up Teddy. He was sopping wet – him and his nightie and the cot sheet. He hadn't been changed for hours. I sat down heavily on the bed. He twisted around in my lap, hiccuping, trying to catch his breath for another wail. I shivered in the cold. By now I was crying too, noisily, missing my Mum. I couldn't move, so I had to wipe my nose on my nightie sleeve. It seemed impossible to ever stand up. Teddy was so wet; I felt the drops slide down my leg, inside my nightie.

'Don't cry, Heth.' The bed creaked under me. Dad moved; he was sitting up, behind me. His hands gripped my shoulders. 'Stop it!'

'How could she leave him? Dad, how could she?'

'Don't take on, lovey.' The hands tightened. 'You'll start me off in a minute . . . cats' chorus.'

'How could she leave you?' I blurted out. Meaning: and me too.

'Oh, there's plenty of reasons for that one. For leaving yours truly.'

'She couldn't do it. *Why?*'

The hands squeezed my shoulders. 'Glad I've got one fan. You still love me, after what you heard?'

'Of course I do,' I sobbed. 'Why shouldn't I?'

'For ever and ever?'

'Ever and ever.'

He moved and sat close behind me. I had my arms round Teddy

and Dad had his arms around me, all squeezing each other in a row.

I bent over Teddy's hot head. My mouth spoke into his hair; it was fine, and damp. 'What if Mum doesn't come back?'

'She'll be home, you bet.' His voice rumbled against my backbone. 'She's been away before, remember? Couple of days.'

I nodded. But this time it was worse. 'What if she doesn't want us any more?' I took a breath. 'She doesn't seem to want us, sometimes.'

'Don't take no notice of her.' He pressed his nose into the back of my head.

I took another breath and said slowly, 'What happens if she's gone off to sell our home?'

I felt his body jerk with laughter. 'Heatherbell, she can't do that.' He turned my head. Gently, he pushed the hair from my face. 'Honest.'

I couldn't say: I don't quite trust you any more, when you say *honest*. So I said, 'What if she tries to sell it?'

'Over my dead body.'

'Don't die, Dad! You won't, will you?'

'Hey!' He pressed my head against his chest. My neck was twisted but I wanted him to keep me there, without moving.

'Let's you and me make a pact,' he whispered. Why did he whisper? There was nobody who could hear.

He smiled. 'Let's you and me see she doesn't. Right? Signed and sealed in blood.'

I should have felt better but I felt just as frightened. It was wrong that we should have to make a pact, against Mum. It was wrong that she wanted to leave us. It was all far too wrong for jokes.

'I must change Teddy. He's soaking.' I tried to get up. Dad was sitting on my nightie. 'So am I.'

He shifted, and we all got up and went into the bathroom. Dad was wearing his vest, and his underpants which were like shorts. In the light, I felt shy. I also felt terribly tired – more tired than I'd ever felt in my life. This night would never end. I felt as if big rocks had been dragged through my insides and left me as empty as a sausage skin. Teddy was laid on the floor. My hands, which did not seem to belong to me, were lifting his damp legs and pulling off his nappy. My hands got slower and slower. Dimly, I heard the cock crowing. The frosted window was still black, but it must be nearly dawn.

Dad was lifting me up in his arms and carrying me out of the bathroom. He laid me on my bed, and I could hear him opening my chest of drawers. I heard Teddy squalling in the bathroom, all alone.

I managed to say, 'There aren't any more nighties.'

Hands lifted me, and I was carried back into his room. I was laid on the bed. The cupboard was opened, with a wheezing creak.

'Looking for a shirt,' I heard, miles away. I wanted to tell him where Teddy's nappies were, and Teddy's clean nightie, but my head felt too heavy to raise. I didn't want him to undress me; I didn't have the energy for all that embarrassment.

'I'm all right in my nightie,' I said. 'Do Teddy.'

Thumps and murmurs from the bathroom. He must be in there now, doing Teddy. At last he must have managed it; dimly, I saw him carrying Teddy in, blocking the light at the door. He lowered Teddy into the cot but Teddy started yelling, perhaps at meeting that wet sheet.

'Teddy-weddy, wettee-bedee,' he murmured, and he put Teddy into my arms. My nightie must have dried by now, or perhaps Teddy and I were past minding. I was snuggling down between the sheets, and the bed was sinking as Dad climbed in beside us. The door was open and light shafted into the room. I wasn't exactly asleep, as I held Teddy, but I was too exhausted to do anything except lie still and be pleased that Dad wasn't going to change my nightie.

Teddy kicked my stomach.

'Ouch!' said Dad. He'd kicked him too. Teddy lay between us, spreadeagled like a starfish. Between my heavy eyelids I could see that these curtains were too short as well. I'd never noticed that. Grey glimmered beneath them; the cock crowed again.

60

Dad's breath on my face . . . 'Night, night.' His moustache pressed against me; his lips touched mine, which were closed and dry. I remember feeling that we'd done this before, though it was too far away to remember when. I didn't want to know. In fact, I don't want to tell you about this now; but I was too tired, then, to resist, and it's certainly too late now. He put his arms around me . . . Teddy was a hot restless body between us . . . Dad's breath was in my mouth. His tongue pushed into me.

'You smell of fruit gums,' he murmured.

I frowned. 'I haven't eaten any.' I tried to wriggle away. 'Honestly I haven't.'

He took a deep breath and let it out, shakily. 'Everything sweet,' he said, '. . . sweet and new . . .'

We lay there, us three, clasped together. Teddy stopped kicking; he was lulled by our warmth. That big strange bed was our place . . . safe and sound. Not strange now. I was too sleepy to get up; by now I didn't want to. The three of us were tucked into our raft, with that space all around, the awful possibilities . . . the draughty, fearful possibilities, like the floorboards being removed. Mum might not come back. Mum might not love us enough ever to come back . . . She might sell our home, just like that. That's how much she minded . . .

With all the kicking, my nightie was rolled up around my waist. I was sorry that I hadn't worn my knickers, but then I hadn't known I would be here. Teddy's knee was poked into my stomach. His nightie was rolled up too; I held his fat, bent leg. His nappy felt loose because Dad had pinned it. How could Mum not want our Teddy? I did. Dad wanted us too . . . I could feel his hand enclosing me, rubbing my leg so gently, and rubbing my tummy. Nobody had ever comforted me so much.

'Oh pet,' he murmured, 'oh my pet.'

It meant as much to him, because he was breathing shakily. He loved me, you see. I'd always known that, about my Dad. He was rubbing Teddy's soft legs, then he was rubbing mine again, and then his hand moved round between them . . . his finger lay on my warm place, my own warm slit where I was not allowed to touch . . . His finger lay there quite still, gently pressing against the skin.

He seemed short of breath . . . His finger was stroking me there, oh so gently . . . I didn't know what to do about this. I didn't move. My Mum had slapped my hand once, in the bath. I'd been touching myself like that . . . But it must be all right, mustn't it, if he did it? He knew, after all; he was my Dad. I could trust him.

He'd stopped kissing me; he was breathing heavily, his face pressed into my hair, with Teddy's head jammed between us. This was uncomfortable but he didn't seem to notice. He seemed to have difficulty taking breath, snorting into my hair like this.

His face was heated . . . But he wasn't going to die, because he was saying, 'My pet . . . my dearest', in a strangled sort of voice. He'd never called me *dearest* before. I was confused, but I was so pleased too . . . I wanted this to go on, and yet I terribly wanted it to stop.

Then he cried out, sharply.

'Teddy!' I admonished. 'Stop it.'

Teddy must have kicked him. Dad lay still. Down there, his finger moved away. What had I done wrong? He was gripping my shoulder, hard, his face still in the pillow.

And then an awful thing happened. I didn't realize it for a moment. I thought he was trying to catch his breath, in gulps. I lay, trying to convince myself, even after I knew.

But he was sobbing.

I didn't move. With each spasm, his hand clenched me. It hurt. I didn't realize that until next day, when I couldn't touch my shoulder. I lay rigid, staring into the grey room. I stared at the cupboard, with its piled boxes on top. I kept my eyes on it. Perhaps Dad would be packing up his boxes too, if I upset him like this.

I've described what happened, as best I can. But I can find no words for how I felt at that moment, hearing my Dad sobbing, with my arms around him doing no good. The only word that gets near is fear.

After a while he spoke, his voice muffled in the pillow.

'Heather, Heather . . . don't be angry.'

'Of course I'm not.'

'Don't be angry,' he moaned.

My arms should be helping him, but I didn't know how to. I wanted him to put his arms around me, strong and safe, so I needn't hear him. I wanted him to be recognizable.

But he just went on making that noise, as if his insides were being pulled out through his throat.

'I tried not to,' he mumbled. 'I did, honest . . . I didn't mean it.'

He didn't mean to call me *dearest*? I wanted to block my ears.

'Honest to God,' he said, 'didn't mean to.'

Teddy jerked against my stomach. I tried to think of words to make it all right, but I didn't know what words to use. My head felt so dizzy. I must stop that noise he was making.

'Mum'll be back,' I said.

He jerked up. '*What?*'

'She'll be back, I know she will.'

He stayed like that, his head reared up.

'You said she will,' I went on. 'So none of us need worry, you or me or Teddy.' I kept my arms round his shoulders. The bed smelt animal-warm, and sour. 'It's tomorrow already, so she might be home today.'

My voice sounded as if it came from another person, not me. But my words soothed me, as if somebody else was doing the comforting. I hoped I was having this effect on Dad.

Perhaps it had done the trick. He lay still. Then he said sharply, 'You lock the door?'

I opened my mouth to say no. I was going to say: I left it open, for Mum to come in.

But then, inside me, something happened. It happened as I lay there, pressed against him, and realized what we must look like. Somewhere in my soft middle, it felt like a lid beginning to lift. It was a sick feeling.

'Did you, Podge?' he asked. 'Lock it?'

I lay rigid. His voice made me nervous. More than anything I wanted Mum to be here to stop this happening. But he mustn't know that.

So I said my first lie. 'Yes.'

Mum didn't come back the next day, or the next. At one point I thought, pettily: how could she do this on my half-term? I felt ashamed for that crossing my mind. She went to work, though. We found this out because Oonagh's husband was a mate of my Dad's; he worked at the Gas Board sports ground, out towards Staines, and my Dad visited him there. He said Mum was living with them and coming home each night. Calm as calm, as if they were us. Dad said that he and Vic laughed about it: *women*, they said. But I didn't understand how they could.

Whether Teddy noticed I couldn't tell. I tried to comfort him. He gazed at me, then he transferred his gaze to the apple branches above my head. He couldn't be minded at Oonagh's, of course, so I'd park him under the tree. I used to think he understood everything, but all of a sudden I was not so sure. I loved him just as much, but I was seeing him more clearly now: he was ever so young, with that blank look babies have, and his expression changing like the clouds for no reason. He was suddenly disappointing. Nothing interested him beyond his own fingers and his mouth. He'd worked out how to do this best. He'd suck his two middle fingers; this left his forefinger free to pick his nose. Even at three months he'd worked this out; Teddy was like that.

My Dad and I were very much alone. Those thousands of cars passed us each day and I knew none would ever turn up our drive. The weather was heavy, and hot, and grey. It weighed like lead. When my Dad was out I'd go into their bedroom and pull out the drawers. Mum's folded clothes were still there; she hadn't taken much. She must come back. She'd left her turquoise coat, too, so what would happen when winter came?

I didn't want to ask him about her; something was stopping me. I didn't want to ask him any questions, because I could no longer trust what the answer would be. Back in April, after that first time, I told you that I felt I didn't know him so well. It was worse now; I felt it all the time, this wariness, with something else nudging behind me. This was the suspicion that in fact there was some answer, some fearful grown-up secret, that he was waiting to tell me. I didn't want him to.

I tried to stop him by the power of thought. I was good at that. I could sit beside the road, for instance, with my eyes closed and will the next car to be red. When I opened my eyes, it was. I could do this with Smarties too – which colour would rattle out next. I willed Dad with my eyes open, otherwise he might ask me what was the matter.

The best thing was to keep out of his way. Alone, I could will myself not to think about what was happening. If I did I would start to work it out and that was the last thing I wanted to do.

The best place was the big field behind us. They'd planted sweet corn in it this year and by now the plants had grown as tall as me, if I stayed bent. I'd park Teddy under the apple tree, where I could hear him if he cried. Then I'd creep into my forest . . . Not too far, but out of sight. When I sat down I was hidden. I was podgy, yes, but I could fit myself into a small space. I'd sit there amongst the stalks; when the wind blew, the leaves rustled. There were the tiniest tassels in there, already; they were silky to stroke. I stayed there a long time. I told myself I was an explorer and this was New Guinea, because it made me feel better if I called it a game.

I slept in my Dad's bed the next night, and the next. You see, Teddy cried if I wasn't there. That was part of the reason. But there was another part, which is more difficult to explain. My room didn't seem mine, as much as it used to; not since Dad had made a habit of going in there. Nowadays I was always having to open the window, he worked up such a fug. And since Mum had gone I was frightened at night. If I slept in my own bed I might wake up and find everybody gone. There might be strange people in the lounge, rearranging the furniture. There might be no furniture at all.

But the main reason was that I wanted to please Dad. I wanted to stop him feeling sad. So the night after the one I've described I tucked myself up in my own bed, but when Teddy started yelling I got up. This time I put on my knickers, underneath my nightie, and my dressing gown on top. I didn't want to leave Kanga. She didn't have Roo any more, because he'd got lost. I haven't told you about this, because I don't know exactly how it happened. One day he was there, and the next day he was gone. I'd spent a week searching but I couldn't find him, and by now my tears were all dried up. I asked everyone, but Dad didn't know, and Teddy and Kanga just gazed at me.

So I took Kanga in with me, for both our sakes. Dad was carrying Teddy into the bathroom. I was glad to see that Dad was wearing his proper pyjamas tonight. We knelt down on the floor together and pinned Teddy's nappy. Then Dad carried Teddy back to his cot; but when Teddy started yelling, as I knew he would, Dad put him into the big bed.

'You'll be wanting your sis, then?' he asked. 'Your big sis?'

So I took off my dressing gown and laid it neatly on the counterpane, and put my slippers side by side on the floor. Dad yawned; in his pyjamas he looked more reassuring. It would be ordinary tonight; I needn't worry myself. Nothing was going to make him cry.

I snuggled down and made a fuss of Teddy, ticking him off for being such a cry-baby, and arranging his frilly collar. Dad kissed me, swiftly, and I lifted up Kanga.

'Look, Dad. Kanga didn't want to be left out.'

I smoothed my nightie over my legs and yawned loudly. Dad stroked me, just once. When his hand reached my bottom it stopped; it must have felt my knicker elastic through the nylon. I yawned again, and turned to face the window. Soon I heard his breathing lengthen, raspingly, and he was asleep.

Something happened in the middle of the night, but I pretended so hard to be snoring that I convinced myself, next morning, that we'd both been asleep. I can almost convince myself now.

When Teddy and I woke up, Dad was still slumbering; he'd always been a late riser. Mum used to complain about it. He wandered in when I was feeding Teddy in the kitchen, and telling him he was a naughty boy because I'd found a stain on the front of my nightie. I'd only washed it yesterday.

'Who's my bad boy?' I crooned. 'Bad, bad boy.'

'What's that?' said Dad.

I turned to show him, pointing at myself. 'Look what that naughty baby did.'

Dad stopped, and barked, 'I'll take it.'

I stared. He started fiddling with the lid of the Nescafé jar. It was probably jammed. He paused and said, in a more conversational tone, 'Just off to the launderette, see.'

'Pardon?'

'Just off, after me breakfast. Time for a wash. Give it me and I'll take it.'

I gawped. He'd never done this before; he'd left it to Mum. Then, sinkingly, I realized that perhaps, from now on, neither of us would be able to leave the washing to Mum.

You're never changed when you expect to be. It's not that neat, is it? At some point during those days I realized that what was happening was wrong. I didn't put it into words; it was just a prickling, shedding feeling. It was like looking around, one day, and realizing that all the leaves have fallen and the branches are bare. I wasn't old enough to have the words for this. If there's just two people – Teddy didn't count – then, if neither of you says anything, and you don't want to, then you can hold it off indefinitely. To admit it to yourself, you'd have to recognize it happening; and both of us, during the day and the night, pretended it wasn't.

I realized it on day number three. This was when, for the first time, I talked to someone outside our home. Until then I'd been around the yard – I remember wondering, for a moment, what those little dents were in the earth, over there beside our bungalow. Then I remembered that I'd dug them. I sat in the forest, and looked after Teddy, and hung up the tea cloths outside, like a housewife. I wanted Dad to be pleased with me – I always did – but I didn't want him to be too grateful. I probably looked quite normal, but one thing was different: I was aware, for the first time in my life, of exactly where my Dad was – in the sheds, in the house, in the field. Ask me, any moment of the day, and I could have told you.

He'd gone off a few times, on errands, or to change the bins down at the Skyscape Hotel, but I hadn't gone with him. I told him it was easier for Teddy and me to stay. Besides, what would happen if Mum came back and tried to collect more of her clothes?

Three days was the longest she'd ever stayed away. I was dreading the next morning because then I was sure that, clothes or no clothes, it was going to last for ever. Dad was out; he was driving our weaners to Slough. I'd watched them leave, squabbling and squealing, their pink skin pressed against the slats of the truck. Mentally I told them goodbye. When he'd gone I pushed the pram down to the main road. Mum would be at work now but I still watched all the cars, just in case. That morning I didn't feel like talking to Teddy.

On the left was the petrol station. The Indian man sat in his booth, as usual. I felt I hadn't seen him for weeks. I bumped the pram along the verge, in the other direction. Every few yards I looked back, to make sure nobody was turning into our drive.

I reached the lay-by. Today my friend was there.

'Look who's here,' she said, bending over the pram. 'And how's little Spotted Dick?'

'They're gone,' I said. 'I rubbed on some cream. It was just heat lumps.'

'Koochy-koo,' she said. Teddy grasped her finger. 'Who's a lucky boy then?'

'Lucky?' I felt like a foreigner, just learning the language.

'Needn't be coy with me, dear. Can't hide it from me.'

'Hide what?' I stared at her.

She just winked. 'Can she?' She picked up Teddy. 'Can she, pudding?' He gazed at her, unblinking. Suddenly I pictured him opening his mouth and telling her. Just speaking it out . . . How I'd been lying in Dad's bed, of my own free will . . .

How Dad had cried real tears.

68

It was then that I realized how wrong it was, what I'd been doing. I felt the heat rising up.

'She's blushing!' She was speaking to Teddy. 'She's going to pretend she never raises a finger . . . Ah, but I've been watching.'

'What have you seen?' I blurted.

'I've been watching . . . and you know what your sister is?'

'What?' I said, urgently.

She pinched my cheek. 'Know what you are? You're a good deed in a naughty world.'

I didn't know what she meant; I couldn't work it out. She said, 'And you tell that to your Mummy and Daddy.'

I nodded.

'Tell them I said so. That this little pudding's lucky to have a big sister like you . . . So you tell your Mummy, when you get home. Promise?'

I nodded again, blushing hotter with my untruthfulness.

'Go on, give her these from me.'

To my alarm she was lifting some carnations out of their bucket.

'Oh no!' I cried.

'Oh yes.'

'Please don't!'

'Don't worry.' She winked. 'Himself up there . . .' she jerked her head back, 'his lordship . . . No skin off his nose.'

She wrapped them in paper and laid them in the pram. 'Tell her they're from a mum too – a mum who's always wanted a nice little girl like you. Had to bring up my two all on my ownsome, didn't I . . . What I've been through . . .'

Thank goodness she started talking about her boys then, and her flat where the council never came to mend the damp, even though they'd done the flat downstairs, and how her boys were always too busy . . . stories I'd heard before and which at that moment I longed to hear again. Something waited, at the back of my mind; I could feel it lodged there but I needn't think of it yet.

On the way back, though, I had to put it into words. I pushed the pram, watching the pink blooms jolting . . .

Mum knew what was happening. I could will things, with my eyes shut. Why couldn't she do it too? She'd willed herself to be there, in her own bedroom. She'd opened her eyes and seen me in her bed. She'd seen how terribly wrong it was . . . That's why she was staying away. She was disgusted with me.

It was all my fault. I'd always known this, but never so clearly as now, with Teddy calmly looking up at me, next to his shivering carnations. It was up to me to get her back, if I possibly could, if she would ever consider returning. It was up to me because I had caused it. It was me who must plead with her and make it all right. If she came home, and I did everything I could to make her forgive me, then we might be a proper family again, like we'd been after Teddy was born; we'd almost been like Gwen's family then.

I knew she worked at Terminal Two. That afternoon, when Teddy and Dad were having their naps, I set out. Neither of them would wake for hours. The airport entrance wasn't far down the road but I'd never walked there. As I said, nobody did; I'm sure you haven't. Everybody travels there in buses and cars; that's how I'd been there before, in the van . . . Down the slip road, where the motorway joined, round the roundabout and through the tunnel with its huge letters, WELCOME TO HEATHROW.

I crossed at the lights, beyond our petrol station, and hurried along the other side of the road. Cars and lorries swooshed by. Alongside me was the high wire fence of the airport. Fir trees had been planted along it; they were grey and dusty, they jerked beside me as I ran. Words I could use rolled round and round my head. Would she believe me? Through the fence I saw the main airport city: the control tower, the terminal buildings, the big blocks with slits round them, like narrowed eyes watching, that must be the multi-storey car parks. She was in there, somewhere.

It seemed so far away. I paused at the first big junction. I had to keep my wits, because cars were speeding towards me from all directions. Signs loomed above me, saying 'Maintenance Area 3' and 'Cargo Depot' and 'M4 Motorway London and the West'. I ran along the slip road, down towards the entrance roundabout where the motorway traffic came in. In the truck there was no time to notice this road, we'd sped along, but it took ages on foot. I passed all the litter they'd thrown from the cars. Some of the cars slowed down, to look at me.

At last I reached the roundabout; there was the tunnel mouth . . . I was dreading going in; it would be dark and blowy, the traffic scraping past me belching fumes. Somebody was sure to report me to the authorities.

But when I reached the tunnel mouth I found a smaller entrance marked 'Pedestrians'. In there it was suddenly quiet; just the rumble of traffic through the wall. I couldn't see the end of the tunnel, it curved away ahead of me . . . A concrete tunnel, dimly lit. It was empty, though there were some crisp packets lying around so other people must have once been here. It was chilly; my footsteps echoed. I hurried. Somewhere, round that corner, I'd get to my Mum. I didn't dare look back in case somebody was following me. I didn't run because that would make me feel frightened. My sandal buckle had worked loose; it rubbed my foot but I didn't stop to adjust it.

Now I was running along towards the square of daylight. My feet slapped on the concrete. I tried not to think of returning this way, back along the tunnel. With any luck I'd have my Mum with me, so I could hold her hand.

I ran up, into the daylight. It was suddenly noisy, with traffic lights and airline coaches streaming past. I climbed over a barrier and edged round a flower bed; taxis brushed past me. I dashed across another road and climbed another fence. There were no pavements here. Horns hooted at me. The huge 'Terminal' signs pointed in all directions, up ramps, across the traffic.

Terminal Two. I got there, at last. Now I was amongst people and parked cars, and nobody was looking at me any more. Electric doors slid open.

Inside was a big hall; it was bright and hot and loud, with people pushing to and fro and calling out to their children . . . Like bird-calls, echoing.

'*Heather!*'

I swung round. No . . . *Deborah*.

A sign pointed up some escalators to Arrivals, so I went up. I usually ran up escalators but today I stood still. A loudspeaker was booming out about *passengers for flight something to Frankfurt proceed to the Departure Lounge*. I slid uphill, rigid with nerves. My face must be brick-red, from the running. Now I was here, the words had all jumbled up inside my head: I couldn't trust what would come out. I wanted to go into a ladies' to see that I looked neat. But then that might be the ladies' where my Mum worked.

I stood still instead, trying to decide where to start. A man and a lady flung themselves into each other's arms. Three children hared across the hall shouting '*Daddy!*' People put down their suitcases to greet their families. My Mum must be used to all this; she saw it every day on her way to work. I felt dizzy with the happenings and the noise.

I looked for the ladies'. I didn't know which one she worked in, because Dad and I had only dropped her outside with the taxis. I found a door, with a skirted sign above it.

I didn't dare go in. Now I was here I felt sick. I stood holding the handle.

'Heavy, is it?'

A lady smiled down at me.

'Let me give you a hand.'

She pushed open the door and waited for me to go in, so I did.

It wasn't Mum in there, it was an Indian lady. She wore overalls and she was swooshing water round one of the basins.

When I was breathing normally again I looked at the row of white basins and, beyond them, the doors of the WCs, some open, some closed. This is what she does, I realized, all day. Now Mum wasn't here and I could pause, I thought: she wants these basins more than us.

I didn't dare speak to the Indian lady, in case she didn't understand English, so I went to the toilet instead. I needed to, being so tense. I sat there working out words. *We miss you so much. Teddy cries for you each night. Don't be angry with me . . . I'll die if you don't want to come home . . .*

Outside the ladies' I hesitated. I couldn't ask anyone, because they'd direct me back here; they'd think I was mad, asking for *another* ladies' convenience. So I hurried across the hall. Teddy or Dad, or both of them, would soon be waking up. Teddy was safe, in his cot, but I must get back before Dad found out I'd gone.

I found another ladies' and went in, my heart knocking. Looking around, I couldn't see anyone. Then I saw the little room, with its window. Inside was a glimpse of overall. Someone was in there, sitting on a chair.

I walked up and peeped round the door. The person turned round.

'Something the matter?'

She had red curls, and her eyebrows raised.

I couldn't get the words out.

'What is it, dear?'

'Is there another toilets here?' I asked, in a rush.

She paused, her eyes merry. 'This one not good enough for you?'

I stared, trying to sort out my words. 'I'm looking for my . . . for a lady. She's called Mrs Mercer.' I paused. 'She works here.'

'Here?'

'At Terminal Two. I know she does.'

'In the washrooms?'

I nodded. She thought for a moment.

'Mercer . . . Ah, you must mean Coral.'

'Yes!'

''Fraid you can't get to her.'

'Why? Where's she gone?'

'She's not gone, dear. She's here.' She paused. 'She is here and she isn't, so to speak.'

'Why?'

'She's in the toilets, right.' She was still smiling. 'But the toilets in the Departure Lounge.'

'How do I get there?'

'Can't. Not unless you've got a ticket.'

'Ticket? Where can I get one?'

'A plane ticket, my love. And you'll be needing a passport too.' She looked at me. When she saw my expression her voice changed, and she explained to me what she meant.

Mum did come home that day. It was long after I'd got back. Dad and I were eating pork pies. I've never seen anyone eat them like he did; he'd nibble off the top first so you saw the grey bumpy insides, like brains. Then he'd spread mustard and pickle on the top and say, 'Fit for a king.'

Rinty barked, but less wildly than for a stranger, and there she was, giving the door a shove, where it was stuck, like she always did.

'Must get that fixed,' she said quite calmly. Her hair was newly set, in stiff, spun rolls. That was the only sign that this was an event. She seemed smaller than I remembered.

If I was younger I'd have flung my arms around her, but I knew by now that she didn't like that sort of display.

Dad's voice. 'How about fetching another cuppa, Heth?'

He took her out later to the pub, which was their only sign that anything unusual had happened. Much later, as I lay in bed, I heard her gasping noises through the wall. I gripped Kanga against my chest; without the bump of Roo, she seemed flabby and in need of holding. I thought I'd forgotten what those noises sounded like, it was so long since I'd heard them. I didn't want to hear them, of course. I was part of that now.

If you press one ear against the mattress, with its lobe folded over, and press the pillow hard on top, against the other ear which is folded flat, you can block out anything. I'll show you how; I'm the expert. If you want to make absolutely sure, you hum as well.

Here endeth my childhood. The next term I went to the big school, where they called me Porky. When I had to pass on a book in class they'd wipe their hands with a shudder, as if they knew.

Part Two

Chapter Six

Thirteen years old. Did you stop being friends with your body then? It's betrayed you, hasn't it, sprouting spots and thickening, lumpily, just where you don't want it to thicken. You don't notice your body when you're little: you *are* it. I remember Gwen aged eleven, prancing around and snorting, tossing her brown pigtails like a pony. She *was* a pony. To be exact, she corrected me, a palomino stallion called Caspar, that nobody could tame. I wasn't that keen on ponies myself but I knew what she meant. Your body was what you did things with, what made them possible, like your own soul made elastic. You didn't think of it as separate, except when you scraped your knee or you had a sneezing fit (I had hay fever, being the pink, allergic type). When I was young, as I said, the only way my body let me down was by blushing. I learnt early that I was a blusher; but that was because I'd learnt so early about guilt.

I looked at my body in the bath. I was thirteen, and inspecting it as if I'd never seen it before. At this time my Mum was working at the airport coffee shop, the late shift, so my Dad and I were alone in the evenings. But he was usually down at the pub, so that was when I had my bath. I'd wedge the chair against the door handle, just in case, and fill the room with steam. The one thing that worked in our house was the geyser. Then I'd lie soaking for an hour. Those days baths were the nearest I came to contentment, in our home. I'd lie there, propped, too sluggish to worry or even to think, feeling the badness soak out of me. 'Open your pores', said *Woman's Realm*, 'to "breathe out" the hidden grime.'

Radio Luxembourg would be playing, but not too loud, so I could hear if the porch door slammed. The corroded geyser spout hung above my toes. Through the DJ's chatter I'd gaze at my reddening thighs, submerged in the water. I knew, by now, that I was overweight. My tummy went into rubbery creases when I sat up, so I'd lie down again. Being fair, my skin was sensitive to heat and cold and turned blotchy with either extreme; my hands went mottled mauve in the winter, and bright pink in the bath. Pale hairs grew down my arms and legs, and there were light brown, coarser hairs between my thighs. My breasts looked fatty, with big, pale nipples. Once, when I lifted up Teddy, he pressed them and sang,

'Jellies on a plate, jellies on a plate –'

'Shut up!' I hissed. My Mum, and, much worse, my Dad, were in the room.

'Wibble-wobble, wibble-wobble, jellies on a plate!'

But here in the bathroom nobody could see except me. I could look at myself with a horrified interest that dissolved, with the heat, into steamy langour. I carried this body around but it didn't belong to me any more. I rubbed the mist from the mirror and looked at my spots – not many, just two or three crimson blobs on my chin. I narrowed my eyes and my face went swimmy in the glass. I blinked, and opened my eyes wide, and blinked again, tight, telling myself it was all a dream and next time I opened them my face would change. I wouldn't be Heather any more.

I willed it. Then I opened them and there I was, large and pink, with the moisture sliding down the mirror like tears.

I suppose all teenagers feel like this, but I didn't speak to them on the subject. My only friend was Gwen and she did most of the talking. She was the one who told me about my little piggy eyes.

I'd developed earlier than her but she was the bossy type; she'd seen me in the cloakroom at school, slipping my package into the bin. I'd hoped nobody had seen, but she grabbed my arm.

'Porks, you spoilsport! There I was, telling you what my Mum said, about periods,' she glared at me, 'and you'd started already!'

I willed someone to come in, so she'd stop. But then, knowing Gwen, she might tell them too.

'You told your Mum?' she asked.

I nodded, truthfully, because I was sure Mum knew, though it hadn't been mentioned. She'd taken me out shopping to buy my two bras, some months before, and had asked me, in the bright embarrassment of the changing room, if they'd told me about feminine hygiene at school. I'd nodded, untruthfully, and that had been that. She must have glimpsed me at home, as furtive as herself, but I knew she wouldn't let on that she'd seen.

'You lucky thing!' breathed Gwen.

I stared at her. 'What?'

'Don't look so superior. Look at little me.' She turned to the mirror and smoothed her cardigan flat. 'Not a sausage.'

She started bemoaning her fate then, so I began to relax.

Dad was the one who touched my breasts, not me. I looked at myself for hours in the bath, and sideways, standing on my bed, but I never touched that area except when I adjusted my bra. I knew it was dreadfully wrong to fondle yourself, there or below; I knew this one rule and I kept to it, through all my confusions, because it became so important. It was the one thing I could do – rather, refrain from doing – myself.

This soft, pink body that I had to carry around . . . I didn't want to admit it was mine, yet it was. And it was the only one I'd ever have. At primary school we'd chanted a rhyme:

> It's a strange, strange thing, as strange as can be,
> Everything Miss T eats, it becomes Miss T.

Yet Dad, when he stroked my breasts, he called them 'bubbies'. They didn't belong to me, then.

'How's them little bubbies?' he'd murmur in that shaky voice. 'They're liking it, see? They're liking it when I do this . . .'

They weren't mine. I never called them that; I never ever would. But I'd lock the muscle in my head, and let him. I didn't stop him . . . I knew I wouldn't.

Then sometimes when I was alone, sitting in my bra and knickers, I'd wonder if the other girls felt just a bit like I did about my body. The trouble was, I'd gone too far now ever to find out. What I was doing was so deeply wrong that I'd never know; I'd lost track of Gwen and Co. One of the many casualties of all that happened was that I never knew how a teenager was supposed to feel.

But then teenagers were meant to be mixed-up, weren't they? My magazines said so. Perhaps I was getting confused about something that was quite normal. Looking back to when I was eleven and I'd slept with Dad those nights, I knew I'd felt anxious. But I'd also felt that surely there wasn't anything to worry about, because he was my Dad and so he must know the right thing to do. If I couldn't trust him, who on earth could I trust? It was all my fault that I was muddled. And later on, during the next couple of years, when things had become much worse, I still wondered if I wasn't making a fuss about nothing. I still felt he must know.

By then I'd visited Gwen's home and seen how different it was to mine – I've told you about that, and how upsetting it was. But there were a lot of girls who might not be like Gwen – that was the point of school, wasn't it, to meet all these different people when you'd never met any at home? Perhaps at Janet's place, or Margot's, I would glimpse some clue that would make me feel better.

But I never did – I looked, all right, you can be sure of that. I never did, and I never knew them well enough to ask.

I said before that realizing something's wrong doesn't come at the expected moment – when you're doing the wrong thing, or even thereabouts. In my experience, anyway, it doesn't. It happens during some humdrum moment; it might be days or months later. My first inkling had been when I'd lied to the flower-lady; something had shifted inside me, then.

The second stage was more complicated, and gradual. It wasn't until I was thirteen, and Dad and I had been having sexual intercourse for a year, that I let myself begin to realize what was happening. Pretty stupid, you might think. It may seem odd, not to dare for so many months, but it didn't seem odd at the time. It seemed the only way I could manage to walk down the drive each morning to catch the bus, and sit just like a normal pupil in class, and mooch around the playground, one of a huddle, just like the others, and help my Mum just like an ordinary daughter without a care on her mind, trotting down to the phone box to call up the electricity, sucking my Biro over the shopping list and even chiding my Dad, oh yes, quite jauntily, when he trod mud across the lounge. And loving Teddy, who kept me sane. Slapping him, and getting maddened, but loving him all the time.

It's a wonderful object, the mind. What you can stop it doing. For months I did manage to keep myself separate – just – from what was happening. I was still innocent, you see, somewhere deep inside. It wasn't so bad, in the beginning. During my first year at the big school he sometimes kissed me, in that hot, uncomfortable way, and fondled me as he had in his bed. It didn't happen often; not even once a week. He didn't have that many opportunities because those months Mum was working early and she was home by four. And I'd also got to know the signs. I'd be in the hen-house, for instance. The hens were my job. I'd be crouched down, searching for the eggs, when darkness fell. He was behind me, standing in the doorway and blocking the light.

'What we'd do without our Heth,' he'd say. 'You're a good girl, know that? What would your Dad do without you?'

Then he'd come in, all affectionate.

So I stayed away from the hens. Now I was in the big school, in Class One, I had homework to do, so I stayed indoors in the lounge. Mr Talbot was ever so pleased with my progress. He said,

'Heather's an example to you all.'

Another thing I did was to use the toilet at the garage. As I said, our bathroom door didn't lock. Dad wouldn't come in, I was nearly sure of that, but I never felt quite safe. I could get down to the petrol station without being seen, by wriggling through the hedge and trotting down the depot road; it ran alongside our drive but it was hidden by the hedge.

The toilets were out of sight of the booth; nobody seemed to use them, and the attendant had to stay at the pumps. A few years later the garage was modernized into a self-serve. This struck me as appropriate; after all, I'd been doing it for years.

Sometimes I'd wander into the forecourt, all *insouciante*, and look at the bags of sweets on the swivel stands. There was a shop, with plush Snoopies in it and car deodorants on golden chains. The walls were covered with that plastic panelling I told you about, which Dad had nicked for Kanga's house. The attendant I remember best was the Indian one. He didn't seem to mind me wandering around; he was just right – not too aloof and not too familiar. In fact, he once gave me a packet of Polos. I felt relaxed at the garage. Nothing was demanded of me. I was reassured by that big public road.

I wasn't exactly escaping. You must remember that in those days, when I was only twelve, I still loved my Dad and felt I shouldn't be avoiding him. That's why I did it on the sly. If he knew, then he might turn cold on me and I couldn't bear that. I still adored him being pleased with me and taking me on his knee. I kept my wariness well hidden and I soon learned to distinguish the times when this was safe – in company, or when he was being vague and ordinary, sort of breezy and *known* – and the times when it wasn't.

I want to get on to when I was thirteen, a teenager. I don't want to talk about the first time it happened. By it, I mean the sexual intercourse. I want to tell you when I began to change in myself, which was later. Still, if you want to know the facts, it happened first – only partially – when I was twelve, and four more times that year. I don't want to remember when, or where. If you were a psychiatrist you'd be stopping me here, I bet. You'd be asking me questions and pulling me back. That's why I refused to see one. With you, it's easier. If you're still there, listening, you'll only hear what I can tell you, and if it's too painful for me, then I'll stop.

82

It wasn't hard to pretend nothing happened, because half an hour later everything was back to normal, just like that. Another thing I must say: I was never forced to do anything. I didn't have to be, because he was my Dad.

I do remember the exact moment when I lay soaking in the bath, aged thirteen, and realized how wrong it was. Not just wrong of me – I was used to that feeling – but wrong of him. I'd suspected it, of course, for ages, but I'd never dared admit it. Can you understand why? If you can, you'll know why I lay there without moving. And why I didn't move as the bathroom grew dusky, and the bath water grew cooler and cooler until it was quite cold.

Teddy used to break things. He snapped all his crayons in two, and he smashed the shed windows. He'd go into the field and pull up the cabbages. I wasn't like that. Nothing showed, with me. When I was young I was an open little girl, I trusted everyone, but I'd long since lost that. Even if they were the noticing kind, which they weren't, nobody in our house could tell that I was changed that evening and afterwards.

I didn't behave differently; I just felt different, through and through, because I'd realized: *it's his fault too.* I didn't dare repeat it to myself in those words. But as I climbed out of the bath, those words were spreading and settling inside me.

The next day, Saturday, I had a dentist's appointment. The surgery was in Staines. I went there early, on the bus, because I wanted to do some window-shopping. But there wasn't a bus back so my Dad said he'd pick me up.

I was terrified of the dentist. Nobody likes going, of course, but I didn't know if my fear was normal. As I said, I couldn't tell if I felt like everybody else. I was nervous of the pain, oh yes, but the terror came from the dentist finding something out. I felt this with anyone official who examined me. The doctor, for instance, and even our games teacher, who'd discovered a verruca on my foot.

My mouth, surely, could give no clues – logically it couldn't. But the pitiless, antiseptic smell, and the white coats, and that probing light inside my throat, and the way he paused, with his

pointed instrument in my teeth, and frowned, and looked closer
. . . Then the way he turned to his assistant, who was standing
right near me, and said something in code which she wrote down
in a file. Perhaps you can understand that when it came to rinsing
out, the assistant had to hold the glass against my lips because my
hand was too trembly to do it myself. Pink water splashed out of
my mouth.

'All shipshape.' Mr Downes smiled. I'd had an injection, and a
filling. He laid his hand on my shoulder. 'All over now, Heather.
Okey-dokey?'

I nodded.

'Never as bad as we'd expected, is it? You're a brave girl – just
one hole, but a biggy.'

I was given my coat.

'Anyone picking you up?' he asked.

'My Dad.'

'Ah . . . the elusive Mr Mercer. Janice, you've sent him a remin-
der, haven't you?'

'Two.'

Dad always threw them away; he was like a child about the
dentist.

Then my heart stopped. What if they gave him gas and he
started talking? People said things, under gas; he'd told me so. *All
your little secrets*, he'd said, *all pouring out*.

'Janice can pop down with you. Is he downstairs?'

'No!' I lied. 'He's waiting miles away!'

'Miles?'

But I was clattering down the stairs.

Dad was sitting beside the reception booth. 'What's the hurry?'
he said. 'After you with his drill?'

I was outside now. I ran to the truck. Wrenching open the door,
I caught my breath at last.

We drove away. For the first time, out in the open, I thought:
it's not just *my* fault that I can't look Mr Downes in the eye. It's
not just my fault that I've behaved so oddly. It's yours too. Why
did you let me get like this, when you're my Dad?

On the way back he had to stop to see a mate of his about a dog – Rinty had been run over the week before. Perhaps that's another reason for my behaviour; I'd loved Rinty.

I stayed sitting in the van. The sun was setting and the sky was streaked yellow. I should feel peaceful, now the dentist was over. The road was a cul-de-sac; there were bungalows down one side. The other side was a field, clumpy with gorse, and beyond it the raised bank of the reservoir. There was no real countryside around us, I realized: just forgotten fields like ours, scruffy and neglected.

The sunset was so beautiful; it seemed a waste that I was feeling this way. Farther down the field someone was trotting round and round on a pony. Behind them stood the electricity sub-station; a brick block with wires criss-crossed above it. It was all spoiled, our countryside, with its ugly buildings. I wound down the window to clear the fug. Near my face the hedge was cobwebby with old man's beard, draped around the branches; on the black twigs the berries looked like beads of blood.

'Up, down, up, down . . .'

A woman was shouting at the girl, I could hear them now. I recognized the girl on the pony: it was Sandra, from my class.

'Toes up! Heels down!' The voice carried on the autumn air.

Girls at school had pets, I realized – Gwen with her guinea pigs and tortoise – and I just had animals. I was different. Another thought struck me. Perhaps the dentist thought Dad couldn't read – that's why he wanted to remind him about an appointment. You see, my thoughts were clear and unwelcome that evening.

Dad climbed into the cab.

'A bitch.' He shut the door. 'Never told me it was a bitch.'

'What's wrong with a bitch?'

'Too temperamental. Moody, like, when they're in heat.' He inserted the key. 'Have half the neighbourhood sniffing round our door.' Then he turned. 'How's Heth, then? He filled your teeth?'

'Just one. He said I'd been looking after them very well.'

'That's my girl,' he said vaguely, patting my knee.

The drill had hurt. I so wanted to be comforted. Sandra and Gwen would have been.

'I had an injection, but it still hurt.' That was the wrong thing to say, because his voice softened.

'Poor old Heth . . . Hurt a lot?'

'Not really,' I lied, willing him to start the engine.

'Poor old Heatherbell . . .' His hand was rubbing my knee. 'Poor old mouth.' He pushed back the hair from my face.

'Up, down, up, down!' yelled the lady.

'Poor old mouthy,' he said again. His face came close, his breath warm. 'Daddy kiss it better.'

I drew back. 'They'll see.' I raised my eyebrows, jerking my head towards the bungalow. 'Your mate will.' Then I said, 'And my friend Sandra's in that field.'

A silence. His hand remained heavily on my knee. I'd said it aloud: I'd spoken about what we were doing.

Stunned by my words, I couldn't move either. I remember counting the wires against the streaked sky. I didn't dare look at anything closer. At that moment I was apart from my Dad, because I had spoken about us. And that made us terribly together. I felt so old.

He reversed the van, abruptly, and turned it round. We drove up towards the main road. I've been trying to pin-point the stages, telling you how I was losing my innocence. This was one moment. And – see, he wasn't even touching me. But as I said, it happens when you least expect it . . . lying in the bath, and then sitting in the cab. My body had been violated before then, oh yes, but not my spirit. And, please take it from me, it's the spirit that matters.

I watched Sandra as we drove past. She held herself so straight and proud; her hair floating up and down.

On the way home he pulled into a lay-by. The sun had set; the passing lorries had already switched on their headlights. He turned off the engine. There is nowhere on earth as lonely as a lay-by. In my heart I'd wanted him to stop; I knew, now, that this was all the consolation that I deserved. It was the only comfort we could give each other.

A field stretched to the far motorway, with its raised arc lights. We were under the flight-path; in the field stood beacons, too tall for their surroundings, dwarfing the bushes. They were as tall as telegraph poles, with lights on top. As he drew my head on to his shoulder, as I knew he would, I was thinking that they must be put there in some pattern, a lit grid that made sense to planes in the sky, but that down here they were just big stupid poles.

'I've been a bad boy,' he mumbled into my hair. 'That's what you said . . . I've been a bad, bad boy.'

He meant it, but he was also working himself up. I knew both those things, now. 'Will my Heatherbell forgive me?'

I didn't nod, but I didn't move away either.

His voice thickened. 'Does she know how much I need her?'

I nodded then. I did know.

'How lonely I am . . . how blooming lonely?' He rubbed his nose up and down in my hair. He paused. It took him some time to speak. 'Both of us is that, aren't we?'

He rested his head against mine. 'Ever so lonely.' We sat quite still. 'Whatever's going to become of us, Piglet?'

I couldn't answer this.

'I'd do anything in the world', he said, 'to stop you being harmed . . . never want you hurt, in all your life . . . You know that, don't you . . .' He pushed back my hair, strand by strand, and then he kissed my ear. 'You're so precious, that's why. My precious . . .' His voice grew thicker. 'Even if I'm a bit of a naughty boy . . .'

His hand moved inside my blouse. His hand was big, and dry, and so warm. 'They know it too, don't they . . . so soft . . .' His voice was almost inaudible now. 'They're wanting me to give them a kiss . . . so they're knowing for sure . . .'

His mouth closed over my skin; his moustache tickled. His mouth was very soft; he was never, ever rough. You must believe me. He paused, and murmured,

'Your little heart's beating . . . beating like a bird, a wild, wee bird, trapped in there . . .'

He straightened my blouse again, carefully. Outside, in the

dusk, a heifer rubbed itself against one of the poles. The traffic rumbled past; nobody was stopping. He rested his head against my chest. As always I felt awkward about my plump stomach, beneath his chin, but I also knew that he shouldn't be the one to rest his head there; my plumpness shouldn't belong to him . . . But my lumpy growing had been under his touch.

'There's someone else wants to tell you too . . .' His breathing was quickening now. 'Someone else needs you . . . you know he does . . .'

His hand closed over mine. It stayed there a moment. The van shook as a lorry thundered past. Then he lifted my hand and carried it down to his trousers. 'So lonely, he is . . . there's only one person can take his loneliness away . . .'

He was undoing his buttons. I didn't help, but I didn't stop him. The fabric sprang back.

'. . . just one darling girl can do that . . .'

I kept my head turned away from him; I kept my eyes on the field with its tall lights. The heifer was ambling away. My fingers, guided by his, felt skin. It was tucked away, bulging, but he was tugging at the last button. I never knew what to do with my fingers; they were useless. The trousers were open; it sprang up. It still shocked me, when it did that. It was too big and sudden.

'See . . .' he murmured, 'he's all ready . . .'

He couldn't put it into me, not here in the cab, beside the road. I was glad about that. He was holding my hand, guiding it up and down, as if I were doing it all by myself. I was squeezing my eyes shut now, and clenching my brain. His breath was making fluttery sounds so I knew it would soon be over . . . the seat was creaking with his movements. I bit my lip and it hurt; the dentist's numbness was wearing off.

My eyes were wet, but when he finished I kept my head turned away, as I always did, so he wouldn't see. If he saw, he would be certain to start sobbing in that horrible way. I couldn't bear us both to be crying.

Besides, I needed to keep something to myself . . . something of my own, that belonged to me, even if it was just my tears.

88

I had changed, that day. I'd become tougher. Do you know how I can tell? Because, though this sort of scene, and more, had happened several times before with my Dad, this particular evening is the first one that I can bear to describe.

Chapter Seven

If you're wondering why I didn't stop my father, for all those years, I'll tell you the answer: if I'd stopped him, he might have stopped loving me. And nobody else would.

You might be wondering other things by now. What about my Mum? And didn't I know the facts of life?

If you think I'm keeping my Mum out of this, you'd be right. But remember, she kept herself out of it – out of anything that went on, whether it was something she might have been sharing or not. She hadn't run away again, but she seemed as removed in spirit, nowadays, as if she'd been out of the house. She was at work, of course, a lot of the time. But even at home she hardly spoke to my Dad, and when she did it was with that taut look on her face. Sometimes I thought this was even worse than their flare-ups. She sat tight, scattering ash.

When I was younger she had been pretty, but it was hard to believe it now. About once every six months I heard those noises through the wall; but there she was in the morning, waxy-yellow and thin-lipped as ever. Sometimes she softened with us children, especially Teddy, but most of the time she left us to our own devices. She complained of aches and pains and spent more time in her bedroom with the door closed. Teddy barged in but I didn't dare, which was probably my fault. Occasionally she took in her magazines with her, but often she didn't even bother. It worried me terribly that she didn't want to watch the TV; I once suggested that I brought it in but she just looked at me and said,

'Why?'

I did try to get close to her. As I said, I think she wanted it as I grew older but by then my secrets made it impossible. She didn't encourage it, and children don't know how to take the initiative. 'Shy' sounds sweet and soft and vulnerable, but truly shy people, like my mother, they've long ago learnt to cover that up. Vulnerable means they can be approached, but that's the last thing they want. So they become wary and cool, and awkward. Oonagh, who heard all Mum's woes, probably knew more about what went on in her heart than any of us. Even Teddy, who wasn't the sensitive type – even he, aged three, when he sang his favourite song,

> Yum, yum, bubble gum,
> Stick it up Heather's bum

even he often substituted 'Dad' for 'Heather', but never, ever 'Mum'. Even at three he knew it sounded wrong.

One good thing, by this time, was that I no longer felt entirely the cause of this. Aged thirteen I still felt responsible, but not in such a sharp way, because as I grew older I realized it was our life in general and my Dad in particular which might be more of a cause than me. You can imagine the relief. What I was doing with Dad made me feel just as bad, and in some ways worse, but at least I realized that I wasn't the sole reason for Mum's unhappiness. When you're young you're egotistical, aren't you? You think the world revolves around your little self.

I'm sure she suspected nothing. I say I'm sure. I don't want to think about this. If she had suspected it, and still left us alone together without doing anything about it, without being upset, or appalled, then the last shred of sense would have been taken away from my life.

As he grew older, the only person I had to watch was Teddy. He was a sharp kid. He had this knowing, grown-up look. At the age of three he'd pick some grass and weeds, put them into beer bottles and take them down to the main road. He'd sit on a cushion and shout at the cars to stop.

'Five pound!' he'd shout. 'One pound!'

He was always up to something; no wonder he got into such trouble later. The hens were too silly to keep out of his way; he'd chase them with sticks, shooting as he ran. He'd collect twigs and bits of pipe which he called his weapons and store them in the caravan, which long ago had been the Rosy Arms. Its door had fallen off now. Once I found a tin of cracked eggs, which he'd pinched from the hen-house and forgotten about, and which he called his bombs. I'd been upset about that and slapped him, which made me feel worse.

There was even more junk around now for him to play on. Being too old to play myself, I was now old enough to feel some of Mum's weariness about this. Nothing got moved; instead, more stuff was added. Dad was always going to repair the things, but soon the nettles grew up through the machinery. Teddy bounced up and down in his disintegrating car.

I wish you'd seen Teddy; I was proud of him, even though he was so wild. He had a crew-cut and he was really beautiful, because he didn't know it. Despite the tough talk, from the back he never realized how young he looked, with his tender skull showing through, and his delicate neck. He'd rush about for hours, breaking things up, then he'd drop asleep, just like that – he'd drop asleep wherever he happened to be, as if he were in a fairy story. With the cats stretched out beside him, sunning themselves, they looked as if they'd been put under a spell.

But once, when Mum was out and he'd fallen asleep on the carpet, Dad started cuddling me. I moved my head and there were those two round eyes, staring at us. He was picking his nose, calm as calm.

One day, when I was fourteen, I went out shopping with him and my Mum. There was a parade of shops about a mile up the road. First you passed our car park field, then the flower-lady's lay-by, then the pink placards. 'Bulbs!' they said, and 'Manure!' because it was autumn. Then you passed the market garden drive-in, then the Kodak laboratories, then a big brick factory called Delta Flexed Products; after that you passed the Skyscape Hotel, which had been fields when I was younger. Then you came to the big roundabout and traffic lights; if you survived the traffic you reached the shops.

I remember each detail of that day, you see. Most of the shops were called 'Ford Spare Parts', and 'Cargo Shippers', it wasn't that neighbourly, but there was a greengrocer and a post office. I was helping Mum to carry the shopping. We went into the post office to collect our allowance. It was a Saturday, and crammed with people, but nobody talked. While Mum waited in the queue I perched Teddy on the shelf with the Biros on strings, because he was demanding it. On the blotting paper he drew a picture of Micky, our dog, and something that didn't look much like a fire engine. Then he drew a person, one of his stick people with a big round tummy. Inside the circle he did a scribbly shape, he was a careless artist, then he announced in a loud voice,

'This is Hevver with a egg in her tummy.'

A silence. I stayed absolutely still, leant up against him to stop him falling off. Mum was at the grill, collecting the money . . . Thump, thump, went the man, stamping her book. In a moment she was beside us.

'Get him down!' she hissed. She slapped Teddy's arm. 'You wicked boy, sitting up there. It's not allowed.' She turned to me, two pink spots on her cheeks. 'You know it's against the rules!'

'I know.' I lifted him down. 'Sorry.'

'You know it's not allowed!' Her eyes were bright, and looking right into me. 'Can I trust you?' she whispered. 'Can I, Heather? Sometimes I wonder.'

My throat closed up, with no air getting through. 'I'm sorry, Mum,' I said in a low voice.

Outside the wind was blowing. Mum wheeled Teddy's old pushchair, piled with shopping. At the lights I held his small,

93

treacherous hand. I knew she wouldn't mention it again. Her head, in its tightly-knotted scarf, was bowed against the wind. Teddy was chatting to me, though the traffic snatched away the words.

He'd been an egg once, inside my Mum. Out of the corner of my eye I saw her, bowed and smaller than me, and the maroon blur of her coat. So had I, great big me. Dad had put us there. What was he putting inside me?

You probably think I knew about this long ago, what with all our animals. But for one thing I had a basically innocent mind – Teddy, as he grew up, was far more knowing about that than me. And for another, not a lot of it went on. Birth, yes; mating, no. Our dog was single; our pigs were all sows, and when the boar man visited I'd always stayed indoors because I feared him more than anyone – he was a huge, leery man with a skin infection. Sometimes our cock jumped on a hen, with some fussed fluttering, but I didn't connect that with big, bald humans. Teddy would, but I didn't.

No, like everyone else, I'd learnt from Yvonne. Last year she'd told all our class – her friends first and then, because she couldn't bear to keep it from the rest, her second choices, who she grabbed with a ruthless, sudden intimacy. She was like that. I never trusted her; and, after that afternoon, I've never forgotten her.

'You mean you don't know?' She raised her plucked eyebrows. 'No? Honestly?'

Gwen and I shook our heads. We were sitting against the wire mesh of the playground. Thirteen, and we still thought babies came from kissing.

'That the man puts his thingy up her bottom? Didn't you know, Porky?'

I must have shaken my head, because she seemed satisfied. Inside I had turned to water.

'It's terribly painful the first time, of course,' she said in a weary voice. 'Absolute agony.'

'Is it?' asked Gwen eagerly.

'Apparently. She has to lie on a towel,' said Yvonne, 'for the blood.'

94

Gwen swung round to me. 'Imagine!'

'She's blushing,' said Yvonne. 'I knew I shouldn't have told her.'

I couldn't speak. I thought, I didn't have a towel, and there hadn't been any blood. For a wild moment I thought perhaps it hadn't been the real thing.

'No, I shouldn't have told her.'

Pain: yes.

'You're probably too young to understand, you two.'

'We're not!' said Gwen. 'Go on, please.'

'He says he loves her, and things. And then his sperm goes in.' She added, patiently, 'That's the seed.'

'I know that's the seed!' said Gwen.

'Then it goes up her tubes, and she says she loves him too.'

He hadn't said anything. Neither had I. Then he had made that choked noise; then he had banged his head against the straw, again and again.

'But I thought she doesn't like it?' Gwen's voice came down a tunnel, far away.

'She has to do it, doesn't she?'

'You mean, that's what my parents do?'

'*Absolument vrai.* Every night.' Yvonne yawned. 'On the dot.'

After Yvonne had gone, Gwen wanted to talk about it. I said I had to tidy my desk. I knew she thought me priggish but for once I didn't care.

The classroom was empty. I sat at my desk, my hands damp and my heart thumping. Thank goodness nobody came in. Me, Heather: I was doing what people's mothers did. I'd known it, of course, but it was such a shock, Yvonne telling me . . . Nobody did it at my age; nobody's father would, in a thousand years. Nobody's but mine. And that's how babies were started.

The bell rang. As they all trooped in I remember one small, trailed-off thought: I wished it hadn't been Yvonne who'd told me.

So you see, I'd had a year to live with the knowledge, though I'd suspected it before. You might think that this made a great difference to me. It did, and it didn't. I knew we'd been doing something far too adult and terrible to think about, sanely. Nothing could make it worse, even knowing the words for it. I'd just become more confused, so I'd stopped it getting into my mind. At times I panicked, when I realized that this was how babies began. But in some curious way I still trusted my Dad. You might find this hard to believe, but it's true. It vanished later, but when I was thirteen and fourteen there was still some left. A child's trust has the stubbornest roots; it takes far more digging than you would expect, to pull out every little piece – it surprised me at the time, I remember, that I still relied on him. You can dig and dig, and there will still be some buried. And so I trusted him to be somehow doing it safely, in some special way he knew about, being grown-up and my Dad. I also remembered the health visitor's words, years ago, about it being impossible. She'd just been starting to say 'thirteen and fourteen', hadn't she, before she looked at her watch and hurried off?

So I shouldn't have been so shocked in the post office. But I was: I was terrified. Did Teddy know? Did Mum? As I said, I made myself go blank when I was expecting something to happen; I locked myself, inside. But I could still be caught unawares, at the stupidest moment.

The week after Teddy and the egg I stayed the night with Gwen. She called it a sleepover, because she was pen-pals with a girl in Detroit. We'd never mentioned it, but it was understood that these sleepovers took place at her home and not at mine. She obviously preferred that too. I felt secure in her house, but lonely as well.

Gwen pulled out the rubber band and brushed her long, brown hair. We were going to the pictures with her Dad. We'd planned in advance both to wear our frilly blouses. They were from C & A; we'd bought them together in Staines. Hers was yellow and mine was blue, on account of my blue eyes.

'Two little twinnies,' said her Dad as we sat in the car.

'Big,' corrected Gwen.

'Big. Aren't I the lucky one tonight, with two young ladies to escort?'

'We're sisters,' said Gwen. 'Go on, we're pretending.'

They had a lovely car, it was spotlessly clean. Her Dad worked at the airport. In the cinema foyer there was a shop.

'Please can we have some chocolate?' asked Gwen.

'Gwen!' he said. 'You know you're not allowed it.'

'Please. For a treat.'

'Your teeth. You know the rules.'

'Porky's allowed sweets all the time,' she sighed. 'She's so lucky.'

'She's with us now. Aren't you, Heather?'

He bought us some peanuts.

In the cinema he sat in the middle and put his arm round each of us, giving us a squeeze. The film was *The Railway Children*; I'd thought it sounded babyish but Gwen had insisted. She ate her peanuts with one hand; with the other she held his. Up on the screen, the father of the Railway Children was being taken away; two men in hats ushered him out of his front door. Now the children were crying.

Gwen was sobbing, too, noisily. Her Dad passed her his hanky and held it while she blew her nose. He put his arm around her and she buried her face in his jacket, keeping an eye on the screen. Gwen was a great sobber. Up there, the children were exploring their gaunt new home. Gwen had both her arms flung around her Dad now and he was patting her shoulder, gently, and mopping her with his hanky.

'Daddy!' she moaned.

'There, there,' he said in a smiling voice. 'Silly billy.'

'I can't bear it,' she croaked. 'Hug me tighter.'

He hugged her tighter. 'Funny way of enjoying yourself,' he said.

'It's so beautiful,' she squeaked, 'it's so sad.'

They sat there, Gwen clutched round him as if she were drowning.

'You OK?' He leaned over. It was too dark to see me.

'Yes,' I said.

'You're far too sensible,' he said, and went back to Gwen.

It was only when the lights came on that they saw my face. Gwen stared.

'Why didn't you say?'

Her Dad looked at me. 'You poor thing. My handkerchief's sopping wet, thanks to this silly girl here.'

'Don't worry,' I said, hiccuping, trying to stop. I couldn't. He put his arm round me and wiped my face with the back of his hand.

Gwen had recovered the moment the lights came on.

'It's only a *story*,' she said. 'It's only a film.'

People were standing up along the row, waiting to pass. I could get to my feet but I couldn't stop sobbing. We shuffled out, bumped by the other children. I was making a horrible noise, like an animal, I was frightened by it myself; I was usually so controlled.

'Poor old thing,' he said, ruffling my hair. 'It's not real – it's not *true*.'

I thanked him and agreed. But that wasn't the point, of course. I wasn't crying about the film. I was crying about Gwen and her Dad.

Afterwards Gwen was sitting at her dressing table. She'd taken off her blouse and was looking at herself in her white bra – she wore one now.

'Kevin almost kissed me, you know,' she sighed. 'He was going to. I could tell.'

Kevin was in the next class. This event, which I'd heard a lot about, happened at the monthly disco.

'Wonder what it's like, Porks. When they do.'

I was sitting on the bed behind her. My throat was sore.

'Where will I put my nose? Wouldn't it get in the way?'

Some answer was required by now, even for Gwen.

'I suppose it fits somewhere,' I said.

'Wonder who'll be first.'

'Pardon?'

'To have it done to them, dum-dum. We're lagging behind.' She pushed back her fringe and smiled at herself, like that, then let the hair fall across her forehead. Then she pushed it back again. 'Sandra has, Yvonne has, all that lot has. Betty let Dave put his hands on her bra. On the inside.' She looked at me in the mirror. 'I told you, didn't I?'

I nodded.

'She says you can tell they love you when they kiss your eyes.' She closed hers. 'Ever so gently . . . Strong and gentle. I shall shut my eyes and lift my head and see if Kevin does.'

'Do they have to?' I asked urgently. 'What if they don't?'

'It's the test, I'm afraid.' She pursed her lips in the mirror. 'Betty knows, you see.' She turned her head sideways, her lips still pursed, and kept her eyes on her face. 'My olive complexion – know what it shows?'

She paused and turned round.

'I said, know what it shows?'

'No. What?'

'That I'm highly sexed. I look a bit like Jenny Agutter, don't I?'

'Yes,' I lied.

'This greasy panel won't last long. It's only down the middle, you see. It's not real acne, that's what Dr Moss told me. Just a greasy panel.' She swung her head back, tossing her hair. Then she turned and swung round again, watching her hair settle. 'Betty said her nipples tingled.'

'Pardon?'

'Do stop blushing, Porks. Nobody can hear.' She moved her eyes back to herself. 'I won't let Kevin do that. Not until we're going steady. I'll just let him kiss me, and kiss my eyes, and tell me that he's mine and I'm his.'

She padded off to the bathroom, then, to do her teeth and put on her pimple ointment. I sat down on the dressing table stool. Its warmed plastic sighed beneath my weight. Behind me stood the shelf of dolls Gwen's Dad had given her; his friends the pilots brought them back from all over the world.

I gazed at my wide, pink face, still blotchy from crying. I'd worn mascara this evening but it had all washed off. My eyes looked piggier than ever. Actually my features were more regular than Gwen's; her mouth was too small and she had a receding chin. If I lost weight I might look all right. But that wasn't the point.

I'd dressed nicely for this evening. Below my face was the blue nylon flounce of my blouse, with the dear little buttons done up. I'd set my hair yesterday, to give it height; it was naturally fine and flat, like blonde hair often is, but it looked quite pretty tonight. It was held in place by my matching alice band.

I sat there, gazing at my face. Boys were supposed to be kissing it soon, cradling it in their hands. They should be looking into my eyes, unable to speak, and then kissing my closed eyelids, one then the other. They should be tracing round my lips, too moved for words. This face, my face, the only one for them. *I want you here in my arms, for ever.* There must be someone, somewhere, who would want to say that. For every girl, there's someone.

Quite often, spurred on by conversations with Gwen and the others, I found myself thinking like this. Thinking just like they did; joining in. 'Is my hair better up?' they'd say. 'Like this? Or like this? Don't I look nice with it parted on the side?'

Just for a moment I'd be swept along. Will they love me if I look like this? Will they?

Until suddenly I'd realize: nobody will, ever.

Gwen came in from the bathroom. She stopped when she saw my face.

'Gawd, she's off again,' she said. 'Niagara Falls.'

Chapter Eight

I t's dark outside now. It has been for some time. Heaven knows
what o'clock it is; I haven't switched on the light. I don't like to
catch sight of myself in the mirror over there. Besides, if I turn on
the light I'll have to get up and start some sort of evening. I'd
rather stay here, in the dark. The only thing I've done is switch on
the electric fire. It takes ages; the bar's just reddening now.

I must have been fifteen before I stopped trusting my Dad. Trusting him meant loving him, and some time during that year my love
was at last extinguished. It had taken a long time, hadn't it? I've
told you how stubborn and stupidly persevering it was.

Gwen had a Saturday job at a kennels. You know how our
place was surrounded by hotels. More were built each year . . . By
the time I was fifteen, along our road you could walk to the
Skyscape, the Excelsior, the Heathrow, the Sheraton . . . Flags
fluttered in front of them like some celebration that nobody had
told me about. Signs said: 'Heathrow Hotel Welcomes Glaxo
International'; the letters were changed daily, like menus. Along
our road, nowadays, you saw more courtesy coaches than Green
Line buses. And far behind us stood the Post House Hotel, a block
in the fog.

It wasn't just the humans who were temporary, it was animals too. They stayed at the Orbital Boarding Kennels. It was out beyond West Drayton, beyond Gwen's house, and next to the Orbital Trading Estate. Gwen was potty about cats and dogs and she earned £5 a Saturday. I knew what she was saving up for, because she never stopped talking about it: a tan suede coat with a fake-fur collar. Poor cows had died to make that coat, I told her, but she didn't see it that way. Cows weren't pets. I didn't see it that way either, but then I wasn't animal-mad. The coat was in the new boutique called Poppets, it cost £37.95, and I wanted one too – more than I remember wanting anything from a shop. This was OK with Gwen – as I said, we liked wearing the same things, it was one of our pacts. £37.95 was far beyond my reach, of course; nobody in my family had that sort of money. If Dad had it, and he was in the right mood, he would have bought the coat; he was indulgent like that. But he hadn't. On the other hand, Gwen's father could buy it easily, they had plenty of money, but he'd told her she must save the pennies herself.

'Old fogey.' Her crimson mouth was pursed; she'd just replenished her lipstick. 'He said, "I love you too much to buy it for you." I ask you!'

I decided on a plan. I'd get a Saturday job too, at the Skyscape's staff cafeteria. There was a vacancy, Betty's friend said so, because someone had just been sacked. If I had a job, I could save up for one of the coats myself.

So far so good. Simple, you'd think. But you must remember that during this time, when I was fifteen, Mum was working daytimes. Each day except Sunday she was back at four. This only left Saturday when my Dad and I were alone. By this time the physical thing was taking place regularly, and it was on a Saturday. Teddy would trot across to the garden centre where his friend Ross lived, who had more weapons and a bigger TV than ours. Dad would come into the house, where I was dressmaking, and say he was shagged out and what a thirst he had on him. I'd make us some tea.

I told him I was going up to the Skyscape, to ask about a job. I told him when we were alone; see, I was learning a little more each day.

'You're what?'

'Just the Saturdays,' I said. 'It's seven pounds.'

'The Saturdays?' He busied himself with his baccy tin. He rolled his own fags now because it was cheaper.

'Then I can pay my way.'

His eyes slid up to mine, then down again. 'You're needed here.'

'Why?'

He wiped his nose, and mumbled at the carpet. 'You're needed, aren't you? Let's say no more about it, eh, girl?'

'For who?'

'Who?'

'Yes, who? Who am I needed for?'

His big, stiffened fingers held the Rizla packet. He turned it over and back again in his palm. The paper poked from the slit. 'Your little brother . . . The house, and such.'

'Teddy's off all day now.' I paused. 'Look, I'll ask Mum. She'll agree.'

The packet stilled. 'Leave her out of this. She's got a lot on her plate at present.'

'I need money of my own. I can't ask you for it, you haven't got any. There's this beautiful coat, for £37.95. All the girls do it.'

'Not my girl.'

'Why not? Why am I so different?'

He kept his eyes down. 'I'm not having it, that's why.'

'Why am I different, Dad?'

A pause. 'Need someone around . . . To get the dinner . . . watch the car park.'

At the feebleness of this even he stopped. If we were lucky there was one car a week in the field, due to the increased competition. Three more hotels had built off-airport parking lots.

There was a silence. We both knew what we were talking about; what was really at stake. During these months there was a growing air of conspiracy about what we were doing. We never spoke of it, of course, but it had become so regular that neither of us could pretend it wasn't planned to time with Mum's absences. Never mentioning her was a conspiracy too.

Both of us were thinking hard. I wanted that job badly. Any job, to be out of the house on a Saturday, with a proper excuse. And I needed the money, of course – not just for the coat, but for the reason everyone needs it: independence. Gwen and Co were always going on about independence nowadays, too, but I couldn't tell if the word meant quite the same to them. As usual, I didn't feel in step.

On the other hand, I felt anxious about what Dad would do if I took away our Saturdays.

At this moment he might have leaned towards me, his voice softening, and said what was poor old Dad going to do without his girl, didn't she love him? But I'd planned this talk for when Teddy was around. We could hear him in the yard, being a police siren.

'Mum would be glad of the money,' I repeated.

'*Da-daa, da-daa* . . .' wailed Teddy.

'You would too, wouldn't you?' I asked.

He didn't answer. For the first time in my life I was feeling a tingling in my scalp, a quickening of my pulse. What I was feeling was the beginnings of power.

'Got to push off,' he said. 'Got to fetch that big end.'

'*Da-da, da-da,*' wailed Teddy.

'We'll talk about it tomorrow.' He laid his hand on my arm. 'Let's keep it to ourselves. Right?'

The next day he took the lorry out and he wasn't back until evening. Mum was in the bedroom. He shuffled around for a bit, taking off his jacket and blowing his nose. I was stretched out on the settee pretending to do my homework. In front of me lay my geography book.

' "Eighty per cent of the population" ', I read out, ' "don't know which state the Grand Canyon's in." '

A clump as he took off his boot.

'Go on, guess,' I said.

'What's that?' Another clump.

104

'Which state it's in.'

'In America, isn't it?'

'Arizona. Most people say Colorado.'

His feet, in their socks, came nearer. For a wild moment I thought he was going to look at my book and actually ask me more. He'd never done anything like that. But he leaned down and put something on the page. It was four ten-pound notes.

'That'll do you?'

I didn't speak. Just then the door opened and Teddy rushed in. In the draught, the notes floated to the floor. I grabbed them but too late.

'What's them?' he shouted. 'What's Hevver got?'

'Nothing,' I said, snatching them up.

'You've given 'em her. Why's she got 'em?'

'Shh!' I hissed, looking at the bedroom door.

'Gimme some too!' he shouted.

Dad slapped him across the face. Teddy burst into tears.

'It's not a present!' I said. 'Don't cry. I was owed it.'

'You wasn't!'

'I was. Shut up, Teddy. I did something and he paid me.'

I stopped. I looked at Dad . . . His mouth hung open.

Teddy went snuffling into the kitchen. I hadn't even comforted him. But Dad followed him. His voice was high and strained.

'Didn't mean to do that,' he was saying. 'Didn't mean to hit you, boyo.'

I hid the notes in my geography book. Looking back now, I realize: it wasn't just me who'd been losing my innocence. In a strange way, Dad had been losing his.

As I said, it was such a gradual process that I can't pin-point one occasion. But that winter's day I first felt the stirrings of power . . . the realization of what I could do.

Corrupt, see? Oh yes, I'd been a victim, but nobody stays a victim for ever. They learn. That little girl was older and wiser now.

Around that time I started looking clearly at my father. I never had before. One thing I saw, with surprise: he was as confused as I'd been, by all this. He wasn't a bad man, you see. If they found him out, people would say he was bad, but they didn't know him like I did. Another thing I allowed myself to admit: he was a big, blundering, inadequate person. His body was harmful but inside he was as weak as a baby. He was the laziest person I'd ever known. A jolting thought: perhaps it wasn't love for me that had made him do those things – perhaps he was just too lazy to get up and find somebody else. I shut this one off.

Mum was right when she called him a slob. In fact, I might be feeling some of the things she'd felt years ago, when she still loved him enough to be disappointed. I saw now that she'd given him up, for good.

My timid, blind love was finally slipping away. I didn't mourn its going. In an arid way, I was relieved.

If you think I stopped feeling guilty, you're wrong. I had even more to be guilty about now, and it was sicklier and more complicated. But I just buried it deeper, where it did more damage.

A few weeks later I visited Gwen at the kennels. I hadn't got a Saturday job, of course. The £40 had stopped that. He'd given me another £20 the next week, too, so I knew I couldn't try.

The dogs barked at me, flinging themselves against the wire. I was standing in one of the pens, leaning against the netting. I wore my suede coat. Heavens, I felt grown-up in it . . . The tight, buckled belt around my podgy middle, and around my chin that furry sophistication. I ate too much because I was unhappy; it was all stodge because we were poor. I was going to lose weight. I was going to get out of all this. My coat had helped me make this decision.

'Let's go up the Sheraton tonight.'

'What?' Gwen leaned on her broom and stared. 'Why?'

'Pick up a couple of millionaires.'

She gaped, then her face relaxed. 'Gosh, Porks. For a moment I thought you were serious.'

She went on with the sweeping. I was serious; at least, now I'd said it. I was wearing my cream high heels, which pinched. I shifted on to the other foot and watched Gwen ducking through the door and pushing out the straw. Her jeans were muddy, just like my Dad's trousers; the floor was wet, with tan streaks. The kennels was a gloomy place; at least I thought so. It was hidden from the road by evergreen trees and woven fencing, mostly broken. It reminded me of home. Between the pens ran a concrete path; it was slimy with moss where the water butt leaked. The animal stench was familiar.

'All this for a fiver,' I said. 'Why don't you go somewhere nicer?'

Gwen lifted her face; it was radiant. 'I love it.'

'It's filthy.'

'I like a wallow.'

If she weren't so busy she might have added: no wonder you don't like it. At your place it's wallow, wallow, all the time. Gwen said things like this; she thought she was allowed to, being my best friend.

Thinking this made me angry, even though she hadn't said a word. She was untying the lead of a hefty brown poodle. It started passionately licking her face.

'You're such a goody-goody,' I said. 'I'll have to go with Sandra instead.'

'Go where?'

'The Sheraton.'

She turned, her face blazing. 'I'm not a goody-goody. Mum and Dad wouldn't let me.'

'Why should they know?'

'Would yours?'

'No.'

'Wouldn't they mind?'

'Oh yes,' I said quickly, hoping they would.

'Darling Bennie.' The poodle was standing on its hind legs now, showing its bald underparts. Its woolly arms were around her neck. 'Who's a lovely boy-boy?'

'Go on. Say you'll come.'

'Who loves his Gwenny-Wenny, then?' His pink tongue slurped over her smile. 'It'll be full of old men.' She gazed at the dog's face. 'Won't it, Bennie? You know what they'll be after . . . Only one thing.'

'So's Bennie, if you ask me.'

'Porky! You're getting awfully coarse. You never used to be.'

'I'm just facing up to the facts of life.'

'You didn't even know them, two years ago. Hey steady on, Ben.' She struggled with the arms. 'Remember Yvonne? Us two little innocents?'

'Yes.'

'Anyway, it's Sue's party tonight. Remember?'

I followed her as she collected dogs down the pens, opening one gate after another. Four large dogs bounded ahead, dragging her along. Through the side gate, a cinder path led down towards the canal. I hobbled after her on my high heels. On one side lay the school sports ground; on the other lay the riding-school field, with jumps made from oil drums. The dogs howled with joy; a piebald pony lifted its head and lowered it again. It had never crossed my mind to take our dog for a walk; none of us ever had. Gwen laughed as the dogs pulled her along.

'I can't keep up!' I shouted.

'See you tonight!' she called. 'I'm wearing my blue midi.' Her voice grew fainter. 'Can't wait to see Nick's face.'

Nick was her so-called boyfriend this term. I watched her from the back. The sun caught her hair clips. A smaller figure now, she half-skipped, half-ran. She wore her usual Saturday gear – dirty, Snoopy-patched jeans. I felt empty inside. I felt this most of the time nowadays. I watched Gwen, skipping down her sunny path.

Back home Dad said, 'Where've you been, then? I been worried.'

Dads should say this, of course, if you've gone off somewhere without a word.

'All dressed up,' he said.

'I went to the shops, then I went to see Gwen.'

'All dressed up and looking so pretty. Let's see my girl.'

His hand was on my buckle. Dad's hands were the ones that always undid my coat. Too big, his hands; too wrong. Gwen, who had bought her coat too, said that Nick tried to unbuckle it in the bus shelter but she'd slapped his hand and said, 'Naughty, naughty.'

'Dad, don't.' I was pressed against the fridge. 'Got to unpack the shopping.'

'Oh, Heather.' His voice was already hoarse. 'Give us a hug.'

He was humped against me, trembling. Lately he'd become more urgent.

'I can't. Where's Teddy?' See, we admitted this now.

'Still with his little mate . . . Heth, my love, I've been waiting here.' His breath was hot on my face. 'Waiting for my darling girl. Just sitting here on my ownsome.' His hands ran up and down my jumper.

'You been having a drink?' I was the only one who could ask this, and only when we were embracing like this and he daren't be angry.

'Just the one, Heth.' He was speaking the truth, I could tell by his manner. 'Waiting for my girl.' He pushed up my jumper. 'Waiting for my Heather-flower to come home.'

His hand stopped. 'What's this?'

'What's what?'

'This thing here.' He nearly touched my bra with his finger, and stopped.

'I told you, I've been shopping.'

I gazed down at my new brassière. It was black.

He paused. 'Don't know I like this.'

'It's not yours to like.' I kept my eyes on the black, lacy cups. 'It's mine. I was bored of white.'

'That's for bad girls. That colour.'

I didn't reply: *but I am a bad girl, and who made me it?* I said, 'I am fifteen, you know.'

'You been a bad girl, Heth? You been naughty?' He clenched himself against me, his voice muffled. 'You been doing something you shouldn't?'

Him daring to say that – it took away my breath. How could he? Head buried, he was fumbling with the new bra clip.

'You got a boyfriend, then?'

I shook my head. He was still fumbling; the bra was a front-opener, but I wasn't telling. I felt buzzingly blank. I'd bought my bra for all sorts of reasons, but not to make him talk this way. He was kissing me more roughly than usual; inside my mouth his tongue pushed round, thick and muscular. I'd wanted to change my bra before I saw him but I hadn't had time. I'd wanted it to be a new secret, just for myself. On second thoughts, perhaps I'd bought it to put him off, so he'd realize I was grown-up now.

Oh, I don't know why I bought it . . . I just wanted it. Now he was spoiling it like he spoiled all my clothes.

He was moving me towards the door. 'Come and give us a kiss,' he murmured. 'You big bad girl.' Still clenched together, my black breasts squashed against him, we were edging towards my bedroom.

'There's a party tonight. Must wash my hair.'

'Just five minutes,' he moaned, as he always did. 'Just a little five minutes.'

As we sank on to my bed, I realized that I wasn't feeling entirely blank. Something was stirring.

It was disgust. Disgust that he wasn't shocked by my bra, as he should be, but aroused. What had I hoped for? Wasn't I stupid, still to hope?

Later that evening, when Mum and Teddy were back, I asked him to give me a lift to the party. Such an ordinary request never sounded natural, when I asked it. The words had an edge, as if we both knew he had something to pay. Driving me a couple of miles was scarcely an equal bargain, but now I was older a threat hung in the air: *dare not to*. Of course he never dared refuse.

As I climbed into the cab I thought of the twenty other girls; I knew them all and they all thought they knew me. All of them were being given lifts by their Dads; they wouldn't have the first idea, not in a hundred years, what I meant by repayment.

110

'You're the smart one tonight.' He looked at my dress. Afterwards we always acted normally together, even when we were alone, as if nothing had happened. 'It's nobody special you're meeting?'

'Just the same old crowd.' I rubbed the cinders off my heel.

In fact Jonathan was there, as I knew he would be, and he was fetching me a rum and Coke, as I knew he would.

'You look glam,' he said, sitting down beside me.

'Couple of these and I'm anybody's,' giggled Gwen, plonking herself on the arm of the settee. This was a blatant untruth. She was nobody's except Nick's, and hardly his at all. She let him do her homework for her; he was much cleverer than she was. She let him kiss her, at the suitable moment, and hold her hand. The rest of the time he sat around while she cleaned out her guinea pigs and parked herself for hours at her dressing table, asking him rhetorical questions about her looks.

Jonathan, my one, was incredibly tall and narrow. He was Nick's best friend and both of us, I suspected, felt an air of obligation about getting together. He'd already held my hand in the pictures, when the four of us went together. Tonight we were due for our first kiss.

There was a special room for this, of course. Sue had got rid of her parents and turned off the lights in the lounge, where the snogging was already in progress. Jonathan and I were dancing to the Bee Gees – this was two years before the Sex Pistols and anyway we were an old-fashioned bunch, you've seen how we hadn't known the facts of life until we were thirteen. We jiggled about, wooden-faced like the others, avoiding each other's eyes. The lounge door was near us; when the record stopped we could hear the dark, concentrating silence within, and somebody choking on a cigarette. After the third dance, though we'd hardly worn ourselves out, he said, 'Phew.'

I'd caught him pinching his digital watch, to see the time. We all knew that Sue's parents were coming back at twelve.

'You whacked?' he asked, looking down from his height.

I nodded. He took my hand and led me into the lounge.

'Ow!' said a voice.

'Sorry,' he said, and squeezed my hand.

We stood still for a moment. The bodies in there made it stuffy; it smelt of smoke and everybody's different perfumes. It was pitch dark.

'Laurie!' someone whispered. 'Don't!'

Somebody else giggled.

Jonathan leaned down and whispered, 'That's Janet.'

'Wasn't it Yvonne?'

'Nobody on earth giggles like Janet.'

'That's true.'

He shifted his hand, lacing his fingers through mine, and squeezed. We stayed standing there; we felt, rather than heard, the room creaking and sighing around us. It was like being in the middle of a hedgerow. Those faint, scratchy sounds were girls, in their micromesh tights, rearranging their legs.

Jonathan leaned down and whispered, 'Shall we get out?' He paused. 'Do say if you want to stay – it's difficult because I can't see your expression.'

'No, let's get out.'

'What a relief!' He started edging through the bodies, towards the french window. 'Hold on tight. I don't want to lose you.'

I gripped his hand as we felt our way round the armchairs, and the warm bulk of the humans in them.

'Whoops,' said Jonathan. 'Sorry.'

We arrived; it was easier to see here, because of the street lights beyond the gardens. He fiddled with the catch and opened the french window. We stepped out. We stood on the chill, dewy lawn. He breathed deeply, then he whispered,

'Blessed is thy silence, oh night, after all that snapping elastic.'

The garden was bathed in a dim, white light. Behind us stood the house, packed with people; music thumped, as if its heart were beating. We stood silently, breathing the sharp winter air, then he crooked his arm.

'Ready, darling?' he drawled. 'Let's inspect the dahlias.'

I put my arm through his and we scrunched slowly down the path.

'Useful chappies, gardeners,' I said. 'What ho.'

'What ho indeed.'

He stopped, and plucked something from the wall. 'Have a peach.'

I opened my mouth and he pretended to pop something in. My lips brushed his fingers.

'Scrumptious?' he asked. 'Spiffing?'

'Sooper-dooper, darling. Here.' I copied him, plucking air from the wall. Against my fingertips his mouth felt warm.

I put my arm back into his. We proceeded around the garden. It was so small we had to go slowly, or we'd arrive back at the french windows.

We stopped at a row of canes, with dead stalks still clinging.

I touched them. 'Not quite ripe.'

'You mean the grapes?' he drawled.

'Quite so.'

'Do hope they'll be ready for when the Duchess comes to dine.'

I sighed. 'Oh, this social whirl.'

He stopped and picked a cabbage leaf, rolling it up and slotting it into the buttonhole of my dress. I did the same for him, poking one into his jacket.

'Let's give them the slip,' he said. 'What a spiffing wheeze. Let's hop on the yacht.'

'Madeira, yet again? . . . What about Majoorca?'

He squeezed my arm.

Suddenly he lunged off to the bottom of the garden. A garage stood there. Against its wall was a heap of bricks. He climbed to the top and held out his hand. I climbed up. He hauled himself on to the garage roof and sat there, panting. Then he hauled me up. In his normal voice he asked,

'You all right? Tights OK?'

I nodded.

'My little sister climbs like a monkey, you should see her. She's only eight.'

'What's she called?' I asked.

'Maxine. Awful name, isn't it? She hates it too. You'd like her.'

'Do you climb with her?'

'When nobody's looking. Are you freezing?'

I nodded and he put his arm round me. We sat hunched, looking at the lighted windows of the houses.

'Have you ever had an Advent calendar?' he asked.

'No. What is it?'

'Little windows and doors; you open each one and it's the most magical sight . . .'

We gazed at the assorted yellow windows.

'I'll buy you one before Christmas,' he said. 'It's not too late to catch up.'

We sat there in silence. I hardly dared breathe, in case I let out my joy. He touched my nose.

'Hmm, as I thought: icy.'

I touched his. 'So's yours.'

He tilted my head round and kissed me, terribly gently. I don't know how long it lasted. I heard the wind soughing through the garden trees, miles below.

Finally he drew back.

He said shakily, 'I've been longing to do that for two terms.'

I couldn't reply straight away. I said, 'Have you?'

'Haven't had much practice, though.'

'Haven't you?'

'In fact, none at all.' He rested his head on my shoulder. 'Zero.'

'Why not?'

'Never met anybody else I wanted.'

There was a long silence.

'Girls are more experienced than boys, aren't they?' he said. 'I mean, being mature earlier . . .'

I stayed rigid. I couldn't reply.

'One of the things about you . . .' he began, and stopped.

He wanted me to speak. At last I whispered, 'What things?'

'You don't seem like most of them . . . sort of brash and giggly . . . pretending to be all experienced.'

114

At last I said, 'Don't I?'

'No. You seem – well, innocent. *Proper.* Just right . . . as if you don't have to pretend anything.' He stopped. 'You're shaking. Here.'

He was struggling out of his jacket.

'Don't!' I said sharply.

He stopped, one arm in and one out. 'But your poor teeth are chattering. Listen.'

'Please don't!'

He stood up. 'I'd hate it if you caught pneumonia. Your parents would never let me see you again.'

I stood up too. Inside me, something screamed: *stop this! I can't bear it!* It made me desperate, hearing him talk this way. Didn't he understand . . . couldn't he *see*? Couldn't he tell that underneath my clothes my nipples were sore from my Dad rubbing them?

Just then he took something from his pocket and knelt down. It was a piece of chalk. On the garage roof he wrote, swiftly, in huge childish letters: I LUV HEVER. He stood up, then he dropped to his knees again and added: FOR EVER AND EVER.

Back in the house I told him that I was going to powder my nose. He said he'd make me a hot rum, and went into the kitchen. Perhaps he just thought I was too frozen to speak. I paused for a moment, looking back.

'Wotcha, Jon,' said Terry, nudging him. 'You been somewhere?'

But Jonathan ignored the remark, and eased his way through the crowd.

More people were dancing now. I found Gwen glued to Nick. Her father was going to pick us up; we'd arranged a sleepover at her house.

I grabbed her arm.

'What's the matter?' she asked. 'What's the hurry?'

'My Dad's turned up,' I hissed. 'I'm going home with him.'

'OK.' She closed her eyes again, in bliss.

I snatched my coat and was out of the house before the record finished. Clutching my fur collar I started running, clattering along the street. Tears were streaming down my face. I had no idea where I was going. My heart bumped against my ribs.

I left the houses behind. I couldn't run any more; my shoes were crippling me. Now I was walking fast along the lane, with bare hedgerows either side. It was foggy out here. In the orange sodium mist the lane looked like some nightmare when you can't close your eyes. Eventually I reached the main road. Headlights swung round; I was at the big roundabout two miles from home, right the other end of the airport.

It would only take half an hour to walk down this road, our own A4, back home; but home was the last place I could face. Opposite stood the Cosmos Hotel. It's built like a concrete tower; you've seen it if you've been down here. I looked at my watch. I thought it had stopped and held it to my ear. It was still ticking. Amazingly enough, it was only 10.45.

I crossed over the road. Inside the foyer there were plenty of people milling around, and suitcases stuck with airline stickers. It was too big and anonymous for the reception men to catch my eye, thank goodness. On the walls hung lights like slabs of rock. I found my way to the ladies', to calm down. Two women stood at the mirror, painting their lips.

'I could tell he was mad at me,' said one, 'because he started picking on Barbara.'

Sitting in the lavatory, I inspected my tights. There was a hole on the thigh, where I'd grazed it climbing down from the roof. My high heels were streaked with mud; I spat on some toilet paper and rubbed it off. My heart would not stop thudding.

The women had gone. My hair was flattened, damply, from the fog. I brushed it. Jonathan had kissed away my lipstick so I renewed it, painting a crimson mouth. I kept on my coat, as security I suppose.

The bar was dimly-lit. Some people sat at a table, roaring with laughter. Otherwise the customers, mostly men, were scattered here and there. I looked so adult, in my suede coat, that the barman scarcely paused.

116

'Rum and Coke, please.'

Beside me, two men turned back to their conversation.

'It was Wolverhampton.'

'Should've told me. I have influence in Wolverhampton.'

A snort of laughter. 'I was under the influence in Wolverhampton.'

The other one patted him on the back. 'Must toddle. Patrick's waiting in the lounge.'

He left. There was a silence. The barman brought my drink. The only money in my purse was a ten-pound note – if you remember, my dad had given me twenty pounds recently.

On the next stool the remaining man watched the transaction. His eyebrows rose.

'Ah . . . a kept woman.'

A pause. I could think of no reply to this.

He leaned over and patted my shoulder. 'Only my little joke. Don't mind me.'

I put all the change, all the crumpled notes, back into my purse.

'Drives my friends bananas,' he said.

I looked at him for the first time. He was nearly bald. In the dim light his face was as round as a moon. He had loosened his tie.

'All forgiven?' He must be waiting for a response. 'Shake hands and kissy-kissy?'

He held out his hand. I shook it, and turned back to sip my drink. Trouble was, I had difficulty lifting the glass. I don't think anyone noticed.

'Now we've got that straight, may I introduce myself? Name's Jim.'

'Hello.'

'And who do I have the pleasure . . .?'

'Heather.'

'Heather . . . lovely name for a lovely girl. Use these, Heather?' He offered a cigarette.

'No thanks.'

'And what's a girl like you,' he flicked his lighter, 'doing in this den of iniquity?'

I shrugged.

'Don't tell me, Heather – you knew I'd be here.' He snorted with laughter.

'I live down the road.'

'Do you, Heather? Can't say I know this area myself. Pass through it often enough.'

'Where are you going now?'

'Well, Heather, as my Nan would say, I'll be popping up to Bedfordshire.'

'Bedfordshire?'

'Beddy-byes, for my beauty sleep.'

'I thought you meant you were going there . . .' I gulped down my drink.

'What, me?' He snorted with laughter – it was a snort, I can't think how else to describe it. I told myself it was jolly. 'No, no, I'm off to Eytie-land. Six-thirty at the airport.' He looked anxious, but added, 'Still, always time for a drink with such a charming young lady. That need freshening?'

He swung round on his stool and clicked his fingers. From the side I saw his stomach, plump in the white shirt.

'Rum and Coke for the young lady, and a tonic water.' He turned back, tapping his head. 'Got to keep my facilities, as they say. Big day tomorrow.'

He took the tonic. I'd hoped he was going to be drunker than this.

'Big day, Heather. Got to be bright-eyed and bushy-tailed.'

'Why?'

'Heard of Milan, Heather?'

I nodded.

'That's where our fair's held. Bang in the middle of pastaland.' He paused, his voice sombre. 'Seriously, Heather, that man you saw me with just now – that man is Bernard Goodall, our vice-chairman.' He paused. 'Bernard and I get along fine, you might have noticed that. I think he enjoys my little jokes . . . Know why you have to have a few jokes, Heather?' He paused. 'So you'll be remembered.'

I glanced around the room. The barman was clearing the tables now. There were only two other men left; I couldn't start all over again. In the corner of my eye, I saw this man looking at his watch. How many months ago had Jonathan pinched his watch, to look at its light?

'I'm a lucky man, Heather. Bernard usually stays at the Sheraton, but there was some balls-up – pardon my French. Double-booking I expect. So he's here. As you saw, Heather, we had the opportunity for a good chin-wag. On a social, relaxed, level. That's very important, you know. I always say: one hour in the bar's worth eight hours in an office situation.'

I drained my drink. Thank goodness my head was starting to feel swimmy. It had taken long enough.

With a clunk the grid crashed down. There was a silence. I gazed at the caged bottles. Sue's parents would be home soon. What would he be doing?

'And what do you do with yourself, Heather?'

'Oh, this and that.'

'Well well.' There was another long silence.

'You're staying here?' I asked.

'For my sins.'

'Are the rooms nice?'

'Sure. All mod cons. Oh yes, Bernard appeared satisfied. May not be the Sheraton, I told him, but what can you expect for twenty quid a night?'

'I don't mind.'

There was a dead silence. As Gwen would say, you could hear the dandruff fall. This man was too bald for that. For some reason, I suddenly started giggling. I couldn't control it; I clutched my fur collar, juddering.

A hand touched my shoulder. 'I say, are you all right? Did I say something funny?'

My giggles had gone as fast as they'd come. 'Can I see it?' I said this quickly. If he didn't reply, I'd make a getaway.

'Sure, Heather. Sure, if . . . er, that's what you'd like.'

'Oh yes please.'

'Fine, fine . . .'

119

'What floor is it?' I asked wildly, for something to say.

'The third . . . Now where are those keys?'

He rummaged around, fiddling with this and that. He spent some time searching for his cigarettes. 'Where are the blighters . . .' he said.

We went outside. In the bright corridor he looked older. The pink skin hung on his face. He looked terribly tired. I wondered what his polished head would feel like under my fingers.

'Er, let's take the stairs.' He led me that way. By avoiding the lift, I saw, we also avoided passing the lounge, where his boss might still be sitting.

We walked along the carpet. Two hours ago I'd been scrunching along a garden path. Hard to believe, really, that it had happened at all.

'Bit of a pigsty, I'm afraid.' He was fiddling with the keys. 'Wasn't expecting . . .' He cleared his throat, 'er, such charming company.'

'It doesn't matter,' I said politely. 'Honestly.'

He opened the door. I went over to the window while he shuffled behind me, humming determinedly, pulling suitcases off the bed and doing something furtive with the underwear on the chair. He must have had a shower, all unsuspecting, when he'd arrived. Outside lay the airport, twinkling, and black office blocks. I suddenly thought: from Sue's upstairs windows they could read I LUV HEVER on the garage roof.

No doubt it would soon rain; it was a filthy winter. I pulled the curtains closed; they hissed like indrawn breath.

The chair was ready now. He pulled it out for me to sit down. He'd switched off the main light and put on the bedside one, with its tasselled shade.

'Nice and cosy,' he said, rubbing his hands and trying to sound happy. The poor man just wanted to get to sleep. 'Afraid I can't offer us a nightcap.'

He sat down on the bed, which creaked. 'Phew,' he said. 'Hot, isn't it?' He jumped up and took off his jacket. 'Shall I help you off with that, Heather?'

I unbuckled my coat and he took it.

'Nice piece of skin, this.' He was feeling the suede. 'How much did this set you back? No, wait, I'll hazard a guess . . . Thirty-five?'

'Thirty-seven.'

'I'm in the leather business myself, Heather. The skin trade, ho ho . . . On the wholesale side.' He hung my coat behind the door. 'Shame I didn't know you sooner. Could've got it at cost.'

'Thank you.'

'No trouble.'

He sat down on the bed again. There was a silence.

'Yes,' he said, 'nice piece of skin.'

'My boyfriend bought it for my birthday.'

At once the atmosphere eased.

'Boyfriend, eh?' He patted the counterpane. 'Come and tell me about him, Heather.'

I went over and sat beside him.

'What's he doing, letting a lovely girl like yourself out on her ownsome?' I felt an arm slide round my shoulder.

'He doesn't know.'

'Naughty naughty. You're how old? Sorry, I know ladies don't like to – '

'Eighteen,' I lied.

'A lovely, well-built girl like yourself.' He kneaded my woolly red shoulder. 'When you sat beside me, Heather, I can tell you now, yours truly couldn't believe his luck.'

We sat side by side in silence, gazing at his suitcases. They must be full of skins. I imagined them packed away there: bald brown skins, tan skins, blue skins, folded on top of each other.

'Shy, are we?' he murmured. 'Let me tell you something, Heather; I'll be frank. I'm not really in the habit of doing this either . . .'

He turned my face, to kiss me, and paused. 'Something's caught in your dress.'

I helped him pull out the cabbage-leaf. It tore, and the stalk stayed stuck in my buttonhole.

'Fancied a bit of gardening, did you?' he said, smiling.

I scrunched up the leaf and leaned forward to throw it in the bin. Behind me the bed creaked as he moved back, at long last, to switch off the light.

I shifted back, close to him. It was dark now. The one thing I didn't want was him to kiss me, so I started stroking his thigh.

'You do that to your boyfriend?' he murmured. 'Like that?'

I shrugged, pretending to be casual. His hand was round me, stroking my woolly breast.

'I'll be gentle, Heather . . . If this is what you want . . . If you're sure . . .' His voice was shaking now. 'Trust me . . . you can trust me . . . I won't take advantage – '

I moved my hand up his thigh. He gasped. My bold hand worked on. I felt for a button but he wore different trousers, proper tailored ones, with a metal clip. He was breathing hoarsely.

'Hey . . . Heather . . .'

My hand worked swiftly. I slid open the clip and pulled at the zip. It grated down. His underpants felt big and straining. I was breathing heavily too; for the first time in my life, I wanted it. He was shaking and very hot. Perhaps he'd get a coronary – salesmen did, didn't they?'

He shifted his position and I pulled down his trousers and underpants, right down to his ankles. I think both of us wanted to get it over quick. I kicked off my shoes and we keeled over. He pulled up my dress and I wrenched down my tights and knickers, dragging them off my feet.

'Jesus . . .' he muttered.

I was still sore from my Dad, that afternoon, but I wanted this so much I didn't care. I took it in my hand and it slid in easily. My face was burning and my mouth was full of saliva. He was trying to kiss me but I twisted my head away. I didn't want to touch any of him; I kept my hands on his clenched, surprisingly smooth buttocks, pressing him in. He was a short man and not as heavy as

122

my Dad, on top of me. His stomach was soft and he smelt of perfume. My Dad just pushed in and out but I knew what I wanted now. I gripped this body against me, wrapping my legs around him, and ground him into me, backwards and forwards. Heat was spreading through me, hotter each time, right up to my scalp. He was trapped around the ankles, his trousers hobbling him; up above, his shirt rubbed against my bunched dress. He pushed inside me harder now and then suddenly he cried out, a high, dying wail like a cat – a weirder sound than I was used to.

He lay panting, and much heavier.

I tried to nudge him on; I tried to keep grinding him against me. He mustn't stop. But he didn't seem to notice.

He stroked my hair. At last his breathing settled.

'Well, well,' he said, 'you're a hot little number, aren't you . . .'

He couldn't stop like this.

'. . . super little mover.'

I lay under him, rigid. He planted a kiss on my forehead.

'I don't think I'm flattering myself,' he murmured, 'if I said that you seemed to enjoy it too . . .'

I remained silent and in a moment his breathing grew deep and regular. In the pillow, his lips made a rubbery noise as the air blew out.

I offloaded him. We both grunted but he stayed asleep. I lay there, gazing into the blackness.

At some point during the night I think I slept a little. The room smelt stuffily perfumed, and sour. It seemed an age before the light showed dully behind the curtains. I climbed up and went into the bathroom. Then I came back and pulled on my tights. The room was growing visible. One of my shoes was kicked under the table. As I knelt down, I saw his order forms on the table; I'd jogged the leg and they'd shifted. Underneath lay his wallet.

He must have hidden it when I stood at the window. I looked at the plump little man lying there, curled up, his trousers round his feet. He'd actually hidden his wallet, just in case.

I opened the wallet. No, he needn't have worried, I wasn't going to pinch his money. I found his business cards and held one to the light.

Walter, he was called. Not Jim. South Midlands Sales Representative for El-Dee-Kay Modern Leathers.

I pulled out a photo and went to the window. It was a colour snap. He wore a paper hat, and on his knee sat a little girl as plain as himself. They were both smiling, their eyes red as rabbits in the flashlight.

I put it back, put on my shoes and took one last look at him. Not Jim, but Walter. He hadn't even told me his name. I didn't feel anything; just numb.

As I tiptoed out, I wondered idly if he'd remembered to set his alarm. He did have to be bushy-tailed, next day.

I didn't really mind; it was no concern of mine.

I bet he had set it, though. He was that sort.

The rest of term I avoided Jonathan. He tried to stop me in the corridor.

'What did I do wrong?' he cried, in front of the whole Lower Sixth too.

I just shook my head and pushed past, holding my books like a shield. He sent me notes; I read them and hid them in my bedroom. Once he actually came to our home. I saw him, tall and sudden in his black school blazer, walking up our drive. I ran to the caravan and crouched amongst Teddy's sweet wrappers. My Dad bellowed for me but I stayed there in the rubbish.

In the end Jonathan had to give up, and I learned where not to look in morning assembly. Summer came. In June I passed four O-levels and left school, and left those friends I had long outgrown. Or who had outgrown me.

Chapter Nine

Y ou're probably feeling less sorry for me by now. I can't help
that. In fact I couldn't help anything. When you're young it's
obvious that you're helpless, isn't it? But when you're older it
doesn't show, and people don't know how to be sorry for you
because you don't let them. By the time I was sixteen you wouldn't
have liked me so much, not if you'd met me. Somebody said I had
a 'blank look'; this was helped by the thick black eyeliner I used
then. Another man, who I met at the Holiday Inn, said I was dead
from the waist up . . . But then his pride was hurt and he was
saying all sorts of things. None of them guessed that I was so
young. Most people took me for twenty-one, which is what I told
them if they asked.

If I'd had a stronger personality, who knows, I might have
overcome my past. But misfortune doesn't just happen to people
like that; it doesn't choose people who can cope. In my *Golden
Book of Bible Stories* there was a tale about a man who'd lost his
sheep, and his ass, and his children, and his house, and still
managed to forgive everyone and become a nicer person. He knew
that God was waiting to reward him. On the opposite page there
was this beautiful painting of a staircase into the sky and masses

of clouds, all molten, with the steps leading up through them, through a golden gap. When I was small I loved that picture. But soon I stopped believing in God, and later I even stopped believing the picture, which was more of a wrench. Unlike that man, I didn't become a nicer person.

By now I was clued-up, of course. I'd read magazine articles and I knew it was called incest, and I knew that it happened to other people too. This was the most wonderful relief, you can imagine, as if doors inside me had opened to let in the fresh air. But it was also disturbing, because the people were described as 'cases'; they were separated off from the human race. Even more worrying, they'd all gone to court to tell the grisly details. I read those details, you bet, with an echoing sense of belonging. But what happened if someone found me out? In the photos their faces were blocked out, like criminals.

Things with my Dad had changed. I wasn't so frightened of him now, you've probably seen that. I knew he couldn't hurt me any more than he'd already done, it wasn't possible, and I knew that he wouldn't tell. But he was never sure about me, so I grew more powerful. There was this uneasy conspiracy between us, though we never put it into words. I'd realized by now that he was stupid, and pitiful – oh, I'd come to see so many things about him – but I was in too deep to stop it.

In too deep. Can you understand what I mean? That's the only way I can describe it. *Entangled* sounds lightweight, as simple as string. Snip, snip and you're out.

I was bound to him, I was in there with him, body and soul. I told myself that he meant nothing to me, that he was crude and inadequate, that he'd not treated me as a father should. But deep down I knew we were still bound together. We'd opened up our raw insides, the place nobody else would ever see, and what had happened would affect us until the day we died. Remember, he'd never had to force me to do anything, ever.

The sexual side was different, now. Mum had chronic stomach trouble; she knew when the pains were coming on, and how to lie hunched until they passed. It had been like that, for me; a series of episodes that I learned to expect, from the gathering signs, and to bear until they were over. I bore them because I loved Dad and wanted him to love me. But that leather man changed this. I learned soon enough that he'd been no great lover, compared to some other people, but his body had given me pleasure. Men could do that. Dad must have done that, to Mum. I felt this wonder about them, and the dark core of their marriage: the closed place I should be forbidden to touch. He said she'd never been interested, but I suspected he was lying, to make me sorry for him. Perhaps he'd forgotten; he had no powers of memory, he just went sentimental about chosen moments; most of the time he just lived in the present, like one of his animals.

I didn't let Dad give me pleasure; I didn't give him that power. I had some instinct of self-preservation, you see. I had to keep something separate and intact. Oh yes, I wasn't that stupid.

I had to get away. That's why I left school, though they told me I was fairly bright and might get an A-level if I stayed, like Jonathan stayed, into the Sixth Form. I didn't want any of that. I wanted to get work for myself, instead of dawdling at home, smelling the pigs when the wind blew from the west. I wanted a place of my own, oh so badly; a place where I'd never have to feel guilty . . . Where I'd feel my right age. I'd sit and watch the planes slicing up into the sky, the molten clouds opening for them just like the clouds in my Bible book. I suppose I felt like my Mum, pausing in the drive; but I didn't dare compare my feelings with hers; I shut my mind to that.

I was younger than Mum; I could do it if I tried. We'd had another offer for the land. Remember how anxious I'd been, years ago? This time I urged Dad to sell, telling him about all the possibilities that money would bring. I wanted my childhood home to be bulldozed into the mud. But he wouldn't budge; he was that obstinate.

All he did was to sell the car park field. They brought in the piledrivers. A crane rose above the pigs' field; it bent down, as if inspecting us with a weary, superior look, before it swung away. It carried a huge slab of concrete. One day, I thought, it'll swing right round and drop a slab on us. Instead, over the hedge I saw the scaffolding climb up into the sky. He must have got a lot of money for that land, but not nearly enough. Dad was the original soft touch; he was a child when it came to business and I realize now that they cheated him. They got him drunk, you see, and he signed it away when under the influence. Mum didn't know that. Despite her complaints she was an innocent, too, when it came to that sort of money.

He bought us presents: a bike for Teddy, *carte blanche* up the West End stores for Mum and me. He bought us a new telly and a music centre with dials like a mission control; none of us knew how to work it. He abandoned his old lorry, which joined the other vehicles behind our yard, and bought a new one. He talked for hours about his plans. He'd set up in the big-time haulage business; he'd clear the junk out the back; he'd build greenhouses and grow orchids for VIPs.

But the money melted away. He'd run up huge debts at the taxi rank, I discovered later, and he spent more time there now, losing in greater style. He was a useless poker player, being so emotional.

Then he had a visit from a couple of smoothies who said they ran an investment company. They persuaded him to part with a lot more cash. They were setting up a leisure centre in Swanage: Space Invaders, TV games, all on the rental system; that was the new thing in 1976. It was a high-risk business, they said, and only people of a special calibre had been approached. Dad fell for that one. My heart sank when he repeated this conversation, in an important voice, shortly after he sobered up. He didn't dare tell Mum.

The project fell through, of course; that's what they told him.

He lost £5,000. By the time the building was completed in our field – it was a big car showroom – we were near enough back where we'd started. It was autumn again now, and I'd found a job. Each morning I walked down the drive like my Mum. Ahead, the first planes were taking off. Down one side stood the showroom, all glass and yellow brick, with the trees rising behind. Some mornings were dirty-dark; on others the mist rose through the trees and the glass glinted in the early light. On the other side stood the garage whose toilets had meant so much to me. It was 24-Hours open now, its Mobil sign glaring throughout the night, and they'd expanded the forecourt to display used vehicles. There were usually four or five, and they each wore a placard on their roofs saying '£2,999 and I'm Yours'. I was saving up for driving lessons. Waiting at the bus stop, I'd look at my getaway cars. One day there was a Mini that cost '£499 and I'm Yours'. I had to meet its eye for four mornings. But the next week it had gone.

Coming back from work, looking out of the bus, I'd see the tall, skeleton poplar trees around the factories, and the sky streaked red behind them. In the hotels the bedroom lights would be switched on and the curtains closed. Shadows moved in there. Soon they'd be making their getaway; soon they'd be closing their curtains on the other side of the world.

I spent as little time as I could at home, and then I stayed indoors. Mum was for ever complaining about the mud; you should have seen it. Out the back it had always been muddy, except in summer, when the weeds grew tall and cotton wool blew from the willow herb. The caravan was only made of plywood and its panels had warped now. More than ever, our back view looked spoilt, and temporary, and submerged.

Out the front, though, we'd once had a patch of grass. Trouble was, the veranda roof had collapsed, breaking the panes, and Dad had hauled a new load of bricks and planks right across the lawn. He never did rebuild the veranda – like everything else he started it, and fiddled around, on and off, for years, but he never finished. So the front of our bungalow looked like a building site, too. He'd covered the planks with plastic, but as time passed the plastic got torn, through natural causes aided by Teddy's penknife, and it flapped in the wind like wings.

I remained indoors, in my room. I was confident enough by now to know the door would stay closed. I'd told Dad I didn't want him in there and nowadays he meekly agreed with what I said. The décor hadn't changed much. I hadn't painted my room because I'd set my sights on leaving it. The only thing I'd done was buy a blind for the window, which I could pull right down so no gap showed.

I'd given Teddy most of my unsuspecting toys. Under his ownership they hadn't lasted long; if they were hard he took them to pieces and if they were soft he disembowelled them. I just kept Kanga. Both her eyes were gone now; a grey sack slumped on my pillow, she mourned blindly her lost son. I'd pinned up some film posters; Sandra's brother worked for Rank and he'd given them to me. They covered the damp patches. My wardrobe was nowadays crammed with clothes. Its sliding door was stuck and my crimson dress poked through the slit like a tongue.

If you're wondering what I did, all those hours alone, I'll tell you. I inspected my face and I played my *Let's Speak French* cassettes. I didn't need to keep the tapes low, because the telly was so loud. Just once there was a bout of shooting, then a hush. Everyone must be dead. I was just replying to my tape,

'*Oui, je suis étrangère.*'

My words were clear as clear. But nobody asked me, later, who I was talking to, not even Teddy. I don't think they took in anything while the TV was on.

I'd passed my O-level French, quite well actually. You needed a foreign language to be an air hostess; the British Airways form said, 'One foreign language would be a great advantage', and I knew the competition was fierce. I'd set my heart on that job, though I had to wait until I was eighteen. So I worked my way through the course and I was up to Cassette Six now. I stored the tapes in the chest of drawers, under my woollies.

It wasn't just my face I inspected; it was all over. I shut the door and tilted the mirror this way and that, each time jumping on to the bed to inspect the next portion. You can see why I needed the blind. That winter I was slimming in earnest. I had a weight chart which I kept hidden amongst my underwear. I had to be slimmer if I was going to get anywhere in life.

All day I worked with food, which you'd think would make it harder. But it didn't. By the time I got home the smell of cooking nauseated me and it was easy not to eat anything, even though I often fried the tea for the rest of them. My thighs stayed plump, I've always hated my thighs, but by the spring I had got my waist quite small. My heavy breasts still embarrassed me, even though the leather man had seemed to like them. So had the man at the Holiday Inn. *Have them*, I'd thought, keeping my head turned away. You'd call my figure ripe and old-fashioned, I suppose, like those Edwardian ladies you see undressed on postcards.

I lost weight in my face, which was the best thing. Mum actually said I looked peaky. My face was no longer a pink pudding. It stayed pink, but its shape showed now. My features weren't remarkable, but they looked neat enough. I had to tie back my hair for work, but in the evening, with my fair hair brushed around my face and my make-up on – then I actually looked pretty. This sounds egoistical, but you must realize that my looks were all I had. Some people better themselves through their brains, or their high-powered connections. Some people, like Gwen, wanted to be vets. I wanted to get out.

The only person I let into my room was Teddy. I haven't really told you how much Teddy meant to me. The simplest things are always the hardest to explain. I loved him. It frightened me, how much I loved him; it was the only pure emotion I had. He was the reason I could bear to stay at home.

He was a real toughie by now, with his crew-cut bullet head. Like me, he wanted to be off. At six years old he was roaming miles. You couldn't do anything with him. That lovely, clear face would seem to be listening but then, the moment you turned your head, he'd be off again. He told such tales, the little liar, that you could never find out where he'd been. Sometimes he came back covered in mud, or tar. He talked about the gypsies under the flyover. Once he came back with a roll of photographic paper, so he must've been up at Kodak. I hoped he hadn't nicked it, but it was no good asking. I think he went round the back of factories and looked appealing. People would take him in and give him their sandwiches.

When he came home hours later, exhausted but still swaggering, it was to my room that he swayed. He'd drop asleep on my lap, just like that, as if a light had been switched off in his skull. He looked so beautiful, sucking his fingers, his face streaked and his nostrils bubbling. He did, honestly.

One day in spring, though, something terrible happened. I'd just got home from work. Teddy's school bus dropped him off earlier. With the lighter evenings he was often off somewhere by the time I arrived back. Dad was over at the garden centre, doing a labouring job, so I presumed Teddy had wandered away in that direction.

I went into my room. As I said, Teddy liked going in there, and I saw the usual evidence – the armless torso of his Action Man, propped against the chair leg, with his guns lined up in front of him. Teddy had long ago lost the uniform so the doll sat nude behind his weapons. I was going out later that evening, so I started to pull off my shoes. It was then I glanced at the Action Man again, and saw what he sat on.

It was my pills – my foil panel of pills . . . You know, birth control pills. I kept them in my jewellery box. It was next month's supply.

I snatched up the doll. The panel lay there. Its three rows of blisters were all popped.

'*Teddy!*' I screamed, and rushed out into the yard. '*Teddy!*'

Micky, our dog, started barking. Otherwise, silence.

'*Teddy!*'

Twenty-one pills, he'd eaten. I ran round behind the garage to look at the depot, jumping up to see over the hedge. Teddy sometimes went there. The doors were shut and the cars gone. The reception window was dark. It closed early on a Friday.

I was just going to search the outbuildings when I remembered his bike, so I rushed into the garage to look. It was gone.

That ruled out the market garden. Dad was working far off, in the middle of the field, building a tractor shed. Teddy wouldn't have bumped across that ploughed earth on his bike. He must have gone off along the road.

I ran down to the petrol station. The attendant hadn't seen

132

Teddy so he must have gone the other way. I ran along the verge. The lorries roared past; someone wolf-whistled. How long before he died?

My footsteps thudded. Oh God, what had I done? There was nobody selling flowers today, not even the boy who'd replaced my friend. I stopped outside the car showroom. Round the side, by Parts and Accessories, men in orange boiler-suits were horsing around, punching each other. It was knocking-off time, and Friday.

The space was so wide, between me and them. At last I reached them.

'Have you seen my brother?' I gasped.

They paused. 'The little boy?'

'On his bike.'

They shook their heads. 'We've only just come out. Ask Len. In front.'

I ran back, past the miles of plate glass. Cars on plinths stood in there. I pushed through the front door and asked the man in the showroom. He hadn't seen him, but he'd been busy on the phone.

I ran on down the road, stumbling over the glass. Tears were streaming down my face, because of my wickedness. It took an age to reach the Flexed Products factory. Cars were reversing, and queuing up to get on to the road. I ran past. They were leaving the Kodak factory too. There was no bike; he wouldn't be there now, with the factories closing. I ran on.

Ahead, parked on the verge, stood the snacks caravan.

'What's up?' The man leaned out of the window.

'Have you seen a little boy on a bike?'

He pursed his lips, considering, screwing tight a ketchup bottle.

'In a blue anorak?' he said.

I nodded.

'Seen you with him before,' he said. 'Your son, right?'

'My brother. Have you seen him?'

He jerked his thumb. 'That way. Going like the clappers.'

I ran on. My legs were dragging now, heavy as concrete. My darling boy, my darling Teddy . . .

I reached the hotel. It seemed to take an hour, my feet dragging in their slippers, to get past the car park. I kept my eyes on the road. Where would he collapse? Would his dear body swell up? My head roared . . . I could hardly breathe. Ahead of me, in the sunlight, I saw the roundabout and the parade of shops.

An AA caravan was parked on the verge. It had been there for years; there were flower beds around it, planted with tulips. Across the road, I saw Teddy's bike lying on the grass.

Cars hooted as I ran. Brakes screeched. I was over the grass now, and leaping up the steps.

A man sat at a desk, with Teddy beside him.

'*Teddy!*' I shouted. 'Did you eat them?'

Teddy looked up calmly. He was cutting up a brochure with scissors.

'I'm a member,' he said. 'He said I'm a member now.'

'Have you eaten them?' I shouted.

'No. Cross my heart.' He rolled his eyes.

'Er, my fault miss.' The man cleared his throat. 'He's not telling the truth.'

'Isn't he?' I swung round.

'Now, little man. You tell her. Go on, or I'll take away your membership.' He winked at me.

'Did you?' I asked.

'Only three.' Teddy pointed the scissors. 'He gave 'em me.'

'He what?' My head span.

'Just three,' said the man. 'No harm done, I hope.'

Teddy wiped his nose. 'S'not my fault.'

'What?'

'You said I wasn't to have sweeties from men I don't met before.'

'Sweeties?'

'But he's my friend.'

'Actually, they're throat pastilles,' said the man. 'Sunny Jim here always likes them.'

I paused, steadying myself. 'But . . . what about . . . the pills?'

'Pills?' said the man. 'What's this?'

134

'The pills,' I said to Teddy. 'The *pills*.'

He gazed at me with his clear blue eyes. I lunged forward and shook him.

'What've you been eating?' said the man. 'You pinched her aspirins?'

I gripped his frail shoulders, digging my nails in. 'Teddy!' I screeched, sobbing.

'Speak up,' the man told him.

'Teddy! The pills in my room!'

Teddy paused, jiggling the scissors. Then he said, 'They're in the bomb store, stupid.'

'The where?'

'The bomb store,' he said patiently. 'Under your stupid bed. You're hurting.'

They were. I fished them out, grey with fluff, and wrapped the twenty-one pills in my handkerchief.

If you think I was too shaken to go out that night, you're wrong.

Oh, I was shaken; you're right about that. I could hardly put on my eyeliner. It kept smudging and I had to rub it off and start again. I'd never hated myself so much in my life.

I went into the kitchen and ate a whole tin of creamed rice, scooping it out with a spoon. Some slopped on to the floor.

I was going to the Spread Eagle disco with Naz, a girl from work. Thank goodness the music was too loud for us to talk. I jiggled about, full of rice pudding. After she'd gone I got into a van with two people. We'd shouted a bit at each other in the disco, in the pulsing gloom. They'd had a lot to drink. I hadn't. The only thing I discovered was that one of them, the skinny one, was a compère at a holiday camp each year. He said it was worth it, for the crumpet. He said he'd had twenty-two last season, sixteen of them virgins. He said it was all to do with the way he held the microphone. He said he had to sing dopey songs for the kids, 'Puff the Magic Dragon', crap like that.

We were parked near the canal. I could hear the roar of the sluice-gates and the roar of the traffic, farther off. I remember telling myself: this is me, sitting here. I sat numb as a doll, but perspiring too. I kept my mind locked shut; if I closed my eyes I saw Teddy swelling up.

Do what you want with me. That's what I told myself, lavishly, but I was sure they were too drunk to hurt me. Giggling, they manhandled me into the back, pressing the breath out of me. My spine scraped against a petrol can.

Despite the bragging they didn't manage it so well; they snorted and swore, they were even more embarrassed than me. An elbow butted my eye. As far as I could feel – and I didn't want to – one of them stayed as soft as a puppy. I ended up half-buried under a tow-rope, in a litter of unpaid parking tickets, all slippery Cellophane, and soon the other one gave up as well. It was too dark for his mate to know – only I did, and I was really afraid then. I thought he'd get violent with me, because I'd known he hadn't managed it. So I struggled up and groped for my handkerchief, to blow my nose. But I took out the wrong handkerchief . . . I felt the pills scattering over my blouse, which neither of them had bothered to unbutton.

They let me out at the roundabout. I realized, with a sick sort of satisfaction, that they hadn't even known my name. I tucked in my skirt and took a breath. Opposite, the AA caravan was shuttered; under the sodium light its tulips, like everything else, were a flat brown.

A week later, when my back had healed, Teddy wandered off as usual. But this time he was driven home by the police. My chest closed when I saw the car bumping up our drive. But there he was inside it, alive. It was one of those blue and white panda cars, and there was a police lady climbing out, holding his hand.

He was as chirpy as ever. They'd found him asleep in a double-decker bus. I knew the bus. You can see it from the road even now, it's parked in a corrugated-iron shelter just off the motorway. Its owner, a mate of my Dad's, was a stock-car maniac.

Teddy was really proud about the panda car; they'd let him

press the buttons. But the next week, as I'd feared, we had a visit from the social worker. I think she called herself a visitor but she didn't fool me. She looked different from the lady who came when Teddy was new-born – she was younger and less hairy – but she behaved the same. Her eyes slid pleasantly round the lounge in just that manner. She wasn't a possible ally now, who might be able to explain things; she was an enemy. I was terrified for Teddy. I was also frightened for myself, and even frightened for my Dad. She gave off authority like a smell.

We were all four at home. She didn't get far with Mum and Dad. As I said, officials turned them into cowed strangers. My Mum shrank, sallow and watchful. Dad, on the other hand, grew bigger and more tongue-tied. They didn't seem to belong to me. They sat there, sharing their smokes.

We'd had a postcard about this, so Mum had prepared the house and told me not to put any muck on my face. For once I'd obeyed.

Mum made us some Nescafé. She wore her beige cardigan, buttoned up, with a white collar showing. With a shock, I realized she looked as old as a pensioner.

The lady – girl really – sipped her coffee and said that Teddy was a super kid, he could twist anyone round his little finger. A clink, as she lowered her cup. But that he was also an unusually disruptive influence at school. After consultation, they'd decided to allocate him weekly sessions with the area schools' psychologist.

'Nothing wrong with our Teddy!' Dad's face was brick-red. 'Just high spirits.'

He kept his gaze on the carpet. I was blushing too. What would Teddy say, closeted with an expert? Psychologists sucked out the secrets, didn't they? They drew them out like dentists' gas. That was their job . . . Especially secrets a person didn't know that he knew. Those were the important ones.

'You can't!' I blurted out. It was me who'd caused Teddy to become like this. Me and Dad. He'd never really seen anything, but that was irrelevant. He'd been squashed next to us, as a baby.

Since then he'd felt it in the air, like an infection, and it was turning him potty.

'He's not potty!' I cried.

'Heather, of course he's not.' She leaned over and put a hand on my arm. 'I do appreciate your anxiety. It won't start until next term, anyway . . . He'll be re-evaluated before we begin.' She paused. 'Meanwhile, we need your help too. At home. You see, every child needs some discipline.' She laughed, hurriedly. 'I don't mean physical discipline – "belting them one" – I mean, well, rules and security. That wasn't the first time Teddy's wandered off, was it . . .'

'That's youngsters for you,' said Dad.

She turned, smiling. 'Well, not quite, Mr Mercer. We have been keeping an eye on him, you know.'

There was a silence, then a hiss as Dad stubbed out his cigarette in his saucer.

Soon afterwards the woman rose to leave. At the door she paused:

'Heather, I wonder if you could see me down to the road?'

I knew, then, what they meant by 'turned to stone'. I simply couldn't move.

'Do you mind?' she asked.

I turned my stone head slowly from side to side.

'Do what the lady says,' said Mum. 'Where's your manners?'

Somehow I lifted my stone legs, and managed to get myself into her car. It was raining and the windscreen wipers slewed to and fro. She drove down to the main road and then switched off the engine.

'I thought it would be nice for us two to have a little chat.'

I watched the drops sliding down the window.

'Ciggy?' She offered the packet. I shook my head.

'Job going OK?'

I nodded.

'I hear you've set your heart on being an air hostess.'

I swung round. 'How did you know?'

'Ah,' she said with a smile. 'Ve 'ave our methods.' She paused. 'Actually, your ex-teacher told me. Melanie Cockerell.'

'Oh yes.' I willed this woman to stop. I'd grown just like my parents. I feared the lot of them.

'Seems a super idea,' she said, then paused. 'I just wanted to tell you, Heather, that it's not just Teddy that we're concerned about.'

Traffic roared past, shaking the car.

'I've spoken to several people, you see, who know your home environment. They're all in agreement about this. You're close to your parents, aren't you . . . especially your father?'

I didn't speak. A lorry passed, spattering spray.

'And fathers like yours . . . well, he is a bit old-fashioned, isn't he? It's fathers like him who often find it hard to . . . well, come to terms with their daughters' maturity.'

I whispered, 'What?'

'You're seventeen, aren't you, Heather? No longer Daddy's little girl. But I think he finds that hard to recognize . . . That you're a grown, sexually mature young woman now.' She paused. 'But then, I suppose you've been forced into that rather early.'

Three lorries passed, spattering us. The car juddered. Then a coach went by, its windows a blur of light.

'Perhaps I'm being presumptuous. Let me put it like this, Heather. From all accounts, you've been taking on a role that young girls shouldn't have to take on . . . not until they're much older . . . Until they're, in a sense, ready for it.' She tapped her cigarette. 'Which means that you've rather missed out on your childhood.' She paused. 'Haven't you?'

I sat there, stone cold.

'I mean the mothering role, with little Teddy. The adult role.'

In the silence that followed I realized that it was impossible to speak. My throat had closed up.

'It might sound funny, coming from me – I'm only twenty-three myself, Heather. But I honestly think that you should – well, have some fun. Like other girls your age.'

Relief had drained my head. I nodded.

'From what I've heard, you've been – it seems a curious way to put it, Heather – but too good for your own good. Why not get out more, meet some fellas . . .' She put on a funny accent. 'Live it up, down the disco.'

She stopped. 'Heather, sorry – I see a blush. It's only a suggestion.'

From then on Dad grew strict with Teddy. When he came home from school, there was Dad waiting. He'd trek across the cabbage field, Teddy in tow, back to the distant tractor shed. Over his tea Teddy would tell me about all the sweets Dad had given him, and how if he was good Dad would raise his pocket money to a pound a week.

Between us, the fair head bent over his plate. He skidded the chips around in his ketchup. As usual, Dad didn't meet my eye. He knew that I knew the reason for this sudden solicitude. If Teddy stopped getting into trouble, he might not be sent to the shrink.

I did it too. I knelt down with Teddy in his bedroom, the old boxroom next to the veranda, and zoomed his cars across the floor. 'Ne-naw, ne-naw,' I whined, making the police noises he demanded. I should have been doing it for Teddy, who I loved more than anyone on earth.

Partly I was. But I was also doing it out of fear for myself.

Chapter Ten

I wonder what you felt about your first job. Mine meant a lot to me. Yvonne, who worked for a surveyor in Staines, called hers a drag. She was always yawny about things – she was engaged, and yawny about her fiancé.

I didn't feel like that. But then I didn't know if my feelings were the usual ones. Most of my class left school when I did. Perhaps they felt that taut, breathless separateness of sitting in a bus each morning, speeding away from their home.

At work nobody knew where I came from, or that they'd called me Porky at school. They knew me as Heather, in my cap and overalls, just the same as theirs. They didn't even know my surname. You'd probably call the work repetitive, but for me it was freedom. And it finally changed the physical thing with my Dad.

This didn't happen overnight, but gradually over that autumn. The best way I can explain is that he stopped presuming on me. My last year at school, when I was learning to use my power, he'd become both meeker and more blustering, but he'd still been sure I was his. And I was his, you know . . . I still am.

But when I became a working girl, this changed. I had my own money in my pocket – my money, not his. More awesome, I had my own cheque book. I paid Mum for my board and the rest I put into Barclays Bank, over the other side of the airport. Believe it or not, Dad had never had a bank account; heaven knows how he was paid for that field, but every other transaction he made was cash or barter. He regarded banks with a mixture of humility and suspicion, as if there might be policemen in there: not for the likes of him.

One night, when Mum had gone to bed early, I was standing at the kitchen sink cutting my fringe. The light was brightest in the kitchen, that was why. He came up behind me. One hand, with its smoking cigarette, touched my hair.

'You'll go easy on that,' he said, 'won't you?'

'Why?'

'Girls got their hair like that at work?'

'They're mostly Asians,' I said. 'I told you.'

'Don't want you to change.'

'I've always had a fringe, Dad.'

'Don't want my girl to change.'

'I'm not.'

He stroked the back of my head gently.

'Your Dad misses you, out at work all day.'

'I was out at school all day before.'

'Soon be off . . . off to the bright lights. What'll I be doing then?'

'You've got Mum and Teddy.'

'Who'll I be talking to then? . . . Get so lonely, see. With no one to give me a hug.'

'Can you shift a bit? You're in my light.'

He shifted, and there was a silence.

'Fine as yours, once, your Mum's hair. Wrap it round my finger, I would, tight as tight . . . all sparkling . . . You'll be off, lovely-looking girl like you. They'll be making you manager.'

'Hold on, I've only been there three months.'

'Brains like yours . . . sky's the limit.'

'Haven't got much brains.'

142

'No time left for your Dad.'

I'd finished snipping. I turned round.

'No time left for a hug,' he said.

'Of course I'll have time.' I put my arms around him. I didn't fear him now; I felt guilty, because I wanted his words to be true.

'I'll be getting your blouse dirty.'

'Don't worry. We wear overalls to work.'

'Don't want you mussed up, do we?'

He pressed his face against mine and released me. He asked so little of me. That was how we were, now.

That was early January. Next morning I was travelling to work. Each year they put up Christmas trees outside the factories: three big ones outside Delta Flexed Products, six along the roof of Abercorn Computers, one giant tree in the Sheraton car park. The bus stopped outside Dataloop Systems. People shuffled off, coughing and wheezing. I rubbed the glass. Men stood on the roof of the factory, disconnecting the neon sign which had blazed 'Dataloop Wishes You a Merry Xmas'. I watched the script being lowered. Down in the forecourt, more men were winching down a tree.

'Six months to go,' said the woman beside me.

'Pardon?'

'Six bloody months, till me summer hols.'

The tree fell into a lorry. All these years I'd counted the trees from Dad's van. Now my childhood was over, at last. I was a wage-earner and I was starting to feel like a visitor in my own home. In that stuffy bus I was breathing the sweet, sharp scent of freedom.

'Six months, day in, day out,' she said.

'Gruesome,' I lied. 'What a gruesome thought.'

You might not realize it, but there's a public road runs right across the airport from one side to the other; a road with bus stops and all, for people who work in the area. Passengers like you, with flights to catch, drive through that tunnel to the terminal buildings. Remember how desperately I'd run along there once?

The road I'm describing, the one I took each day, isn't used much because its sign says 'Maintenance Areas', which puts people off. But in fact it cuts right across, from the A4 one side to the A30 the other. It's a wide, empty road, like a road in a dream. It crosses the incoming runway. As the big planes roar down so close, you think they'll strip off the bus roof like a plaster and leave you staring into space. But the shadow moves over you, and the bus shakes, and three hundred people will be watching the tarmac rise to meet them, tense for the bumpety-bump of Britain.

The place where I worked stood beyond the airport, out along the dual carriageway, between Rank Xerox and a building site. JT Catering was a brick box. Its air-vents breathed out curry fumes. Oriental airlines were some of its customers, that's why. It was mostly women who worked at JT; they came from the estates out beyond Hounslow and they were nearly all of them Asians. Their husbands dropped them off on the way to work; they'd hurry across to the entrance, these ladies, clutching their overcoats around their flapping saris; it was always windy because of the traffic. Some of them drove themselves in Datsuns and Toyotas; three women together, giggling as they bounced on to the verge, to park.

JT had contracts with lots of other airlines; it prepared their meals. I worked upstairs, the first weeks. You have to keep your wits when you're sorting cutlery. The clatter was deafening and it was so steamy that by lunch-break my mascara was down my cheeks. Outside, vans delivered crates of soiled plates. They were pushed through a thick plastic flap. Then they rattled along to the washing-up. Turbaned men stood there, in the mist. I never saw the dirty plates; I never knew what the passengers left on their trays, up there in the sky. By the time it got to me it was clean and slippery-hot. I had to sort out each knife, fork and spoon, according to the airline emblem stamped on its handle; then I slotted them into cellophane sheaths, ready for the next flight.

The days passed in a clattering blur. I forgot everything about myself. It was like school, it was so bright and normal, but it was more restful than school because I didn't know any of the people. Besides, most of them talked in their Indian languages.

144

At lunch-break you could walk to the canteen two ways: one way through what they said was the butchery, and the other way through the kitchens. I avoided the butchery, so it was some days before I met Jock. I preferred the kitchen route.

You would have liked it too. The first kitchen cooked Japanese: all stainless steel, with a strip of fish laid out and a few spring onions. Perhaps it was Chinese; I never liked to ask. The next kitchen was Indian, and quite different. They had these giant vats, bubbling. One bubbled orange and one bubbled brown, all oily on top. The aroma was wonderful; I'd always liked curries. Men stood there stirring them with ladles the size of boat paddles. They'd pause when I walked by, and stare, their brown faces perspiring. As I said, there weren't many English girls at JT and most of them were supervisors and older than me.

The Indian women never looked up. They didn't do the cooking; they dolloped out the food. They stood in a row, and my heart lifted when I first saw those stacked foil containers. The women wore rubber gloves; their caps bobbed as they moved, putting a handful of steaming rice into each dish. Then they spooned in the curry beside it, and pressed one green chilli into the rice, artful as flower arrangers. I wondered if they envied the food the direction it would travel. I did. I don't mean Asia; I mean anywhere. I thought that *abroad* would change me. I dawdled, watching them pinching down the tops. The dishes were slotted into the narrow metal galleys, ready for boarding. See, I knew the jargon, even though I'd never been inside a plane. I repeated the words to myself.

It might sound mundane to you, the work I did. But that money mattered. And there I was, sealed off in that steamy brick box, with my thoughts to myself. I was needed in the way the others were needed. Can you see how much that meant to me? And nobody knew the first thing about me. I was a new person, not just to them but to myself as well. That's what made it alarming, meeting Jock.

I was slimming, as I said, so I didn't eat much lunch. Just some

145

cottage cheese, perhaps, and salad. The food was good because they used the same ingredients as for the flights. There were always curries, of course, for the staff, and fry-ups for the English chefs. I'd soon finish eating and then there wasn't a lot to do. I sat reading magazines; other people smoked but I'd never taken up the habit – you wouldn't, if you'd heard my parents' dawn chorus.

Sometimes I wandered outside, if it was sunny, but there wasn't anywhere to go. Just the traffic out there, slowing down at the lights and starting off again. I wasn't the age to close my eyes and will the next car to be red, or white, or whatever it was – I've forgotten now. I'd watch the planes coming in, their lights winking in the sunshine. But you felt out of place, standing on the road verge. So I usually stayed inside and read other people's newspapers in the ladies', and wandered about. That's how I found myself in the butchery.

Slumped in the doorway was a new delivery, two plastic sacks of meat, the blood pressed against the sides as if they'd haemorrhaged. Beyond it was a stainless-steel room, the same as the others, and a big man turning round.

'I'll be buggered,' he said. 'Frank's little girl.'

He put down the knife and wiped his hands on his apron.

'Sent you round, has he, to check up on me?'

I paused. 'I'm working here.'

'Only joking, wasn't I.' He nodded at my overalls. 'Been here long?'

'Ten days.'

He wiped his hands again. His apron was streaked with brown.

'Now you mention it, your Dad said you was a working girl now.'

Jock was one of my Dad's drinking mates. He was a harmless enough bloke, but it shocked me to see him here.

'Never said it was here, did he? Sly bugger.'

I'd kept it vague, that was why. Dad didn't know where I worked. I looked at Jock's ruddy face. It was as if I'd been in a room thinking I was alone, getting undressed, and then seeing two eyes at the window.

146

'Laugh a minute, this place,' he said. 'Catch me being pre-
judiced. Which bit you on?'

'Department Two.'

'Better keep an eye on you.'

'Why?' I backed away and stood at the rotisserie.

'Catch it if I didn't. You know your old man. Thinks the world
of his Heather.'

I watched the smeared glass window. Behind it the chickens
turned, glistening yellow. They turned, showing the holes of their
bottoms.

'Bashful, eh? He does, honest. Always talking about his little
girl.'

I made my escape. Back at the counter I couldn't concentrate.
That night, most likely, there were the wrong passengers licking
the wrong spoons, up in the black sky.

I hadn't got away, of course. Jock or no Jock, you don't escape
just by taking a job. Not when you're still at home. But it was a
start. I felt like a plane, poised for take-off. But how would I get
off the ground? I had to believe they'd accept me at British
Airways, otherwise there was no point in drawing breath each
day. But they don't recruit from backgrounds like mine; not if it
shows.

It was up to me. I was on my own, as I always was; as I am at
this minute, telling you this. I had to get away, with no help from
anybody but myself. They have to do it through their looks,
women have; people fool themselves if they think a nice face
doesn't help. Once, in a pub with Naz, I was picked up by
someone big in cosmetics. He said I'd make a buyer, a well-
groomed girl like myself, and why didn't he give me a tinkle?
Perhaps we could discuss it over a meal. There was no phone at
home so I told him some numbers out of my head; there's probably some old dear in Hull or some place who had this man
ringing her up in 1977. I told him in a fluster because Naz was
there. But you see what I mean . . . I could work my way upwards,
if I tried.

Concentrating on this, I managed to lose weight. Mumbling into my recorder, I reached Intermediate in my French. I had always kept myself well-groomed, the cosmetics man had been right about that; it was probably a reaction against the mud. So I had some things going for me.

I remember one Thursday, my day off, when I was in the launderette. This was before Dad bought our washing machine. I was sitting beside the dryer, reading the beauty tips in *Cosmopolitan*. In the corner of my eye I saw moving blackness, through the window, which meant that school had finished. All those blazers, dawdling. I kept my back turned. I told myself that I'd left that behind. Kid's stuff, I said. As I emptied the dryer I heard them calling to each other across the street. Soon I'd be living in London, miles from here; that's what I'd planned.

I pulled out my white nylon pullover. Dad's socks clung to it. They were black socks; they stuck like dried-up leeches. I peeled them off with a crackle of static.

Just then someone stopped outside.

It was Jonathan. He was holding hands with a girl I recognized, from the class below mine.

I turned back, quickly. Jonathan's hair was longer now, curling round his ears. I told myself it looked silly. He looked silly, long and gaunt. I waited for a moment; in the reflection I saw their shapes move away. Then I stood up and tried to fold up the white pullover. Trouble was, my legs kept bending; so I sat down again.

When I got home I told Dad I wasn't going to wash his bloody clothes any more.

'I'm not your bloody wife!' I shouted.

We gaped at each other. Outside Teddy was whooping.

'And I'm not Teddy's bloody mother!'

We stayed staring. I'd never shouted at him like that.

Suddenly there was a crash. Teddy started shrieking. Dad and I rushed outside.

Teddy had been climbing the drainpipe; it had come away in his hand. He lay on the ground, beside it. I flung myself down and

148

held him. He gripped me, his arms and legs tight around me. He'd only cut his lip. I squeezed him.

He stopped crying soon, but I couldn't stop. I heaved and shuddered, soaking his shoulder. He clung to me.

'My darling boy . . . my darling . . . ' I gripped his filthy hand and covered it with kisses.

Standing near, Dad was blowing his nose too. When I finally disentangled myself and stood up, my tights were laddered and my skirt muddy. So much for grooming. Who cares about bloody grooming?

You'd think it would be easy, leaving a home like mine. You'd think it would be a relief. But it's never that simple, is it?

Naz worked downstairs, in desserts. That's how I met her. I was promoted, you see, on account of my performance, so two weeks later they sent me downstairs to Tray Prep.

The crockery rattled its way there on a rubber belt. It was quieter downstairs and not so smelly because the only cooking was done at the far end, in the bakery. It was open-plan. The kings worked here: the First Class Chef and the Pâtissier. They'd both come from the big London hotels. None of us dared speak directly to them; messages were passed through their assistants. I was shown around, my first day. In the pâtisserie there were gâteaux, and for Economy Class there were tin trays like at school, full of Bakewell tart and a sticky, nutty stuff that the Middle Eastern airlines ordered, Arabs having a sweet tooth. In the Cold Room, a dark place lined with shelves, there was a row of milky eyes. That was the crème caramels.

I wasn't shown round the First Class section, where the other chef worked. I got to know that only too well later, but when I started all I saw was this tall man, in his white hat, shouting at his underlings. Boxes of lobsters were carried over to him like maidens, their claws bound and their feelers nodding.

I worked at the counter in the middle of the room. We did snacks and light meals. I think I was the only one who read the orders; the others weren't interested. When the supervisor was out of sight I'd go over to her desk, where the forms were pinned. The destinations were written there, with the flight number and the quantity of meals needed. As I wedged in the sandwiches, I knew where they were going. Sausage roll, sealed orange juice and a Jacob's Chocolate Club . . . I thought myself into their flight . . . to Istambul, then to Bahrein. Beef sausage roll, because they were Muslims.

Next counter was desserts. There was an Indian girl there; she wasn't as shy as most of the others and she was a wonderful mimic. She hated the First Class Chef and copied his Manchester accent.

'Call that a roody radish flower!' she boomed. 'You nincompoop!'

We became friends that winter and sometimes went out together on Friday nights, to that disco I told you about. Naz said her family was very strict and they didn't know what to do with her. She pretended to be her father, with his sing-song Indian voice:

'What are we deserving, that you behave like this? Why are you running wild all over town, giving heartache to your mother?'

She wriggled the straw in her Coke, and resumed her normal voice: 'You're so lucky, Heather. You don't know how lucky you are.' She looked at her watch. 'Ten-thirty. Half an hour before he's picking me up. God it's so claustrophobic.'

In my bones I felt the old longing. I was used to it by now. I told myself over again: poor Naz, what a drag. That usually did the trick.

'Poor Naz,' I said.

In fact she wasn't that wild; just cheeky and a bit rebellious. In other words, quite normal. Just like that social worker recommended me to be. It was all talk, like it was with Gwen. All bravado.

She didn't know anything about me and I never talked about my home, or took her there. I wanted her to be separate from all that; I was trying to add more and more things to my life which home couldn't spoil. One night we were down at the Crown, for Golden Oldies' Nite.

150

'Time's up,' she said. Her Dad was waiting outside, as per usual. 'Want a lift?'

I didn't want them to see my bungalow, even in the dark. I could walk back; it was only a mile.

'Oh no,' I said quickly. 'I'm waiting for Tim.'

'Who's Tim?'

'He's my steady.'

'You never told!' She stared. 'You're a sly one! Are you engaged?'

I looked serene, and decided to nod.

'A whole month, and you never let on! I'm hurt.'

'He's a pilot,' I said quickly. 'He's often away, you see. In the States.'

Her Dad loomed out of the cigarette smoke then, so she had to leave.

Dear God, what had I said? Who was this Tim? I'd never lied to anyone I liked before, only to people I hoped never to see again.

I panicked at myself. Sometimes these surprises seeped out, vapours from doorways in my heart that I thought I kept closed.

The next day, to make matters worse, we bumped into Jock outside the gents'.

'Well, well, it's Heth,' he said, buttoning up his trousers. He turned to Naz. 'You looking after our girl, then?'

'She doesn't need looking after. Not Heather.'

'I've been told to keep an eye on her.' Jock winked. 'By someone.'

He meant Dad, of course. But Naz meant Tim. 'Did he?' she said, looking interested.

'See she don't get into no mischief.'

Naz smiled. 'The possessive type, is he?' She turned to me. 'Ah . . . I'm knowing him better every minute . . . our mystery man.'

'She knows him?' Jock turned to me.

I looked longingly at the door of the ladies'.

'It's because he's away a lot, I expect,' said Naz. 'On his flights.'

'Oh yep,' said Jock vaguely. 'Always off, here and there.'

'Heather told me. I'm dying to know more.'

151

'It's the nature of his business, see,' said Jock. 'The travelling. That's the haulage trade for you.'

'Haulage!' said Naz. 'Yes, it must seem like that sometimes. . . Jumbos full of bodies.'

'Poor little buggers.' Jock was picturing Dad's piglets. 'Off to meet their maker.'

Naz burst into laughter. 'Some pilot! I should hope not!'

This had got out of control. Luckily, Jock ambled off then.

As we went downstairs she linked my arm.

'A hoot, isn't he,' she said. 'Your friend.'

I didn't want a Tim, did I? That was what made it so ridiculous. I didn't want anybody. Not Jonathan, not anybody. I imagined this Tim. He was no spectre now, he'd grown solid. He had a sense of responsibility, and he wanted two kids. He had the scentless good looks of an American TV actor. Mum would be overwhelmed at my luck. I didn't want to put a face to any man and here was Tim, risen from nowhere.

That afternoon I promoted him and sent him away on a training course. States-side, I told Naz. Six months. And I didn't want to talk about it, I was too sad.

Work was easy. 'Always a smile,' said my supervisor, 'from our Heather.'

It's simple, isn't it: the jokes, the clatter. I wonder if my Mum felt the same way. Walking in there each morning, I felt lighter.

You live for the brisk present, your fingers busy. You can push everything else aside. I thought I could, anyway. The things I was ashamed of — I closed them away, like the junk in Dad's sheds. It was important to keep work separate; at work, at least, I wouldn't have anything to make me feel confused.

That's why it was such a mistake, the business with the chef.

It was a rainy lunch-time in January that the First Class Chef sat down beside me. With his fork he pointed at my lettuce leaves.

'That keep body and soul together?'

'I'm watching my weight.'

He cut his sausage. It spurted. 'You must be joking.' His voice lowered. 'You might be watching your weight, love, but I've been watching something else.'

A year ago I might have asked: watching what? Now I said languidly, 'Oh yeah?'

The old war machinery clanked into action.

'Looks nice enough to me, the shape you are.' The egg spilled out. 'Not offending you, am I? They tell me I'm blunt.'

'You're from Manchester,' I said, all pert. 'That explains it.'

He laughed. 'I like that. Know something? I think I like you.' He swabbed his bacon in the yolk. 'What else've they told you?'

'Nothing. They're all too frightened.'

'Of little me?' He looked pleased. 'And yourself?'

'Oh no,' I lied. 'I'm not.'

'Good for you, love. Know something?'

'What?'

'That's a girl with spirit. That's what I said to myself, first time I clapped eyes on you.' He slewed his chip in the ketchup, just like my Dad did. He was a big, florid, handsome man. 'Know when it was? When our Eric was showing you round. You stopped him. You put your hand on his arm, like this.' He touched my arm and gave me a squeeze. 'You asked him some question.'

I remembered. It was about night flights, what they ate then, but I didn't feel like telling this man. I wanted to keep him out of all that. I smiled warmly.

'. . . And I thought, here's a lass who won't take yea or nay for an answer.'

The fat had whitened round his plate. I waited, half hoping that he wouldn't say it, but he did.

'Care to join me in a drink?'

I paused, knowing this was a mistake. But I felt stupidly flattered too. 'OK,' I said.

He glanced round. We were yards from the nearest member of staff but his voice dropped.

'Wait outside, love. The red Ford Granada.'

I waited for his sauntering exit; after all, the vans loaded here

153

and he was a married man. We drove down the dual carriageway and stopped at a pub. Along our nowhere roads, pubs have an olde-worlde flimsiness, like stage sets: beams and warming pans and such. I had a Bacardi and he had a double Scotch. In his overcoat, with his greased grey hair, I had to get used to him all over again; without his chef's hat he looked shrunk and ordinary. Perhaps he, too, was adjusting to my outdoors self: my mauve hands and pom-pom beret. We looked so different that neither of us could think of anything to say.

But in the car, on the return journey, he stroked my knee. People do all sorts of things in cars, I've noticed, that they'd never do on dry land. It's a voyage, isn't it – disconnected. It releases you. And you don't have to look at the other person, which makes it simpler.

He rubbed my kneebone. As we drew into JT, however, he removed his hand. He was trying to be reassuring; after all, he was twice my age. I think he was trying to seem fatherly.

I kept him off me for two months. He put my reluctance down to my innocence, as I was only seventeen. He had a terrible temper, worse than my Dad. When he spoke to me he used an intimate, soapy voice but underneath it I could hear the irritation held down . . . It was a strain, being nice to me for so long.

One day he called me into the First Class Cold Room. This was where they kept the seafood and the hors-d'oeuvres' platters. The door clanged shut behind us. In the chill air, his breath was hot on my face.

'Close your eyes, love, and open your mouth.' Something small and rubbery was put on my tongue. I chewed it.

'Ever tasted that before, Heather?'

I shook my head.

'Quail's egg.'

He touched my nose with his finger. 'Know something?'

'What?'

'I thought you and me liked each other. Am I right or am I right?'

I shrugged, pretending to be casual, but I felt nervous. He was such a big man, in his uniform. I looked bold enough, with my eyeliner and pert remarks; I wasn't really, I was helpless. I wished I hadn't come.

'Had a nice chin-wag, the other week. How about a drink tomorrow?'

I paused. 'I'm having lunch with Naz.'

'What, that Paki? Next week, then?'

He moved away. I heard the rustle of paper. He put a package into my overall pocket, and patted it. He gave my waist a squeeze.

'Little prezzie,' he whispered. 'From Cliff.'

At tea Teddy spat it out.

'Ugh! All salty.'

'It's smoked salmon,' I said. Strings of dribble hung from his chin. I wiped his mouth. 'It's ever so posh.'

'It's pooey. It's pooey and salty and wee-wee.' Pleased with himself, he bounced up and down. 'Poo-poos,' he sang, 'wee-wees.'

I kept Cliff at arm's length because he was there. Every day. I couldn't cope with people when they stayed around, getting to know me. That leather man, Walter; I could just about cope with him because his cases were already packed. Next day I pretended it had never happened. The same with that man at the Holiday Inn.

You could do this in our area because nobody stopped for long. Down the verges was all this litter that people threw out of their cars. What did they care? They would never see it again. Teddy used to scavenge round the lay-bys. Once he came home with a dusty thing that he called a balloon; he got such a slap from our Mum for that. Down in the bus shelter someone had chalked up MARION WASN'T HERE. I knew how she felt.

But I finally gave in to Cliff. He wanted me, he was so persistent. I was flattered and helpless, but through it I felt, rising up, that familiar, prickling sense of power. I was learning how to use that. Oh, I was worthless – nobody in their right mind could ever really want me. But he didn't seem to realize that. It was surprising, how nobody could tell.

He took me for dinner at the Skyscape Hotel Roof Restaurant. Gone up in the world, hadn't I, since those days in the yard with the bins. Nobody recognized me, thank goodness, but then staff were always changing in those hotels. I nearly choked on my pheasant bone, though, when I realized that our own pigs would be gobbling our leavings.

'Something funny, love?'

I shook my head.

'Not something Cliff can share?'

'Later,' I lied, smiling across at him.

Underneath the table our knees were touching. The dim light hid my blushes. You wouldn't have recognized me, if you'd known me as a little girl. You wouldn't have liked me. But Cliff wanted me. And once I'd decided it, once I'd changed into this bold gear, with the momentum up . . . Then I could will myself into wanting most men. Things about Cliff that might have put me off – his pompous monologues about himself, his bossiness with the waiters – I blocked them away. I willed them to freeze, just as I'd willed myself, all those years, to numb myself to what was happening.

This large, married man was in my power. During dessert I smiled at him. I moved my knee and slotted it between his legs, pressing it there. His fork shook and the cream slid down to his plate.

What if Dad saw me now? His own little Heth? I avoided Cliff's eye, urging him to hurry up. He'd be too drunk to notice my heavy thighs; he wouldn't notice anything about me. In the dark, we wouldn't even have to talk.

We stumbled into the car. I felt intensely alive; alive down to my toes and my fingertips. He swerved away from the car park, his hand up my skirt. The engine shrieked because he wasn't changing gear.

'We're going for a drive, right?' he muttered. I nodded, dumbly.

We didn't get far. I saw the glaring headlights . . . We were on the dual carriageway. Then we veered off, bumping up a lane. We jerked to a halt in front of a gate. My legs were apart; his fingers were inside my knickers. The headlights shone on a sign: Thames Water Authority: No Entry.

He managed to switch off the lights and then we were out of the car. He pulled a rug from the back seat and I helped him, hopping off-balance because of his hand.

I fumbled at his trousers, pulling him down on top of me. Our breath gasped out grey in the dark. In fact it was freezing, but I didn't notice that until we were finished.

It was then that I recognized the gate. Beyond it, up the bank, lay the reservoir. I'd escaped there, once, when I was little. Mum and Dad had been shouting. I'd run all the way there, and scrambled up the bank . . . I'd lain there panting, watching the water . . . My secret sea, furred by the wind.

Trouble was, of course, that he was there the next day. Cliff, I mean, the chef. There he was, back in his tall white hat. They look comic in them, don't they? Like pantomime cooks. At lunch-time he was waiting in the corridor but I refused a drink. Later he was waiting beside his crimson car, so I crept round the other way.

Next day he managed to speak to me.

'Heather, love, listen . . . I know I shouldn't have . . . Shouldn't have taken advantage.' He waited as some people walked by, and whispered, 'I feel bloody terrible. Am I forgiven?'

I nodded. I hated him seeing me in the daylight. I wished I'd never met him.

'You'll come out for a drink?'

'I'm sorry, I can't.'

Shaking my head, I hurried away. He didn't dare grab me in the corridor, with people around.

That afternoon he shouted at Mo, one of his assistants.

'You stupid bitch!' he roared. 'You bloody stupid bitch!' We could hear him across the room. 'Bloody woman!' he shouted. 'How you got this bloody job beats me!'

157

Mo burst into tears. He stomped away to the stock room. I went over and put my arm around her.

'He's been impossible all day,' he sobbed, 'Mr Billings has. See – then I start doing it wrong.'

Her counter was littered with scraps of ham and salami. She'd been punching out rounds of pumpernickel; they lay like black coins all over the floor.

'I'm all thumbs today,' she sniffed. 'Don't know what's got into him.'

'Poor Mo. Here, use my hanky.'

'You are kind, Heather. It's not *your* fault.'

Later, she took it out on her fiancé. He'd come in his car to pick her up as usual. I heard her raised voice . . . Why was he so spineless? Why did she put up with him? She was fed up, she yelled. I didn't hear the rest because I was on my way to the bus stop, hot with guilt, and the traffic drowned her voice.

Cliff wooed me with giant prawns. Nobody knew about it. I'd find these bulging bags in my locker. At lunch-times, to escape him, I'd loiter outside the building. Indian women, sitting out the lunch-break in their cars, eyed me. The red blobs on their foreheads said: *I'm pure*. I deserved everything I got.

I took the food home. Dad didn't peel the prawns; he ate them whole, cracking them in his jaws with a noise like breaking masonry. I caught Mum looking at me, her eyes narrowed. We'd grown so distant that she didn't ask me where they came from. After all, she'd brought back food herself when she worked in catering. Perhaps she thought I'd nicked it. Teddy was always nicking things; the garage man said that if he saw him in the forecourt shop one more time he'd call the police. Perhaps she suspected a gentleman friend.

I told Cliff that it must stop. He'd get into trouble if anyone found out. I said I wasn't touching the parcels any more. Next day there was another one in my locker. I left it there and by Monday the smell was so strong that people started avoiding each other's eyes. Mo couldn't stand his deteriorating temper; she demoted herself to short-haul lunch boxes.

I found a note in my overalls pocket saying that if I didn't speak to him he was going to tell Mary, his wife.

'Please!' I whispered. 'Don't! You told me she'd divorce you, and what about your kids? It's mad!'

'It's you.' He gripped my shoulder. 'It's you who's driving me insane.'

We were standing in the bakery larder. Behind us were shelves of tarts; it was May, so they were strawberry tarts, winking red in the gloom. He pulled me against him.

'Just one little drink, Heather. Have pity on me.' His voice was as plaintive as my Dad's. 'No harm in that . . . Just one little drink, like old times.'

'Let go, Cliff. Please! It's over.'

'I wasn't any good at it, you mean.'

'I *told* you, it's nothing to do with that.'

'Not as good as your other boyfriends?'

'I haven't got any. *Please!* Someone's coming.'

I pulled away and he readjusted his hat.

Five minutes later, when I was back at my counter, I looked across the room. There he stood, bellowing. When he turned away I saw a splash of red on his white jacket. It looked as if he'd been stabbed in the back. Then I realized that he'd just been squashed against one of the strawberry tarts. It stayed there all afternoon; everyone was too nervous to tell him.

Two weeks later he was fired. They'd found him fiddling the books.

'Whole lobsters!' Naz's eyes rolled. 'Mr High and Mighty. Remember him shouting at Mo when she ate a *vol au vent*? And he'd been pocketing all that, for his own little self. Big self.'

None of us ever saw him again. A new chef came, and I told myself that Cliff had never happened. Perhaps he'll read this. But I still don't know if he'd understand.

My daydreams were of flying far away. But my real dreams, at

159

night, were harder to control. They were the ones I'd had as a child. I was falling, farther and farther, down into a hole that I knew had no bottom. Around me was a thick orange mist. Sometimes there were ledges on the way down, and floorboards, but when I grabbed them they broke off in my hand. I knew they tore my fingers but I didn't feel any pain. I'd shout out and hear my own voice echoing. Sometimes I heard someone knocking and I'd be trying to get up there to reach him, through the thick air. Once, I knew that it was Jonathan . . . But the mist was too heavy. As I tried to claw my way up, through air, I knew I was still falling.

Then I'd wake up, sweating, and hear the drainpipe knocking against the wall. Tap, tap, it called. When Teddy pulled it down the knocking stopped, but the nightmares went on. I'd try to stay awake long enough to stop them returning, but nowadays that no longer worked.

Thank goodness I had employment; not all the people from my school were so lucky. At work I forgot the nights. But during slack moments, when my meals were crated, they rose up again and with them rose the taste of my childhood. Then that big room echoed and the clunk-clunk of the arriving crockery became the knocking that I hoped I'd forgotten.

One Sunday afternoon Oonagh came to our bungalow; Oonagh with the weaselly face and peppermint breath. She'd minded me when I was little, from time to time, and she'd minded Teddy. That Sunday she brought along a small girl called Winnie, who she was minding now. It was a warm day in May, soon after the events I've described at work, and I was outside sunning my legs. Mum and Oonagh were indoors, having one of their long, confidential conversations.

Teddy was busy with one of his drainage schemes, heaping mud into long sausage-walls. Winnie was six; someone had tied back her brown hair with a ribbon. She was inspecting the place, easing her way through the nettles.

I closed my eyes. Light blurred and danced against my eyelids. She was talking to the hens like I used to do, ticking them off. She could be my own, small self. Then I heard her foot on the caravan

160

step, which creaked as usual, and her voice muffled inside.

'Here's our little house, Teddy. You wash your hands.'

Near me, Teddy grunted.

'Wash your hands, it's lunch-time,' she called, her voice clearer, at the doorway.

'Had me lunch.'

'No, in here. Come on.'

My eyes closed, I said, 'Go on, Teddy. Play with her.'

At last I heard Teddy's dragging footsteps, then both their voices inside.

'Who are you going to marry?' she asked.

'Not eating that, I'm not.'

'Just pretend to. Then you can have some ice cream.'

'Where?'

'Here.'

'S'not ice cream.'

'I'll tell you who I'm going to marry. I'm going to marry my Daddy. Finished your ice cream?'

'Isn't ice cream.'

'There, I'll wash it up. I'm marrying my Daddy, when I'm grown up, and we're going to have three children. Two boys and one girl. We're going to call her Sadie.'

'I can whistle now.'

Teddy made whistling noises, off-key.

'My Daddy can whistle,' she said. 'He gives me piggy-backs, my Daddy does. He lets me clean his spectacles. He doesn't let anyone else. Can you whistle "Puff the Magic Dragon"?'

'Enemy approaching!' His flat, walkie-talkie voice. 'Enemy attack!'

'I can sing it. "Puff the magic dragon lived by the sea" –'

'Enemy attacking! Uh-uh-uh-uh.' His machine-gun noise. 'Uh-uh-uh. *Bang! Splat!*'

' "– and wallowed in the autumn mists –" '

'Lie down, you're dead.'

'I'm not!' she cried.

'You're dead.'

Part Three

Chapter Eleven

It's so odd talking to you, whoever you are, and having no reply. If I knew who you were, of course, I wouldn't be telling you all this. But by now I'm wondering about you. It's the hushed centre of the night . . . Not a sound. The whole world is asleep, men, women and children . . .

You've been with me a long time. You might have got bored ages ago, or disgusted. In fact, I don't like some of this story myself. But you can always switch on the telly instead.

I'd like you to know one thing. Far more difficult than listening to this story is telling it. After all, it's what happened to me.

I worked at JT for a year. I thought it might make a difference with my Mum, that I was a working girl now. When I was at work, distanced, I could almost imagine us back home, being companionable, putting up our feet and moaning about our bosses . . . What he said to me, and I said to him, and would you credit it? Home looks simplified when you're away from it. You can arrange it into lamplit scenes to suit yourself, with the right questions and answers, with nobody too busy or embarrassed. You can imagine yourself saying anything.

I had all these conversations like stored reels of film, ready in my head. At work they unrolled, soundlessly, to the accompaniment of the Tannoy and the clump of the meat slice. I asked Mum all the questions I'd never dared. Flickering dreamlike through my head, and for some reason youthful and tender, she gave me the answers I needed.

This evaporated, of course, once I stepped indoors. I remember one evening when I arrived home late. She was still up, darning her tights – she's the last person I've known who actually darned them.

'What sort of time is this?' she said. 'And you needing your sleep.'

'I've only been with Mo.' It was true. Mo's fiancé's friend was a night guard at the freight depot and we'd sat in his booth drinking lager.

'And looking so cheap,' she said.

Usually she didn't notice when I came in. She'd be absorbed in the telly, or she'd be in her bedroom. The night I came back from that van she didn't say a thing. Yet here she was getting all normal, and irritable, and motherly, when I hadn't been doing anything wicked at all. Sometimes I wondered: is she deliberately blind?

'Don't like you looking common,' she said. 'Gives the wrong impression.'

'Who to?'

'Them. You know.' She jerked her head towards the wide world outside.

'Men, you mean?'

She pursed her lips. 'Don't you trust them. All them things they say . . . can't be trusted.'

'I don't trust them.'

She glanced up and said sharply, 'Well, you should. You're only seventeen.'

I would have smiled at the illogicality – she was as bad as my Dad – but I wanted to ask her something.

'What about Dad?'

166

Her needle stilled. 'What about him?'

'Did you trust him?'

She paused, and drew the stitches tighter. 'Don't you say nothing against your father. Won't hear of it.'

I gazed at her, feeling the usual disappointment. I wanted her to speak the truth. If only, just once, she would confide in me. After all, she confided in Oonagh.

'Never strayed, not your Dad.'

'Didn't he?'

'Don't you be pert – '

'I'm not being pert!' I cried out.

'That's not nice talk . . . You know it isn't.'

You see, they closed ranks, her and Dad. Even though they seemed to have nothing to say to each other . . . Even though they'd never got on.

In my dream conversations at work I might have spoken. But you wouldn't have, either, if you'd seen the tight expression on her face. Anyway, could I really bear to tell her the truth? She wouldn't hear anything, if she didn't want to. They both closed me out; there was this loyalty between them. A month or so earlier I'd said to my father,

'Why did Mum never make me a proper birthday party? Couldn't she be bothered?'

Eyes vague, he'd replied, 'Won't hear nothing against your Mum . . . greatest little Mum in the world.' He went on, even vaguer, 'By Jesus, she's a grand little woman.'

Years ago I would have been stunned by this. But nowadays I realized that he believed everything as he said it, and his brain was as weak as water. Our mutual betrayal had silenced us, once. But now it was just the poverty of our words.

I hadn't continued the conversation. Dad, who'd never loved me enough to listen to a word I said.

Soon I'll be an air hostess. That's what I told myself; I clung to those words. The sound gained weight each time I spoke them. Soon I'll be an air hostess, I said, and none of this will matter . . .

167

And that autumn, just a year ago, Am-Air recruited me as a flight attendant.

They call them flight attendants because they're American. I tried Am-Air first because I'd met this trainee pilot in the Sheraton Tropic Room. It's in the Sheraton near me, right by the airport; if you've been there you'll remember it. There's grown trees in there, and humid vegetation. There's parrots singing and a lovely thatched bar. It's the sort of place they film rum ads, to save the air fares. You expect to see bronzed bodies in bikinis, but of course it's all businessmen just arrived off the planes . . . Japs and Germans, wearing plastic name-tags. That reminds you where you are.

This pilot, though, he had a gorgeous tan, and he said that Am-Air were the guys to fly with. He wanted my phone number, but you know I didn't have one; afterwards I pretended I had a car outside, and walked home. He'd just been laying-over one night and killing time with a cocktail. He said it was a people job, and he could tell I was a people person. He said I should give them a buzz, so I did.

They sent me a form saying I should have experience in public contact. JT seemed like that to me; I never saw the eaters, of course, it was more like posting nourishing letters into the sky, but I'd been there more than a year and that seemed like experience. Besides I'd read the order forms and I knew about the special diets, things like that. The timetables danced around my head, the dancing codes of my daydreams. And I knew French, from my bedroom monologues.

So they took me on. They had a building at the airport and I did a training course. I learnt first aid and how to mix a cocktail. I learnt about currency tables and how the air crew always put the passengers first. I can't remember those weeks, not now. We had a lot of tests; if you failed one you had to start all over again. I was so tense that I noticed nothing, just blurred edges around my central, hard concentration.

It's the unexpected moment that it hits you, isn't it? I felt blank, the day I passed, and blank for some days afterwards. My parents

168

didn't help; neither of them could cope with big events. Dad said, 'Blimey . . . Fancy that.' Mum looked warily pleased, as if planes were slightly wicked, but awesome too.

I stood on the bed, wearing my uniform. I turned this way and that; I felt different, but not heart-stoppingly so. It was later that it hit me, in the queue at Boots the next Saturday.

Two women stood in front of me.

'He's a sly one.'

'Thought you said he'd gone to Saudi Arabia.'

'That's what I mean.'

Suddenly I realized: soon I'd be gone. I looked down at my wire basket. A bottle of cleanser lay there, and some lipstick in an embossed tube. Me, Heather Irene Mercer, soon I'd be reddening my lips under a foreign sky. My lips, this lipstick. People would be speaking a strange language around me. And I was being paid good money for going there; somebody thought I was worth paying.

Before I began my job, how did I imagine it? I can't remember. Vaguely, I suppose . . . The golden skies of my Bible stories . . . up into oblivion, the clouds closing behind me like a mouth, closing away the grubby present. I hadn't ever flown, remember, even as a passenger. I'd just seen those big planes waiting, every day of my life.

I told myself it was just nerves, that first flight. All the girls must feel the same way, mustn't they? I sat through the briefing; in my uniform I felt like a dressed-up doll, it wasn't myself sitting there, though underneath the cloth my blouse stuck to me because I was so nervous. The captain was from Texas and he talked real slow. It seemed to take hours, him drawling about the hot shot from Shell, in First Class, and how many vegetarian meals in Economy. I wanted to get to the toilet. A girl called Mary Lou was looking after me. When I emerged she smiled:

'I guess I felt that way too, my first flight. In and out of the john like a goddam jack-in-the-box.'

169

We tap-tapped across the tarmac, holding on to our hats, it was so windy. I told myself: I'm one of a team now. They took me on, didn't they?

If they hadn't, you see, I'd know that they *knew*. This might seem stupid – it was stupid – but it was buried in me, deeper than superstition. I'd felt it at the JT interview, which I'd passed. I'd felt it at my driving test, which I'd failed. JT hadn't found me out, but the driving people had. It was mad, of course, but it blocked my throat like asthma. Standing in the lobby of the test centre, the paper in my hand, I simply couldn't breathe. Then it passed and I was just a normal, disappointed person who happened to have failed her test.

I followed Mary Lou down the cabin, checking the headsets, pillows and baby-kits, like I'd learned in our mock-up. It was a 747, with a spacious, hushed interior that smelt of perfume. Someone switched on the lights and the music. It seemed like a stage-set, waiting; all those empty seats, and those vacuumed aisles.

I clung to Mary Lou, getting in the way as the passengers embarked. I nodded and smiled too. Mary Lou glistened as she greeted them; she was a big, radiant blonde. You'd probably think her bland, but you wouldn't have heard her raucous laugh at the briefing.

'Hi,' I said, nodding and smiling too. 'Welcome on board.'

They glanced at me, smiling; I tried to concentrate but I kept hearing Dad's parting words. *Don't do anything I wouldn't do*, he'd said, patting my bottom. *You be a good girl, see?* I remembered the medical officer tapping my chest, as I lay there in my bra and pants. *You've been on the pill how long, Heather?* Gazing down at me.

Some of the passengers stopped, and caught my eye. Some ignored me, pushing their way down the aisle, lifting their brief-cases as they went. I made my mind go blank.

The seats were occupied now. Faces turned as we walked past, bending across to check they'd fastened their seat belts. As we taxied out I told myself: they don't know the first thing about me. And Am-Air are paying me . . . Am-Air think I'm *worth* paying.

I still felt transparent, though. Kimberley, the purser, was speaking over the PA. In our section, I was doing the demo because it was supposed to be good practice, so I positioned myself in front of all those eyes. I pointed one arm, and then the other, to indicate the masks.

' . . . the oxygen masks will drop automatically . . .'

Avoiding looking at those faces I moved my foolish, clockwork arms. Have you ever dreamed you were standing on a stage, naked?

I clamped the mask to my mouth.

' . . . and inhale deeply . . .'

I mimed inhaling, gripping the mask as if I were dying. The old feeling swept over me. They *knew* . . . They could see right through this uniform to the worthless me inside. They knew about Cliff the chef and how I'd treated him so badly he'd lost his job. They knew about the Heathrow Hotel man pushing me out of his bedroom. And the man at the Holiday Inn.

Actually most of them were reading their newspapers. But only because they could see me for what I was, and they were disgusted, just as my mother would be, if she ever learnt the truth.

My legs felt saggy and boneless with guilt. It caught me unprepared, this guilt, it seeped out like a gas. Where did it come from; what hidden cracks? I was being punished for thinking I could actually do this job, and push Dad right behind me . . . for thinking I'd be changed just because I was being lifted out of England.

Replacing the mask, I smiled at the rows of heads. The smile stretched my skin. We'd been taught to smile, to instil confidence in our passengers. 'Your job, honey, is to reassure them,' the teacher said, 'however lousy you're feeling yourself.'

We were carried along, faster and faster, and then the cabin tilted and we were up, climbing into the sky. A ping released us and I made my escape towards the toilet. Through the porthole, I saw the fields down there. We tilted. A glassy eye stared up at me, flashing in the sun. That was my reservoir.

I'm always cowering in toilets. Remember at school, when I didn't dare come out? All those girls . . . they knew. Now,

171

crouched on the flimsy plastic rim I told myself: don't be stupid. This is just first-day nerves. You'll lose your job if you don't pull yourself together.

Nobody noticed a thing, of course. But I knew then that I couldn't escape, even though I could see the crinkled woollen clouds below me, and the blue void above. It was still the same, heavy old me, pausing there, sticky with fright. He was still beside me, curdling the air.

I felt sinkingly superstitious, that first flight. Five hours later the plane tilted. Below us, buildings lifted into the sky, like fingers pointing. New York literally took away my breath . . . those blocks bathed in rosy light, with shadowed canyons between them.

Dad wasn't down there, in those streets. But it didn't make any difference. It didn't make any difference that he hadn't really touched me for the past year. He was within me, he was in my breathing and the thumping of my heart, and I took him everywhere. I'd take him to the ends of the earth.

I lived in limbo – in a sort of dazzled numbness. Apparently they all did. Korky, another flight attendant, tried to explain it to me over breakfast. We were in Los Angeles three weeks later.

'Boy, does it louse up your relationships,' she said, cracking open the jam sachet. 'Like, you lose the continuity. Love's never having to say you're sorry. But I'll correct that: love's *being* there to never have to say you're sorry.' She flicked the sachet into the bin. 'I never am.'

'Aren't you?'

'Like, you lose your sense of caring. You lose that responsibility, because the next day you'll be gone . . . Kinda weird.'

I thought of the roads at home, and people throwing the litter out of their cars . . . all that untidiness they wouldn't see again. Oonagh's sister, Marie, was a chambermaid at the Heathrow Hotel; she told such stories about the débris people left behind, the intimate débris of their personal lives. What did they care, half-way to Singapore?

After breakfast with Korky I went up to my room to sleep.

172

Outside, the sky was solid blue, as if it had been built around the landscape. The freeway below was lined with dusty palms; it was a wide road sliding with traffic. It wasn't that different from home . . . Just the road wider and the sky bluer, and everything silent because the air-conditioner sealed me in. But just the same . . . Opposite, down there, was the long glass frontage of a Ford showroom, and then a burger joint with lights chasing each other round, 'Fries 50c, Fries 50c'. Nobody walked in Los Angeles either, just like home . . . Farther along stood the Holiday Inn, with blinding white fretwork. Outside it stood a sign saying, 'Holiday Inn Welcomes IBM Convention'. Even the IBM was the same.

This was my first lay-over in LA. Korky said it stretched for hundreds of miles, just like this. There was no centre. You never arrived anywhere, you just drove.

'Back home,' I said, 'there's nowhere to arrive at either.'

'Honey, I've been to Oxford, to your Stratford-on-Avon – '

'Not where I come from, there isn't.'

Upstairs, I showered and hung up my dress in the steam to shed the creases. Remember the shower-cap Mum gave me, long ago? Nowadays I threw them away like everyone else. I drew the curtains and climbed into bed. These hotel rooms were all alike. The décor was either blue, with a nubbly turquoise bedspread and curtains, or orange. Today, aching with fatigue, I gazed at daylight glowing through amber weave. I could be anywhere in the world, except that here they called the curtains 'drapes'.

The weeks passed in a jolting daze of airport coaches and hotel lobbies, of lifting and carrying and pouring and clearing away, the smile plumbed into my face like a bathroom fixture . . . Of foreign coins in my handbag and daylight through the curtains, of midnight arrivals and the sudden blast of foreign heat before I stepped into the bus, of long delays in some brightly lit departure lounge, with the taste of sleep still in my mouth. I felt as blank as my parents looked, watching show after show on the TV . . . I jolted along, busy and passive.

173

Korky was right. I forgot home, not through simple absence – after all I was only away a few days at a time – but through dislocation . . . hazed disorientation. I didn't feel, I didn't think. I slept heavily, with violent dreams.

The only time I felt properly myself was when I bought Teddy a present. I always bought him something; he'd make a fuss if I didn't. I dawdled around the airport boutiques. I was most often at Frankfurt. It's like a futuristic Oxford Street in there, with all the shops. I came to know the Matchbox cars, and costumed dolls like the ones Gwen had, and the spotlit mounds of fluffy bears. Teddy wanted instruments of destruction. He was seven, now, so he demanded more than sticks.

It was in Dallas, one night, that I was standing at the hotel gift shop, looking through the window.

'Hi. Who's the lucky guy?'

'What?'

'Puts a smile on your face like that? You're standing there with this big, beautiful grin.'

I'd been looking at the Atom-Death Bleep Gun. I turned round.

'Remember me?' he grinned. 'I'm the guy you put into an erect position.'

Lots of them say that. I remembered him now; I'd reminded him to adjust his seat for landing. He was muscular, with a square, shadowed jaw. I didn't want to buy Teddy's gift with him there.

'I'm all on my ownsome tonight,' he said. 'You have a date?'

I still can't meet people's eye, however reckless I feel. I gazed at the carpet and agreed to meet him in the Rib Room. I only looked up when he walked away: a loping walk; an utter stranger.

I bought the gun. It was mounted on a card, with a detachable blast-nozzle. I pictured Teddy's face when he saw it.

I persuaded myself that I wanted to have dinner with that man, and the old, tingling excitement and disgust rose up in me. A shutter clunked down in my brain. I shut off Teddy, because I didn't want him to see me now.

It's all so much easier in the dark, isn't it? This man's name was

174

Rod, and he'd turned off the lights. I'd drunk some wine, so the undressing wasn't that embarrassing, and I was half-smothered by him when the crying began.

It was a child crying in the next room. On and on it cried, while Rod grunted and the bed rocked. He kept talking. 'Honey,' he murmured, 'I love you . . . ' I hate it when somebody says that. What do they mean? What on earth can you reply?

The cries went on, dry and monotonous, like a wood-saw. Was nobody coming to comfort it? Perhaps the child lay in darkness . . . The cries grew louder. Rod was grunting into my ear but I didn't hear him. I couldn't bear the sound of that child . . . it was crying urgently now. Didn't this man hear it?

Teddy lay in darkness too . . . Teddy in his damp nightie, bellowing with loneliness. And all the other children . . . me . . . all of them. All of them now, at this moment . . . How many of them were yelling now for comfort? *Shut up*, the lot of you . . .

I tried to shut it out . . . I gripped him, the warmth beating up me, and then the blackness exploded.

When it exploded, shuddering, I forgot everything. I forgot the cries, I blasted all the sadness, all the children crying and the human breakage, I blasted them to pieces . . . Just for those shuddering seconds.

Too swift . . . Always too swift.

Soon afterwards I escaped from this stranger, with his smug recollections and his invitation to a 'togetherness shower' . . . these Americans spend the whole time washing. They must be ashamed too. When I left his room the child had stopped.

Back in bed, I fell into a heavy sleep. I dreamed of searching for Teddy in a huge warehouse full of children. I'd never seen it before but I knew it was in our yard, like my other dreams . . . I struggled to get there through the thick mist . . . All the children wore clothes; they twisted and mewled, a turning mixture of pink cotton and denim . . . The more I searched, the larger the warehouse grew, swelling up . . . I knew he was calling me but I couldn't even hear his voice, there were so many cries. I wanted to touch the children, but I couldn't because somebody had

175

jointed them like meat . . . Inside their clothes their limbs were loose.

You see, my dreams were violent.

Back home, I slept. The banging doors, and the grinding noise as Dad tried to start his lorry . . . As I lay there, drowsily, they seemed to come from the far side of a valley. Dad would tiptoe past my room as if I were an invalid, then bump into the table and swear, loudly. As you know, there wasn't a lot of conversation at our home, and neither Mum nor Dad asked me much about my job, except did I meet anybody famous. They distrusted anywhere abroad, because they'd never been, yet they were awestruck, too. Dad bragged about me to his mates, I heard him, and Mum never told me to do the chores when I was wearing my uniform; she seemed to think I was serving my country, and should keep my strength. Once she asked me what I did, and when I told her she looked shocked.

'They make you do that – just like a skivvy?' She started. 'There's nobody to do that for you?'

Teddy was the only person who treated me the same, rummaging in my duty-free bags for his presents, then pulling them out and shooting us dead.

Time was all dislocated; I'd wake up hungry in the middle of the night; I'd sleep all afternoon. I felt much more removed from home, and out of step, than at JT. Once I got up after lunch and went to West Drayton. When I arrived I realized it was Thursday, and early closing. After California the streets looked cramped, and grey, and amateurish. Standing at the bus stop, I tried to remember how I'd once felt. Over there, in the Wimpy, I'd sat drinking coffee with Sandra – neither of us liked coffee but it felt sophisticated. She'd said, 'Janice isn't a virgin. I can tell because she's had her ears pierced.'

Across the road was the chemist's. Once I'd seen Gwen's family's car parked outside it, and them all sitting there looking at their holiday snaps. Gwen's Dad had just got them from the chemist's and none of them could wait until they reached home . . .

And over there, in the launderette, I'd felt faint when Jonathan had passed.

Now I just shivered in the wind and thought: damn buses.

That winter – last winter – I passed my test and bought a car: a Mini. It was for Teddy and me, to make up for all the times I was away. He bounced up and down in it, he was so pleased. Sitting there, I put my arm round him and squeezed.

'Where shall we go, then?'

He struggled free. 'You pong.'

'What?'

'Your smelly perfume.'

'Don't you like it? It's called "My Love".'

'Pongy.'

I sat still; my throat swelled. How could he? I yearned for him; I wanted to hold him close to me, the two of us in my new car. I wanted to show him the world . . . I wanted to press his head into my breast and keep him safe.

I sat quite still, struck by a thought. Slowly, I thought the words over . . .

Is this how Dad had yearned for me?

It's ridiculous that it had never struck me before. I didn't want to seduce my brother, of course, but that was unimportant. It was simply that I loved him; dear God, I loved that boy. It was the only pure passion I'd ever had. I loved every inch of him, head to toe, inside and out.

And didn't I know the damage that could do? Perhaps it was good that I was planning to move away.

'Everyone else likes the way I smell,' I said abruptly. 'You're an idiot.'

We drove miles up the motorway, past the gravel pits and their cranes reared up, past the Span estates with their young marrieds, Yvonne from school amongst them . . . right out into the country. There were some beautiful, golden days last winter. Teddy sat beside me, just as I'd sat beside Dad, kicking his legs and twiddling the radio. I was the driver now. But Teddy was bolder than I had been; he was the one urging me on. I speeded up. As we drove, I had a rare thought for my Dad. Could he remember our happiness when I was young and sitting in his cab? Or was it all spoilt for him too?

Chapter Twelve

A m-Air 6 flies right around the world: LA, New York, London, Karachi, Singapore . . . It girdles the globe. You fly through twenty-four time zones; you fly faster than the spreading dusk. I signed up for the long hauls if I could; the longer the better. By spring I'd watched *Charlie's Angels* in six capital cities. I also had a tan – faint, because of my fair complexion, but unmistakable. I lay beside bright blue pools. Nobody knew that I'd been fat, once. I didn't have to tell anyone about that; besides, who wanted to know? At some point they usually said, 'Tell me about yourself', but their interest was limited. I stayed behind my sunglasses; every now and then I sat up to oil my legs. I still hated my heavy thighs, but nobody knew that either. I turned the pages of magazines; I seldom read books, I didn't seem to have the concentration. Waiters in monogrammed jackets brought me iced tea; I glanced through menus in their heavy, laminated folders.

Numbed from the sun, I wandered along hotel lobbies. Numbed from the flying, I sat in taxis with lonely men who were far from home. 'Curry Paradise', 'Whisky A Go-Go', said the signs. 'All-Nite Topless!' We stayed stuck in traffic jams, trying to keep a conversation going. It was a relief when they didn't attempt to talk.

I never dated, as they called it, members of the air crews. After all, I'd see them next day. Besides, they were either gay, and off for their beauty sleep, or else family men scared of the risks.

It was a bad idea, too, to date the passengers. I found this out, to my cost. At each landing we said over the PA, 'Am-Air hope you enjoyed your flight and look forward to seeing you again.'

And once I did. It happened one Bahrein–Frankfurt flight. I recognized this grey-cropped head in the aisle seat. It was a German cement contractor. Two weeks ago he'd told me all about his mother. Later, in his room, he'd asked me to spank him because he was such a naughty boy. I'd patted him, blushing, disowning my hand. I'd hoped to forget all that.

But here he was, plucking at my sleeve. Being German, he made himself only too clear. Shireen, another flight attendant, was near enough to hear him saying,

'Why did you not meet me next day, as promised?'

'I'm sorry. I forgot.'

'I am waiting in the lounge three hours. I wait in the hotel thinking: where is my English friend?'

I tried to move away.

'My feelings,' he said, 'you hurt my feelings.'

I escaped. Back in the galley Shireen said,

'Who's that nut?'

'Don't know,' I mumbled, busying myself with the water jugs.

'Jesus, don't we get 'em.'

After that episode I took more care. You can throw the litter out of your car, but it's not so easy with people. Believe it or not, even in my job they cropped up again. If you're laying-over in some city, after all, it's possible to bump into them . . . the main streets and the big hotels, they're usually in the same small area. Once or twice it happened and I felt gagged, panic-stricken, my past rising up in my throat. I didn't want to be reminded of my behaviour. Once, in the lift at the Kuala Lumpur Inter-Continental, the doors

180

slid open and some men stepped in. I recognized one of them. He was a tall, ravaged-looking man, vice-president of something or other, he'd told me. If he recognized me now he wasn't showing it. I looked away, but the lift was all mirrors. Whichever way I turned, there was his profile, splintered into angles; there were his two eyes. The grey cloth of his suit was within touching distance.

'We're talking in seven figures here,' he was saying. They must be going up to the conference suite. 'We need to make that clear . . .'

Yesterday afternoon he'd been suckling me, his face red and crumpled.

'. . . there's no option on this one, gentlemen. Seven figures are the figures we're talking . . .'

Kneeling there, bowed, his mouth clamped to my nipple. My breasts didn't belong to me . . . they were bubbies. That's what I called them. Now he was here, I hated him. I hated us both.

I'd been a flight attendant for nearly six months when I met Ali. We're talking about last March. He was a passenger, so I had to be careful. He wasn't.

I have to pause, here. I'll make myself some coffee.

Bear with me; I've nearly finished. When you hear about Ali, you'll think that I've been saving the worst until last.

But believe me, the worst happened long, long before I met him.

Chapter Thirteen

I saw the dawn just now. I didn't realize that I've been sitting here so long. I saw it out of the side window, when I went to the kitchen: the sky stained grey, with flat clouds laid across like ink spreading into damp paper.

Here in this room it's still dark. The mug is warming my knee. I bought this kimono in Bangkok and I've worn it for the past week, I haven't really got up yet.

I don't know what I should have put in or left out of my story so far. I could have chosen other events, just as random as these. That time in the cinema with Gwen and her Dad, remember? When I felt so sad. It's over now, sealed, now I've said it. I've locked it into the plan of my past, but if I'd stopped and thought, I could have locked in so many others instead. I'm trusting to instinct, telling you the first things that come into my mind. Nobody's taught me to organize my brain, you see. Except for the odd moment at school, nobody's bothered.

My first couple of meetings with Ali were as random as anything else. Try to picture me, last spring, as Ali first saw me. My long hair was puffed up and held in place with an alice band; someone once called me a Barbie Doll. I was a big, blonde girl with spiky eyelashes; I probably looked old-fashioned, but then lots of air crew do. You'd never have guessed anything about me. That's because I was used to small talk, it's the only type I ever heard. I looked ripe and pink.

I can think quite calmly now, of how I looked. If you'd seen me then, you might have thought me attractive.

Ali thought so, anyway. He was flying from Karachi to Bahrein. Muslims either knock back six Scotches or they drink a glass of water. He asked for water. It was a night flight and he stayed awake in his pool of light. When you're working at night, there's a club-like feeling between you and the insomniacs . . . He was reading sheaves of paper; he was very good-looking, and as young as me, with pitted skin. I remember thinking: poor thing, he must've had terrible acne.

That's all I remember. When he disembarked I noticed how slight he was; no taller than me.

I was laying-over. The next night I went to a party. The flat belonged to the boyfriend of a British Airways girl called Cathy; it was crowded, and the air was thick with smoke. English and German men stood around, guffawing; their shirts were stained dark at the armpits. It was mostly men; these parties usually are. They spend the evening comparing booze prices and talking about their next leave. They don't have much in common, except being stuck in Bahrein.

I ate Twiglets. I must have done this a hundred times; life seemed particularly senseless. This being Bahrein, there was a building site outside the window, the scaffolding criss-crossing the sky, and the winking lights of a plane coming in to land.

Then I noticed the Pakistani. He was standing at the other window, a glass of orange juice in his hand. I've always found it awkward, meeting passengers off duty. He looked shy, too.

We chatted a bit; he asked me the usual questions, like did I have permanent jet-lag and which was my favourite city. He didn't ask me whether I had a boyfriend back home and if he got jealous with me gadding about; at this stage of a party someone usually does, but he was too polite for that. He was the well-mannered, quiet type. He asked me to join him for dinner to-morrow, but I'd be gone by then, so he gave me his card and asked if next time I was in Karachi he could show me around his home city.

'My home city . . .' That's how he talked. Someone had brought him up nicely. 'I would be honoured', he said, 'if you would join me.'

I was imagining holding his pitted face in my hands and pulling him towards me. Believe it or not, I'd never done that to an Oriental before. They'd tried all right, but I'd never been chatted up by one I trusted.

Not that he was chatting me up now. I looked at his card. He was called Ahmed something, but once I got to know him I liked calling him Ali, him being a Pakistani. You know, Ali Baba. Anyway, it's better that none of you know his real name.

His father ran a shipping firm, he said. He'd joined it and he did a lot of business in the Middle East. He didn't brag about how sophisticated he was, what a hot shot, which impressed me. He was my age; most of the men I met were older. He talked a lot about his father, and his family; they were obviously close.

'You live at home?' I asked.

'Oh yes. And yourself?'

'When I'm in England.'

'The best place . . . I'm right? Home is where the heart is. At least, in my country it is.' There were damp rings on the glass table. He ran his finger across them. 'I admire my father very much . . . He's a wonderful man. I do so hope, Heather . . . that you will meet him.'

I rubbed the table with my damp finger, thinking how I'd describe my own Dad.

I usually threw away cards, but I kept his, with his office and residence addresses. After all, I hadn't got to know him yet. All we'd done was shake hands in the lobby of my hotel.

Two weeks later I saw him again. It was March; sleet blew into my face as I climbed into my Mini. The yard was slushy from last

184

week's snow; Dad hadn't bothered to sweep it. Closing the door, each trip, I closed away England. From now on it would be corridors and lounges, heated and odourless, with no demands on me except the easy, automatic ones. I would know no weather for fourteen hours, until I stepped off the plane. When I arrived there, home would have dissolved away; and when I was back home, all those cities dissolved away too. You can see the appeal of my job.

I saw him in Karachi and he fell in love with me. Actually, the scent was there at our first meeting, though you would hardly have believed it from the conversation. He had dark, liquid eyes; he looked as startled and pure as a woodland creature. I gazed at his slender brown wrists, covered in hair.

He said, 'I want to show you everything beautiful in my city.'

I wanted to shut my eyes tight. I wanted to slip my hand inside his white shirt and to feel the warm, smooth skin in there. Oh yes, I'd felt like this before, but I wasn't prepared for the effect upon him.

He'd been brought up so religious, you see. The first place he took me was the Quaid-i-Azam's Mazar. The Kaidi What? I asked. It's the tomb of our Founder, he replied, the Founder of Pakistan. His driver took us there in a beige Mercedes. Ali talked about the Muslim State; in front, the driver's shoulders set themselves squarer, in pride. I sat in the back, within touching distance of Ali. I was heated by the sun, and lust.

The tomb was an ugly modern thing in the middle of a round-about. He talked about Islam, and what it meant to him. When he couldn't think of a word he rubbed the side of his nose. I was trying to work out why his scarred skin made him even more attractive. I suppose it stopped him being perfect; it made him vulnerable. He was marked by his youth. On most faces the past doesn't show . . . most people can cover it up.

His family meant a lot to him. He was the only son. He had two sisters and he was worried about their education. There were endless cousins too, and uncles; his life seemed to be one long series of weddings and family reunions. His upbringing sounded the opposite of mine. That family was the centre of his life . . . Until he met me.

I was just laying-over for two days. We went on a boat-trip with his sisters and some girls from Am-Air; we scarcely talked, alone. The next day I was to meet him at the Gymkhana Club. He'd asked me for a game of tennis but I can't play tennis, nobody's taught me, so I said I'd join him later. In fact, I arrived early to get a glimpse of his legs. He was playing with three older men, all of them drenched with sweat. They shouted to each other, laughing, 'You rascal! . . . You rapscallian!' His legs were all I'd hoped; the hairs painted on them like seaweed in the current.

Afterwards we all shook hands. Two were uncles and one was his father. We sat at a table, drinking Seven-Up. The men sucked their straws; with their fizzy drinks they looked as innocent as children.

'Don't trust him,' they said proudly, 'he's a terrible sport.'

The father put his arm around Ali, fondly. The portly one gave him a mock punch in the ribs. Under the milky sky I felt the old envy rise, catching in my throat. I thought I was immune by now.

They turned to me, from their charmed circle, and were polite.

'Your parents must be proud of you, jet-setting round the world.'

'Oh yes,' I agreed.

'But I expect you're glad to get home. To the roast beef of old England . . . Not forgetting the Yorkshire pudding. Your father's in business?'

Yes: the betting and boozing business. 'Haulage.'

I said to myself, 'And pig-breeding.' Just so I could imagine their faces. You can't even mention pigs in front of Muslims; they'd probably faint.

'If he ever travels this way, on his business, we would consider it a great pleasure to show him our city.'

He's lucky to get farther than Slough. I made these silent replies so often, nowadays, that people were calling me enigmatic.

Ali sent roses to my room, but so far the only moves he'd made had been floral ones. We were in company most of the time, either

186

with crew members – my own temporary and forgettable family –
or his retinue of relatives and his driver.

One of us must do something. He was too well-bred for me to
know his feelings. Perhaps he thought I was even more well-bred,
being English. I'd hoped that my being an air hostess would stop
these polite thoughts; most foreigners weren't troubled with
them.

On my last evening he drove me back to the hotel. In the car
park he switched off the engine. You know the moment . . . By
this time most men are loosened by alcohol, which helps.

At least he smoked. He lit a cigarette.

'And tomorrow you'll be gone,' he said in a low voice.

'Gone to London.'

Sleeping cars lay on either side; ahead stood stiff rows of
flowers, bright in the spotlights.

'I can't begin to tell you how happy I've been, these last two
days . . .' Smoke wreathed his face. 'In your company, Heather.'

A silence. Several cars away a door slammed.

'You must hate this damned smoking.'

'I don't mind. I'm used to it.'

'I can't . . . Oh, I don't know what to say.' He paused. 'I wish
you weren't leaving.'

'I'm here now. I'm not gone yet.'

Approaching footsteps. Two men were passing our car; they
carried briefcases and they spoke in loud English voices: '. . . so
she phones up', said one, 'to tell me the bloody gerbil's died.'

We waited, watching them walk into the hotel.

'I suppose this is goodbye,' he said.

I rested my head on the back of the seat. 'For a while.'

In a lower voice he said, 'I can't bear you to go.'

I turned. 'Can't you?'

'I can't bear it . . . I . . .'

I moved towards him. He took my face in his hands and kissed
my mouth, hesitantly. I was released, like a coiled spring; the old
blindness rose up. I grabbed him.

It lasted for a long time. Then he drew back, shakily, and kissed my eyes and my cheeks; I put my hand inside his shirt, at last, and felt his lovely hard chest. I stroked the hairs; I ran my hand over his shoulder, feeling its smoothness. He was trembling, he wanted me so much. My mouth was dry; I couldn't swallow.

I whispered, 'Don't leave me tonight.'

We kissed again, and finally we managed to get out of the car. Dazed, we made our way into the hotel and along the lobby. My legs were so weak that I had to lean against him. We stood at the lift . . . his shirt was unbuttoned but he didn't notice. I always feel superstitious, at lifts. If the lift arrives soon, its arrow pinging, then it will be all right. This time it did. We stood there suspended like waxworks as the lift rose.

I fumbled my door open and slammed it shut. Then we were down on the bed, struggling.

'I love you,' he said. 'Heather, I can't believe this . . . Let me look at you.'

'No.'

I gripped him between my thighs. I'd got his shirt off now and his skin . . . oh, its smell . . . I was rubbing my nose against it.

'I mustn't do this . . . Heather – '

'Come on,' I crooned, unbuckling his belt.

'I shouldn't – please, my darling, please stop me – '

'No,' I hissed in his ear.

'We mustn't – not yet.'

'Yes – now!'

'You see, I love you. Do you understand? I've been wanting to tell you, all this time . . . I didn't dare say it – don't – '

I was licking his chest . . . the salty skin. My tongue stroked him. I grappled with his zip.

'Ever since that party . . . those stupid people all round you – '

I silenced him. He couldn't speak now. I silenced him with my mouth, pulling him into me until I was filled. Greedily I explored his mouth; greedily I arched and fell with him, gripping him, damp with sweat, my legs tightening around him. There was a high humming in my ears, like telegraph wires singing in the wind, higher and higher.

188

He was so passionate. His face was wet with tears, from wanting me so much. Cries came from deep inside him, as if his soul was being dragged up in pain. My face was wet from his kisses; he couldn't stop kissing me . . . we opened our mouths so wide it seemed our faces must split.

We rolled over and fell on to the floor, bumping my hip. The counterpane was pulled down, tangled in our legs. I giggled but he didn't; there was nothing light-hearted about him. We were jammed against the table; its lamp rattled, in rhythm . . . the wires in my head hummed higher.

Miraculously, we finished together. Afterwards he lay holding me tightly, for a long time. I had no idea what he was thinking; his intensity had shaken me. We lay there, skin to skin; he didn't relax. I wondered if I should get us a glass of water.

Minutes passed. Finally he unstuck himself from me, gently, and removed the counterpane as if tenderly unwrapping a parcel. He gazed at me; his dark eyes were like two sorrowful pools.

'We shouldn't have done that,' he said.

'Why not?'

His voice was high and tight. 'Just . . . so very soon . . . too soon.'

He started stroking me, still in a sad way. He stroked every inch of me, gazing at my body. I was used to this, as you probably are . . . a lazy itemization . . . a sated inspection of the goods. But the expression on his face wasn't like that. It was tragic, and reverent. He pulled down a pillow and put it under my head, to make me comfortable.

Finally he got up and put on his underpants. There was a thud and a giggle from the next room. He sat on the bed.

'Want a Polo?' I asked.

He put his head in his hands. 'No thank you.' I fished for the Polos, on the table behind me, and took one. Sucking it, I watched him. He sat there, slumped. I gazed at his walnut body and white briefs.

Then he said, 'Did that mean anything?'

I looked at him, startled. 'What?'

189

'I just have a feeling . . . that I wasn't quite reaching you.'

I paused. 'Really?'

He lifted his head and gazed at me, stricken. 'I love you so much, you see . . . I love you so much, Heather, that it frightens me.'

Chapter Fourteen

T wo weeks later a letter arrived. I read it in the Tesco car park;
I preferred reading letters in my Mini. The back seat was
heaped with carrier bags. Dad was useless at shopping, and Mum
was at work.

It was a sunny Saturday. I wound down the window. Beyond
the fence was the recreation ground, and the squeak of the see-
saw.

My darling Heather,
Your departure has shattered me. It's as if half of myself has
been torn away. Those two days with you have changed my life
for good. Existence before I met you – all twenty-one years of it
– has become irrelevant. I told you it's frightening, didn't I?
And now, life without you is meaningless too. I open my mouth
to talk to people – why? I eat, I work, and I can't see any reason
for it. Believe me, I've never felt anything like this for any
human being. I can't be careful and cool about it, there's no
point disguising my words. I tell myself that you can't possibly
feel the same, it would be a miracle if you did, but I would be
quite happy if, some day, you just felt a fraction of what I feel
for you. Do I dare hope?

I can't concentrate, I can't work, I just remember the scent of your hair. I close my eyes and try to picture your face. If only I had a photo. I go over those two enchanted days again and again, trying to find some moment that I've overlooked. Just now I had a wonderful surprise – I remembered the government shop, and we were looking at handbags and you leant over and said, 'It's such a relief, not having your driver staring.' I remember how happy I felt then. I remember, over and over, what happened that last memorable night. Those words I said: will you forget them? I behaved badly, please forgive me.

I can't exist without you. I must see you. Even being in the same city would help – even if I only saw you sometimes. Please, will you write and tell me whether you will be angry if I come to London?

And please, one more thing, will you tell me exactly what you're doing and what you're wearing, while (IF?) you write to me?

All my love, my darling, in hope

Your Ali

A cracking of branches. It was Teddy and his friends, bashing through the undergrowth. I sat in the car, holding the flimsy blue letter. Teddy stopped, and said to them loudly,

'I kiss my girlfriend's tits before I go to sleep.'

They stood, switching at the bushes aimlessly. Teddy was eight now, and turning into a real thug.

'So do I,' said one of his friends, feebly.

'Smelly-bum!' Teddy rushed at him; they thundered off like elephants through the rhododendrons.

'Tits! Tits!' They raced out of the bushes and across the grass. Toddlers rose up and down on the see-saw, watching them.

I'd never had a letter like this. I couldn't think how to reply, so I put it off until the next week, when I was in New York. He wanted to know what I was doing; I told him that I'd put a mud-pack on my face. I said I was sitting in my hotel room; there were cop sirens on the TV and down in the street, both at the same time. I ended it by saying that I hoped he was well, and that I'd love to see him again, if he came to London, and he must let me know the date. I ended it 'all my love' because he did.

It didn't seem an adequate reply, a bit flat, but I didn't seem to have any feelings except lust and curiosity. I should have been terribly flattered, but I kept thinking: how can he say all that when he doesn't know me? Does he think he knows me? My one fear was that somehow he'd come to my home. I imagined him standing at the main road and realizing that the place with the pigs wallowing in front belonged to me.

Porky, Porky, Poo-ee . . . They'd thought me filthy, too . . . They knew how I felt. This Ali hadn't found me out yet, but what difference did that make?

When my face moved, the mud-pack cracked. I showered, and beige water trickled into the drain. Later that night I met a Lebanese man; I used my Intermediate French with him as he sat beside me, his hand up my skirt, and told me how *très important* he was in the government. Later still, I lay beneath him and gazed up into his nostrils, which were stuffed with hairs. He was pompous and overweight; I hated him.

Gwen used to make herself sick by scratching her throat. I remembered that, as I pressed him into me. *Ali, want to love me now?*

I made my escape through Ali. In April a letter arrived; not flimsy blue this time but a creamy envelope posted from London. He was in Earl's Court; he'd found a flat and moved straight in, the first day. Could he see me? Now that he was only seventeen miles away, the letter was formal in tone.

I met him in a trattoria. We sucked in spaghetti worms, though neither of us was hungry. We only relaxed when he leaned over to wipe my chin, tenderly, with his serviette.

'You look so different', he said, 'with your hair up.'

'Don't you like it?'

'No.'

'Shall I take it down?'

'Not now.'

Our plates were taken away. He said in a low voice, 'The flat looks out on the Cromwell Road . . . you know, the one with all the airport traffic coming in. I've been sitting there imagining that one of those cars had you in it.'

'But I didn't know you were here.'

'London *is* you . . . Then I couldn't wait any longer.' He paused. 'Do you forgive me?'

'For asking me out?'

He shook his head. 'For talking like this.'

'I like it.'

'Only like?' He paused. 'I'm sorry. I shouldn't ask you. I told myself that before I started.'

'What's happened at home?'

He raised his eyebrows, hopelessly. It came back in a rush; how I'd kissed his lovely mouth, how his skin smelt. How warm his hands had been inside my clothes. I melted inside. I wanted him right now . . . all afternoon and all tomorrow.

'Heather, I've broken their hearts . . .'

He lit a cigarette. He didn't see the waiter hovering beside him, holding the menu for dessert.

'My mother cried for two days. Everywhere in the house there were doors opening and closing . . . My uncle was called down from 'Pindi . . . My sister Bibs wouldn't speak to me . . .' He rubbed his head and raised it, with the same sorrow I'd seen before, weeks back in the hotel room.

'They said . . . oh that they'd brought me up to be decent and responsible, and what was I doing leaving the family like this, leaving my sisters . . . deserting the business, running off on impulse, acting shamefully.' He paused. 'I wish they hadn't said shamefully.'

'Are you ashamed?'

He shook his head, as if to clear it. 'I'm confused. They know I'm not just sowing wild oats. They know I'm not like that.'

'They must hate me.'

'Just at the moment.'

'Luring you away.'

'But they're angrier with me. Worse than angry – disappointed. Sad.'

He stubbed out his cigarette. He wore a blue tee-shirt; not one of the smart suits I'd seen him in before. After all, he was unemployed now.

'You've given up an awful lot,' I said. I was imagining rolling up his tee-shirt slowly, taking my time; rolling it up like a window blind.

'I love you,' he said.

Three days later I moved to Earl's Court. Dad watched me pack up the Mini. Now I knew I was going, I'd become more friendly with him.

'It's not Honolulu,' I said. 'It's half an hour away.'

'Beats me what you see in it. Filthy place, London. You're a country girl.'

'Call this the country?' I said, my arms full of clothes.

'Fresh air, here.'

'Kerosene fumes and pig-shit, you mean.'

'It's London makes you swear like that.'

'Dad! It was you.'

I climbed into the car and wound down the window. From here I was level with his belt as he stood beside me.

'Well, Dad . . .'

'Earl's Court, you say? You watch out . . . full of wogs. Wogs and Jew boys . . .'

A silence. Neither of us knew what to say; we never did, at moments like this. I looked around at the yard: his sightless lorry, its windscreen broken . . . the blond grass, swept flat by yesterday's rain. I pictured myself being buried there, and the grass was my hair sticking out. I looked at the caravan, its hardboard panels buckled and peeling.

'Remember when you was little?' he said. 'Couldn't get you out that trailer. Had all them bottles in there.'

195

Remember when I was little, what you did in the hen-house? Twelve years old, I was.

I spoke something to the dirty denim of his trousers. A plane roared overhead.

'What's that?' he said.

'Nothing.'

We paused.

'We'll be seeing you at the weekend, your Mum and me?'

I nodded and drove off, jolting over the potholes. Cars hooted as I swerved into the main road.

I reached Earl's Court in twenty minutes flat, speeding through the lights as they changed to red, and flashing cars that got in my way. Drivers swore at me as I passed.

Leaving the car, I ran up the stairs and into Ali's arms. I pressed my cheek against his scarred skin.

'Are they upset?' Ali asked. 'Will they ever speak to me?'

'They don't know about you. You're two girls called Daphne and Rose, you work for British Caledonian.'

'Should I feel guilty, plucking you from your family's bosom?'

I shook my head, wordlessly. We rocked backwards and forwards.

'I still can't believe it,' he said. 'I can't believe my luck.' He hugged me tighter. 'Tell me about them and little Teddy. I want to know everything about you.'

'I wouldn't bother.'

'You're a mystery girl, know that? I'll find out. We have all the time in the world. I want to know you through and through . . .'

'Stop it, Ali!'

He drew back. 'What a challenging look. Try me.'

I was loved. No doubt about that. I hope that some time in your life you've been the object of such tenderness as Ali lavished on me. He opened out like a flower – honestly, there's no other word for it. He shed his stilted good manners; he bloomed with confidence.

I'm sure you deserved it more than I did. I was used to lust, of course, and to people fooling themselves with the words they were saying when their blood was up. But Ali meant what he said. When he urged me to tell him everything, he meant exactly that. If I'd replied: my father betrayed me, he scrumpled up my childhood and threw it away like soiled paper out of a car window . . . If I'd said that, oh, and a hundred other things, it would have been all right. Ali would have been outraged but he'd have held me in his arms and loved me even more fiercely. He'd have said: trust me.

If only it were that simple. In women's magazines, on the problem page, they always advise: talk to him about it. They're so silly. If you're able to talk – if you want to share it – then where's the problem?

Closing my eyes, I can describe every detail of that flat. I can think myself back into it; nobody can take that away from me. It was on the second floor. Down below was a porticoed porch, with flaking columns. The hallway was silted up with bills and cards for 24 hour minicabs; yellower ones were heaped on the table. It smelt of tom cats and escaping gas. I never saw the people who lived on the ground floor. On the first floor lived a woman who passed me once and muttered in something that sounded like German. On the third floor, above us, lived some Iranian students whose pop music thudded dully through our lovemaking and the rhythm of my bad dreams. There must have been someone called Miss Maguire on the floor above, because letters addressed to that name disappeared from the hall.

Our flat: a big front room, fitted carpet, and embossed wallpaper like an Indian restaurant. Through the nylon curtains you could see down into the Cromwell Road, busy day and night with the traffic coming in and out of London. Amongst the cars came the airport buses, big as queen bees, carried along in the flow. Our first day I realized: it's the A4. This is the road I'd lived on all my life, and I'm still living on it . . . Still here.

There was a partitioned-off kitchen, with a high, stained ceiling, and a bathroom, and the bedroom at the back. It overlooked a dark well of yards. Beyond the houses you could see a church, one of those monster, sooty, Victorian ones, all boarded up. Its spire rose above the TV aerials. At night all the lights came on in the little windows, all those flats where people lived who I'd never meet, nobody knew anyone in Earl's Court, I soon realized, because nobody was there long enough . . . hotel-land, bedsitter-land, foreigners and transients and girls, six to a flat, waiting to get married. So many other girls, you couldn't count the numbers, who'd run away from home. All the lights came on but the church stayed black.

Our flat . . . You probably want to know about me and Ali, but that flat meant a lot to me. We didn't do much to it; it was furnished, and anyway we didn't have the inclination. Someone's child had pasted Flash Gordon stickers to the hardboard where the fireplace had been. Someone else had hung a net frill around the electricity meter; I wondered about that person. The flat never really became ours, though we inhabited it. For days I didn't even know the address. We didn't move the furniture around; it was enough to be there.

That's what Ali said, anyway. He'd say, 'Let's stay here all day.'

'My feet are cold.'

'Darling, your poor toes.'

He lunged over me to tuck in the blankets. The bed was double but the blankets were single.

We'd get up some time in the afternoon, the curtains still closed and the rooms greeny-dim, as if we were wandering around on the floor of the sea.

He couldn't bear me to put on my clothes, after all those hours in bed. He'd bought a paperback book of love poetry, he was romantic like that, and he'd read it out in a special sombre voice that made me blush. His favourite bit was by someone called Donne, a poem about eyes mingling on threads, and another one, which didn't sound so gruesome. It went:

> My face in thine eye, thine in mine appears,
> And true plain hearts do in the faces rest;

Where can we find two better hemispheres,
Without sharp North, without declining West?

He said it hurt when I zipped up my skirt and pulled my jumper down; he was losing a part of himself. He'd press his lips, one last time, against my disappearing skin.

We'd wander outside. He'd flinch at the noisy traffic. It was so brutal, he said, after our silence . . . You see, he told me everything; he trusted me.

We'd cross through the traffic and wander down the Earl's Court Road, doing our shopping. We'd buy some Vick Inhaler because we'd caught a cold off each other. He liked to come with me everywhere, he couldn't let me out of his sight.

Bustling and cosmopolitan, they call the Earl's Court Road. It's always crowded; he'd hold my hand tight. There's robed Arabs, and people in anoraks, just emerged from the Underground, bowed with rucksacks and looking as dazed as Ali. There's plenty of take aways to choose from; that area never closes. We'd buy kebabs in a carrier bag and dawdle back to the flat. In the side street I'd see my Mini, yet another parking ticket on its windscreen.

Ali and I lived timelessly. I only knew it was April because Sketchleys had pasted a daffodil frieze round their window, to promote a spring cleaning discount.

Oh, yes . . . and there was the tree.

Out the back, way below, lay the bare earth belonging to the unknown being in the basement. Nothing grew there, though the students above threw stuff into it; once I remember opening the bedroom curtains and finding a chapatti on our window sill. Out on the front it was paved, with dustbins. But on the pavement the council had planted a tree. It was still young, just a sapling; I think it was a cherry. During our first weeks it was struggling into blossom.

I remember because it was the first time that I'd told him something about my past. I'd fended off the questions until then.

199

But the night before, I'd had a violent dream about my mother . . . I'd been holding her and she turned out to be pieces of chalk in my arms, moaning chalk, her powdery legs squeaking together. She kept telling me she wasn't, but I heard the squeaking. I'd woken up crying, with Ali's arms around me. He'd held me for ages, he was sobbing too because he couldn't reach what was happening inside my head. It was out of both our control. And then we got up and he gave me a bath, both of us frail, like elderly people.

The taste of my mother stayed with me, I couldn't get rid of her, and the feeling that she was lost to me. At lunch-time we went out to buy some breakfast croissants. As we walked, arm-in-arm, I said,

'My Mum brought us home cheese portions. Know something? I've been eating take-aways all my life.'

'Why? Tell me why.'

'She was busy, that's why.'

'Too busy to care for you?'

'Oh, we managed.'

'Tell me about them. All I know are their names, Coral and Frank.' He went on quickly, 'If you'll tell me about them I can know you better . . . Then I can love you – well, more *usefully*. I might be able to stop you looking so sad.'

'Do I look sad?'

'Sad and empty. When you don't think I'm noticing.'

'Then you shouldn't notice.'

'Don't be angry. Don't close off like that, you always do. Just tell me – didn't they love you?'

A silence. I held the warm croissant bag against my chest. 'Of course they did. They were my parents, weren't they?'

I shouldn't have spoken. We crossed the main road.

'You feel a bit better now?' he asked, holding my arm. We were both wearing dark glasses because our eyes were sore. 'Do your eyes still hurt?'

'No.'

'Mine do. That tree . . . that hurts.'

We stopped at the sapling. Its trunk was hooped with wire netting, to protect its growing. Trouble was, people had stuffed rubbish down.

Ali was so sensitive; he was always telling me how he noticed much more, now he was in love with me. He said he'd been half blind before.

'Poor little tree.' He touched its buds. The pink blossom was all bitten away and browning. 'It's trying to flower . . .'

I replied, 'It's got blight.'

I went home for a night, to see Teddy. They made me tea, like a visitor. They felt obliged to switch off the telly, as they had when I came back from my first trip to New York, and we sat around in hopeless silence. I wondered if either of them ever dreamed about me, in the upsetting way I'd been dreaming about them. My mother wasn't made of loose bits of chalk . . . there she sat, thinner than ever; recently she'd dyed her hair a brighter blonde which didn't suit her sallow, ageing skin, though none of us would ever dare tell her. Outside it seemed odd that the sheds were in their same old positions, when I'd known them widened and shifted in the soupy mist of my nightmares.

Dad came out and stood beside me.

'Respectable, are they?'

'Who?'

'Girls you're staying with. They take you off to night-clubs, places like that?'

I shook my head.

'Harmful places, night-clubs,' he said. 'Dangerous.'

I gazed across at the cow parsley, a froth against the piles of timber. Beside me, I heard him scratching his stubble.

'They're not dangerous!' I said loudly.

Most of the time I stayed in the flat with Ali. I wasn't flying that month, because I was due some leave. Down in the hall the phone never rang for us.

A chill wind blew and we sat close together on the floor,

propped against the storage heater.

'Two orphans,' he said. 'Marooned.'

I'd leaf through *Honey* and he'd do sums, working out his dwindling finances. Scattered around us lay the foil containers from our take-away tandooris. I'd told him about packing the airline meals; I'd tell him safe things like that. Once he'd tried to work out, on a chart, whether he'd eaten one prepared by my own fair hand. Being Oriental, he believed in fate. He was sure we were destined to meet, at some point in our lives. We'd sit there for hours, speculating; I worked out airline routes but he called them predestined paths, as if the flights were planned by God. We read each other's horoscopes in the newspaper.

Otherwise, looking back, I can't remember how we passed those days. He took ages brushing my hair, he marvelled at it, brushing it until it crackled. I'd sit between his legs, facing the blocked fireplace, and hear his breathing as he plaited it, then unplaited it, and then held it bunched in his fist as he turned my head sideways to inspect my profile.

I was less relaxed about the other parts of my body being put to this scrutiny. I hated being looked at, with the light on. I pinched my stomach, holding the rubbery fold between my fingers. I wanted him to be shocked.

'You can't love this.'

'I love it.'

'I used to be even fatter. You wouldn't have loved me then.'

'I wish I'd known you. It pains me, the years of you I've missed.'

I liked it better with the sheets pulled over our heads. Everything's so simple then. He was wonderfully ardent. He said he was inexperienced – there had only been a couple of girls before, a French one from the consulate and a Pakistani one from the Hyatt-Regency Hotel camera shop, and he'd felt ashamed afterwards, for them and for himself. With me he was desperately loving – yes, desperate. Sometimes I felt a sort of despair in his passion. Once he'd said he was battering at my soul to get in . . . was there anyone at home?

In these moods I tried to joke him out of it, but he had no sense

202

of humour; he couldn't laugh at himself, that was one of his faults. He was also proud and touchy. And inflammable too . . . oh yes, he was that.

What I liked was his openness. He stroked my face in the street, he openly sobbed. Some people wouldn't like that but I was flattered; nobody had ever revealed themselves to me before. We were together all the time. The only moments he left me were for prayer. I told you how religious he was; his whole family was devout. It was odd, though, after he'd been bending over me, to see him bending down to the carpet. He'd press his forehead down, again and again, amongst our scattered magazines. I gawped the first time, but I stopped when he saw my face. He prayed so naturally – that's what made him suddenly a foreigner. At that moment he wasn't mine at all.

Washing was another part of it. He didn't wash like normal people; he had to gargle and spit, it was part of the ritual, and those bathroom noises came from someone I didn't know. And then there was the diet. Pork's forbidden, of course. You can't even mention the word, it's worse than swearing. And there I was, brought up on Spam. No alcohol either. He wouldn't have forbidden me to drink, but I didn't in his company. He even disliked the odour of pubs. Walking with him, I realized how foul pubs smell if you're not inside them: that stale sourness as you pass the door, as if my Dad was breathing out.

It disturbed me, how deeply he believed. He told me to take no notice, but this hunched foreigner made me awkward. He prayed at dawn, and when he climbed back into bed his body was cool. When this chill man climbed in beside me I realized: here am I, presuming to live with someone. I don't know why it struck me then; I suppose I felt so hopeless.

He asked me whether I believed in God and I remembered my Bible book, with its golden clouds. I didn't tell him about it, though. That was another one of my secrets.

The only time he went out alone was on Fridays, to the mosque. This being Earl's Court, there was one a few streets away. I'd passed it: an ordinary terraced house, it was, as seedy as the rest. It had a plastic sign above the door. Nothing to get spiritual about.

When he came back, one day, I asked him if he'd mentioned me. After all, he'd asked me to marry him and I'd refused.

'Is it like confession?' I asked with a stupid, prodding voice. 'Do you have to say you're living in sin? Are you ashamed?'

He paused, in the middle of hanging up his jacket, and gazed at me sombrely: 'Ashamed? My feelings for you are one of the few things I'll never be ashamed of.'

I was flying to Hawaii in early May. I had to get up at four in the morning. My suitcase lay on the carpet, gaping. I felt detached, putting on my uniform in the artificial light, with the world asleep. I felt like an arrangement of moving limbs. I often felt this.

He sat in his underpants on the bed, watching me. He was trying to stop smoking, but I heard the click of his lighter.

'Will this flat seem unreal, once you're away?'

I couldn't answer because I was putting on my lipstick. I was sitting at the chest of drawers, with the mirror propped in front of my face.

'Or will it seem unreal there, in Hawaii?' he asked.

I blotted my mouth with a Kleenex.

'Will you become a different person?' His voice was as edgy as mine, when I asked him about his religion. We were both jealous. 'Do I know you at all?'

'Ali, I've done this before, you know.'

'But who were you leaving behind?'

'Nobody much.'

'Do you mind now?'

'Of course I mind. I'll miss you.'

'It's watching you putting on your face . . .'

'I have to look attractive or I'll lose my job.'

I brushed my hair – he didn't rise to help me – and slotted in a tortoise-shell band.

'You look so beautiful. When they see you, they must feel the same as I do. They'd be mad if they didn't.'

'They don't. Only you do.'

I snapped shut my compact. I wished he wouldn't probe me . . . pick, pick, tweezers picking into my soul. He was always asking me questions.

I did mind leaving him. But somewhere, well hidden, I felt the old excitement rising. I was already gone, I was already in my Mini, speeding past the first lit windows. Into the airy, anonymous outside world. Nothing closed and trusting about the sky out there.

I went outside, into the chill. I was behind the wheel, my passport in my handbag. I'd be caught for speeding soon, if I didn't watch out. I was always speeding away from something or other.

I did have a dalliance, under the tropic stars, with the MC at the hotel. Well, under the tropic stars of the Ballroom Annexe, when he'd finished his patter. He was a middle-aged alcoholic from Teddington, not too far from my home, and we ended the evening like long-lost friends. We didn't do much; by that stage he was only capable of swaying and lengthy cuddles. I was swaying from sleeplessness anyway. But he wrote me a rambling note, including his address, on the back of my cheque book. The season was over and he was coming back to England soon; he kept on saying how homesick he was. For blooming Teddington? I asked, adjusting my bra. I'd had three vodkas and orange, after my month's denial, and I was swearing like my Dad.

Ali and I spent the Monday in bed. I'd forgotten how beautiful he was, with his polished, hard skin; he seemed so delicate compared to the soft, freckled Americans I'd been meeting. We lay clasped together, motionless.

He didn't go to sleep; he seldom did. As usual I had the feeling that something in him wasn't satisfied. He said it was wonderful but he stayed propped up on one elbow, gazing at me. I wished he wouldn't. I remembered his words about never having reached me, and hoped he'd forgotten them. Wasn't this enough, this

205

filled, sticky langour, the heaviness of our limbs as if we were filled with soup?

Later that afternoon I had to go to the dry cleaner's. He stayed in because he was expecting a phone call about a job. I took an armful of clothes and my keys, that was all.

Walking to the traffic lights, I remembered the message on my cheque book. Ali wouldn't find it, would he? He wasn't devious enough to rummage.

Five minutes later I was standing at the counter. On either side hung clothes ready for collection, sheathed in plastic skins. The woman was heaping my dirty clothes – sundress, Am-Air uniform – on the counter, when I felt the door opening behind me. A draught made the plastic shiver, like silver.

'Heather!'

His hand on my shoulder.

'Wait a moment.' I turned to the woman. 'Is that it?'

Outside in the street he raised his hand to hit me, then he burst into tears. This was Earl's Court, so the pedestrians just carried on walking.

'You'll hate me now!' he moaned.

I put my arms around him and stroked his hair; outdoors it shone blue-black.

'I shouldn't have looked,' he mumbled into my jumper. 'When I read it, I could've killed you . . . You see, you never tell me anything . . . so I start imagining . . . Then, seeing that man's name . . .'

'He doesn't mean anything.'

Ali moved me back. 'But what *does* mean anything to you? What's been happening to you?'

'In Hawaii?'

'Not in Hawaii.' Jostled by the passers-by, he stayed gazing at me. 'Has somebody hurt you? I never ask, because I don't dare. You know, you never talk to me.'

In my brain, the muscle locked. I gazed at him, not hearing. It was as if he were mouthing at me through glass, from inside an aquarium. This was happening more often nowadays.

'You seem so cold,' he was saying, 'so closed off from me. Was it a boyfriend, who hurt you?'

'Yes, a boyfriend.'

'Let me heal it . . . give me the time.'

He pressed his scarred face against mine. We kissed. A dog sniffed my skirt; it was dragged away, its claws scraping. Ali held me tight, for a long time. I stood still as a statue.

A woman stopped.

'Disgusting,' she muttered.

Chapter Fifteen

O ddly enough, I can see it from Ali's point of view now. It is odd, considering what he's done.

But it must have been the most enormous shock, coming to live with me in London. His whole life was turned upside down. Apart from the emotional rift with his parents, the culture shock and all that, for the first time in his life he was poor. Until then he'd lived such a privileged life with his family, his servants, his money and his government contacts. People like Ali live that way, in the East. Sometimes I thought of my mother, taking down the biscuit tin and counting the notes, one by one, as if by some oversight she'd missed one the last time.

In Earl's Court he was cut off from all that. He never complained – he never said he regretted it – but the flat was expensive and he wouldn't let me pay for it. He was too proud for that; he said he wanted to care for me. I suppose, being Oriental, he felt more manly that way.

By the end of May he'd found himself a job. After jet-setting around the world, Bahrein one day, Singapore the next, it must have felt cramped to sit all day in a cupboard. Actually, three cupboards. That was Savewise Travel. In one sat the boss, Farouq.

He was a Muslim from Uganda, with oily hair and a smooth telephone manner. In another cupboard sat Eileen, the secretary, her fingers smudged from thumbing through timetables. And now in the third sat Ali. He didn't fly any more; he planned other people's journeys. Savewise was down the Cromwell Road, and near his beloved mosque.

From then on, the tempo changed. Though the flat still had a temporary air, with my suitcases half-packed, the week settled into a shape, with five working days and then the weekend. I'd forgotten about weekends just as you forget, when you're grown up, how the year used to be shaped around the school holidays. When he was out, I slept. I slept a lot of the time nowadays. You'd think I had everything to get up for, wouldn't you? But I slept.

We rented a TV and on Saturday mornings we lay in bed, with mugs of tea on our stomachs, watching *Swap Shop*. On Sundays we wandered down the streets, past windows with their curtains closed all day, as ours were – windows with 'Freehold Investment For Sale' boards outside, and dustbins crammed with wine bottles and with milk cartons because nobody got around to having a milkman deliver. It was that sort of area.

All Sunday the big church stayed padlocked. There were drifts of rubbish against its fences and cars jammed in its driveway, not for Holy Communion but to save on residents' permits.

'Does nobody believe in God?' Ali asked.

'Only you.'

He kept asking me to marry him. He wanted me to bear his children. I expect he pictured one of those Span houses along the motorway, with him and me in it.

'Why would that change things', I asked, 'when we're together anyway?'

'I want to be sure of you. I never feel sure.'

He was standing in the kitchen doorway. I was chopping up ginger for a curry; I liked Pakistani food and I was learning to cook it.

'I'm never sure . . . that I'm getting there.' He moved his hands, trying to express – what? A vacuum?

'I love you more and more,' he said. 'Sometimes I feel quite desperate.'

When I was little I prayed for things. I prayed to God for patent leather party shoes. I prayed for the sort of party my friends had. I prayed for my Mum to be there when I got home from school. I soon found that nobody had been listening.

I poured seeds into the blender. 'Do you pray about me?' That stabbing edge had crept into my voice. 'Do you, when you're on the rug?'

'Don't put it like that.'

'When you're praying, then.'

'Heather, my prayers aren't like that. I told you. They're not pleas, or confessions. You don't even come into them.'

'Don't I?'

'They're for our Prophet . . . they're adoration, and submission . . . They're – '

'Wait.'

I switched on the blender motor. The engine rasped, the spices rattled round. I leaned on the top, holding it down. Him and his prayers – why did I feel so excluded?

When the motor stopped he said, gently, 'Perhaps you'd love me better if we were married.'

I said flatly, 'You don't want to marry me.'

'I do!'

'I don't believe you.' I peeled the garlic with my sharp knife.

'You think it's just . . . well, physical? How can I convince you?'

'You needn't bother,' I said.

'Don't you trust me?' he asked. 'Darling, you seem to have a poor view of human nature.'

'That's my problem.' I stabbed open the papery skin. 'You needn't worry about it.'

'How can I make you believe me? What can I say?'

'Words never do any good.'

210

'They're not just words . . . they're my feelings.'

'Don't like feelings,' I said. 'Don't like prayers . . . bloody prayers . . .'

He stepped into the kitchen and touched my hair.

'Why do you try to spoil things, when they could be so perfect? What's the matter with you? Suddenly, these ugly words.'

I went on cutting, my knife flashing. My eyes smarted from the garlic fumes.

For the first time in months I dreamed of Jonathan, crow-like in his black school blazer. I'd spoiled that all right. He was probably married now, with two kids. Like Ali, he was the marrying kind.

How could Ali love me? I started dropping hints about my past, hurting him. I willed him to see how worthless I was. One Sunday we went rowing in Hyde Park. He rowed and I lay in my flounced, yellow dress. I felt clammy and painted, but he said I looked as pretty as a milkmaid.

'You've got a funny idea about farms,' I said.

He just smiled at me. He was happy, remembering similar outings under a hotter sky, with his sisters and his aunts and his cousins. I could never count all his relatives. The laughter, he said, the warmth.

He thought he could start another family with me. I wished he didn't. He sat in his shirt-sleeves, pulling the oars. His face glowed. He looked so innocent. His family had kept him that way. I realized: he looked younger than my little brother Teddy.

He was still reminiscing. 'Your new dress . . . yellow's always been my favourite colour. I used to believe that it was invented when I was born.'

'What?'

'That it didn't exist until then.' He paused. 'You know, I've never told anyone that.'

We drifted on. He shipped the oars and we slid silently through the water. I closed my eyes. Willow leaves brushed my cheek, gently, as if blessing us both. I couldn't bear it. I felt stifled, as I'd felt on the garage roof with Jonathan.

'Ever done it in a boat?' I asked.

'Done what?'

'Done . . . you-know-what.' My voice was stupid and pert.

A silence.

'You know I haven't,' he said at last, in a level voice. 'I've told you about my two, unsatisfactory . . .' He stopped. 'Well? Have you?'

I kept my eyes closed, so I couldn't see his face. 'Ever so rocky.'

I heard the oars bump as he fixed them on the rowlocks.

'Shut up!' he hissed.

Then the boat was pushing violently through the water, the branches scraping my face.

That night he was rough, heaving me over like a sack of coal – as if I were heavy, but grubby too. I was grubby; I was worthless. Why had it taken him so long to realize? My face pressed into the pillow as he entered me from the rear, pushing in with difficulty. Behind my head his breaths were quick and shallow. He didn't speak. His hand slid under me, humping me up against him; his fingers sank into me, and it hurt.

I bit my lip, refusing to cry out. My brain locked shut. He went on for ages . . . I counted to fifty, in French, and started again. Afterwards I fell into a heavy sleep, as if I were dead.

Chapter Sixteen

In June, Teddy came for the day. I fetched him in the car. I was terrified that he'd mention the pigs, but I didn't want to warn him because then he'd be sure to.

I needn't have worried. You know how children just talk about themselves; Teddy was full of some war he was having with Darren's gang at school. He didn't notice that there was no sign of two girls in the flat; I knew he wouldn't. In a way, it was a relief that he was eight years old and had grown so tough. I no longer felt that tight, pained protectiveness at the very mention of his name.

I felt disembodied, walking along the pavement with Ali and my brother; my two lives had always been so separate. It felt odd, bringing them together. Teddy clattered a stick along the railings. At crossroads, when the lights changed red and the cars had to stop, he walked in front of them with his hands held up importantly. The drivers glared at him through their windscreens; I knew, from experience, how infuriating it was. Teddy did this sort of thing even when his mates weren't there to giggle with him; that's what made him a ringleader.

Ali had been looking forward to meeting him, though I could tell he was shocked by Teddy's filthy language. He didn't touch me when Teddy was around, he was too polite for that. We were going to the Natural History Museum; clatter-clatter went Teddy's stick.

'Yesterday guess what we did,' he called.

'What?'

'Stole the caretaker's clothes off of his washing line.'

Ali laughed. 'You scallywags. Sounds just like our pranks, when we were at school.'

'What did you do with the clothes?' I asked Teddy, dreading the answer.

'Burnt 'em.'

Ali was silent. The pavement was littered with bones. We were near the Big T Bar-B-Q, that was why. Teddy danced ahead, kicking an orange rib; he zig-zagged, the bone skittering. Couples separated at his approach.

At the museum he hardly looked at the exhibits, which I'd never seen either. He wanted to go to the shop. Ali gave him a pound, but he'd soon spent that. He came out, ducking under a dinosaur poster.

'Got any more?'

'Teddy!' I said.

'Pay you back.'

'How?'

'I'm gonna be rich.'

'Oh yes? How's that?'

He leaned towards me. 'Wanna know something? It's a secret.' Then he tapped his finger on the side of his nose, just like Dad did. 'He told me it was a secret.'

'What?'

'We're sitting on a gold mine, that's what.'

I stared at him.

'We're what?'

'Say no more.'

I shook his shoulders. They surprised me, they still felt so frail. 'What's Dad said? What's happening?'

'Mum's the word.'

214

He tried to look mysterious – a narrowed, peaky look – but I could tell that he hadn't the first idea what he was talking about. He'd just been given hints, like I'd been given them, years before.

A week later I flew back from New York. I decided to stop at our house. Over the summer the garage had been expanded – remember the petrol station down on the main road? They'd built a concrete shell with the sign already up: 'Same Day Exhaust Centre'. Each year there were new developments along our road. It was a golden, serene evening; I remembered those rabbits, an age ago, with the sunlight on their whiskers.

Dad was two dirty legs sticking out from under his lorry. He didn't hear me, on account of his radio; anyway, Mum came home then so I couldn't ask him.

'Let's go down the Magpies,' I said later, when he'd emerged.

He gazed at me, his mouth open. He rubbed his hand across his moustache. Mum had aged but he still looked the same, except for the weight; it didn't seem fair.

'I'll drive,' I said.

'Better smarten myself up,' he said, 'and tell mother.'

Ten minutes later he was squeezed in the Mini, his knees pressed against the dashboard. I drove fast. He sat beside me, trapped in my cramped little car.

The sun was sinking, hazily. I knew this road so well. Ali didn't exist; he had never existed. It frightened me, how he dissolved. Along the banks of the reservoir the gorse was flowering again; above the ridge the sky glowed. I wondered for the hundredth time how much my father remembered of the past, and which parts he'd blurred and softened. I wondered what on earth went on in his mind and knew I could never bear to find out. I wondered if it would be easier if he were dead.

He wasn't. He was here, filling the car with smoke. My eyes smarted. I think he was nervous; he was probably dreading that one day I'd actually talk to him.

I didn't, in the Magpies. For a start, there were too many familiar faces there. I'd changed out of my uniform; I didn't want him to show me off and make me remember how ashamed of him I'd felt . . . Yet it was not as simple as shame. Remember how I'd wanted him to show me off in my tartan frock? I'd longed for him to be proud of me then.

He was drinking more heavily nowadays, Mum complained about it, but he wasn't really a drunkard. He was too erratic for that, and forgetful. But he'd always loved the boozer. He found solace there, in the rosy phoniness of a manufactured home, with the comfort of other bodies but without their demands, with nothing needed from him. Come to think of it, I was becoming like that. I didn't drink like he did but I was spending plenty of time in bars, now, around the world, amongst the false smiles of people who had no need of me, nor me of them. It's like being swaddled in clothes that you don't own – no caring, no repairs, nothing that needs to be fixed . . . No responsibilities . . . It's like living in a hotel. I'd grown up amongst the hotels, and I lived in them now.

We were two of a kind, Dad and me. Wasn't it his fault, that I'd become this way?

Outside in the car park it was chilly, and the street lights were lit. We climbed into the car. Years ago I'd been sitting here waiting for him, but now it was me who held the key. When it was inserted, I paused.

You know that we were two of a kind. I didn't have to speak, because at that moment he started fumbling for his tobacco and said,

'Thinking of selling up.'

'The house?'

He nodded.

'Glad we've got this moment to talk,' he said, 'because I'd been planning on telling you.'

'You're really going to do it?'

I wasn't looking at him but I knew the sounds so well: the scrape as he scratched his cheek; the wheezing breath, through his nose, as he felt for his matches.

'Isn't the same, you see,' he said.

216

'What isn't?'

He paused. 'Home isn't.' He didn't light the match. 'Not now.'

Lights dazzled us as a car swung out. More people came out of the pub, singing. For a moment I thought his mates were going to come over and tap on the window.

'What do you mean?' I said dully.

'Not since you've been gone. Not the same.'

'There's Teddy,' I said. 'And Mum.'

'Don't see so much of Teddy. Always off, he is.' He looked at me. 'It's yourself I'm talking about.'

There was a silence. I don't know how long it lasted; I didn't dare break it.

Then I heard him draw a breath, his lungs whistling, and he said, 'Don't seem much point, you see.'

'What doesn't?' I whispered.

'Nothing don't. Nothing I do. Not when you're not there to see it.'

Another minute passed.

'Even . . . getting myself up in the morning. Knowing that little room next to me's empty . . .'

I tried to answer this. Finally I attempted to laugh. 'You've never been much good at that.'

'At what?'

'Getting up in the morning.'

He paused. 'You know you're the one . . . that mattered. You've always known that, Heth.'

I fiddled with the key. 'Where are you thinking of moving to?'

'Might not have behaved myself . . . once or twice. But I'm forgiven now, aren't I?'

I gazed at the steering wheel.

'All in the past now,' he said. 'All forgotten now . . . Right?'

'Oh yes,' I said quickly.

'Glad about that. See . . . it's been worrying me.'

'You needn't.' I turned the key, and started the engine. 'I haven't told my boyfriend.'

'You what?' He shouted above the motor.

I was reversing now, looking over my shoulder. I said casually, 'I haven't mentioned anything to him.'

'You said boyfriend?'

We swung backwards into the road. A car swerved, hooting. I crunched the gear into first.

'Didn't I tell you?'

'Tell me what?'

'I'm living with my boyfriend.' I turned left. Another car hooted, because I'd forgotten to use my indicator.

There was a silence. Then he cleared his throat.

'You said two girls.'

'That was to spare your feelings.'

'Why're you telling me now then?'

'Well, it's not two girls. It's a boy. We love each other very much.' I was driving badly. I flashed the car in front, to hurry it up. 'So you see, I'm fine. Needn't worry about me.'

'You been keeping it from me all this time?'

'I've got my own life now, Dad. So don't worry about the house.'

He paused. 'You'll be bringing him home to meet us? You planning on marrying him?' His voice was louder.

I said airily, 'I might. At the moment we're just living in bliss . . . Getting to know each other.'

I slewed up the drive; we bounced over the potholes.

At last he said, 'Didn't know about this . . .'

I braked, with a jolt, in the yard. I unstuck myself from the seat; despite the chill I was sweating. 'I've got my own life now, Dad.' I felt sick with my triumph.

Dad was getting out of the car slowly, like an old man. By the time he stood up I was indoors, where Mum sat watching the telly, and where he could no longer reach me.

Chapter Seventeen

Ali and me, living in bliss. That's what I'd told Dad. That's what Ali called it too.

'We love each other,' he'd say. 'Don't we?'

It seems years ago, not weeks, that he was talking like this. It's the end of September now. Blank space separates me from our rented rooms. Our own little kitchen, where I stood stirring the saucepans . . . I liked strong, hot curries too, the hotter the better, and for the first time in my life I was cooking proper sit-down dinners . . . That narrow room, rich with the aroma of our false domesticity.

Ali and me, living in bliss . . . his solemn, handsome face in the candlelight. He bought candles for our evening meal. He believed in it all. This was the beginning of our life together, that's what he believed . . . Mutual love, and trust. He longed for me to trust him.

He knew a bit about my past. He tried to trust me about that. A few times, when he was out at work, I leafed through the phone books downstairs and found one or two old contacts. I dressed myself for a lunch date. A couple of Bacardis, that's all I had, but in the evening he could smell my corrupt, boozy breath. He kissed me without flinching, but I knew he felt queasy. Then he'd ask casually,

'Been out to lunch?'

I nodded and changed the subject. I tortured him by my delay, just as I'd tortured my father by the casual way I spoke in the car.

'Anyone I know?' Ali asked.

'We don't know anyone.'

'I mean . . . anyone special?'

'No, not special at all.'

He didn't dare ask more. He'd been so ashamed that night, when he'd heaved me over like an animal. Next day he'd bought me five bunches of roses, from the man at the tube station. You know those expensive roses that stay buds and wither as buds, their little heads drooping? They'd drooped around the flat for two weeks, until one of us had the heart to throw them away.

He didn't ask more because his response scared him. Me too. In fact, nothing much had happened on my jaunts. A few drinks, a few hints. On their home ground, English men remember their upbringings.

Out of the country it was different. I flew a lot last August – Singapore, Tokyo, LA. There were more opportunities then, and I'd become bolder. During that period there were several delayed flights. On stopover you're living in limbo anyway, but an over-night delay is even weirder. Time doesn't exist. You have this vacuum of hours to fill and then forget. People do things they'd never dare, otherwise, and afterwards my brain was wiped clean. Sometimes I pictured Ali, dancing like a midge at the edge of my vision. He'd be mouthing words at me but I couldn't hear them. And he was so tiny.

You must hate me now. But I'm not really talking to you, I'm telling this to myself. It's just easier, pretending that there's some-one listening. I've made people out of you, to help me . . . I'm still believing that you were once sympathetic.

It could have been such a happy ending, couldn't it? Ali, lifting me away on the wings of true love. He wanted to fly with me to Pakistan, where a house had been built for him. His family would forgive him, real families always do. He told me they would. He said they'd welcome me, if only I brought him home. Already his mother sent us packages of sweetmeats: crumbly marzipan balls that smelt of soap.

He would forgive me my past exploits, the ones he'd heard of. You can imagine the effort this cost him because he was naturally a jealous person, and also terribly proud. But he loved me so deeply he was prepared to do it.

He thought it would be all right; he really did. He believed you could forget the past and start afresh. He thought love could solve it all, because he believed in fairy stories.

The first weeks of September were brilliantly sunny but I stayed in bed most of the time with the curtains closed. We'd been together for four months and he still insisted that he adored me. But I think I knew, by now, that he and I were doomed.

I felt tired all the time; the only emotion I felt was faint surprise that it was taking him so long to find out what I was like. I came back from Frankfurt with bites down my neck. He saw them when I was putting up my hair, ready for a bath.

'Darling, what's happened to you?'

'These?' I stood at the mirror. 'I wish you wouldn't come barging in like that.'

'But what's happened?'

He stopped abruptly, as he realized.

He paused, then he said in a low voice. 'That was rather a stupid thing for me to say, wasn't it?'

'No, it wasn't.'

His voice came closer. 'Somebody did those. Is that it?'

He grabbed my shoulders and shook me.

'Tell me the truth!'

'Ouch!'

His fingernails dug in harder. 'Go on, tell me!'

'It wasn't important. I'd had a bit to drink.'

I felt nervous now. I was naked and his nails hurt.

'What else did he do?'

'Stop it!'

'What else? Tell me.'

'Oh . . . you know. Nothing much.'

He slapped my face, hard. 'You slut!' he whispered. 'You whore!'

'Get away from me!'

I cringed back and sat down, heavily, on the edge of the bath. He grabbed my hair and yanked up my face.

'How could you?' he hissed. 'What goes on inside there?' He jabbed at my forehead.

'Don't!'

'You're a vandal – know that? Just like your little brother.'

'Leave Teddy out of it.'

'But you're worse than him – you do it with people.'

Suddenly he moved away and sat down on the toilet, sobbing. He buried his face in his hands.

'We can't go on like this,' he said, muffled.

At once I panicked. What had I done? I'd gone too far.

I moved over and knelt beside him. If I lost him, I'd have nobody.

'Don't say that, Ali. I'm sorry . . . I won't again.'

He grabbed me and held me close, my face pressed against his shirt buttons. It was awkward, but I wouldn't let him go.

'I try so hard,' he muttered into my hair, 'to make you love me . . . To understand that funny little mind in there.' He paused. 'But just when I think we're close – then you go and ruin it. Why do you spoil everything?'

He squeezed me tighter. 'It's probably my fault . . . I feel such a failure, not satisfying you.'

'You do . . . Honestly.'

'But even . . . well, in bed. You don't look at me, you want it dark. You feel . . . so mechanical – '

'Don't say that!'

222

'I must. Darling . . . You do it so beautifully, but mechanically, as if you were ashamed – as if it was dirty.'

'How can you say that?'

'There's something so cold in there . . . The way you tease me about – you know, the way I pray, and my ablutions. My gargling. It hurts me *so much*.'

He lifted his head. His face was damp with tears. Mine was dry, because his words frightened me. He kissed my slapped cheek.

'I shouldn't have said that . . . Will you forgive me?' He touched my cheek. 'Does it hurt?'

'No.'

I squeezed him tighter . . . Oh, squeezing is easy. It's the rest that's difficult. Why did I behave this way with him? It was beyond my control.

What am I doing? I stood on the pavement outside our flat. It always struck me at this moment, when I was outdoors from our life. Beside me the sapling hadn't yet shed its leaves, though they'd been born dead and stayed dead all summer. There was something wrong with that tree; its mystery blight. The leaves hung down, small and brown, twisted like corkscrews.

Mum had brought that pot plant once, remember? Oh yes, we'd watered it, like the council had cared for this tree, but I'd known its leaves would fade yellow, a slimy, translucent yellow, and fall on to the top of the TV set. I'd *known* they would.

I hitched up my shopping and started for the steps. Up on the second floor our curtains were closed, as if the flat knew us too well, and didn't want to see.

Chapter Eighteen

I 've always had bad dreams. You know that. I'd be lying in Ali's arms; I should have been safe there. He'd hold me, warm in our nest of blankets. You'd think that he could keep the nightmares away.

Nobody can. You'll lie there, pressed against each other, your legs hooked together, cemented. And the tighter you hold each other, squeezing tighter and tighter, the more you're fooling yourself. Nobody can reach you.

I'd wake slippery-wet and shivering. Ali gripped me, rocking me, talking to me, but nothing could get rid of the dreams. They haunted me for days afterwards. I could will my brain shut, locking it, but the nightmares escaped like poisoned air. I was helpless.

In one I was standing in a lift. There was a little girl beside me, wearing a red party dress that was much too big for her. A man was standing beside her, but I couldn't see his face, the air was misty up there. The lift was going up.

'She wasn't precious enough, you see,' he was saying. 'Nobody wanted her.'

I looked at the girl. She seemed perfectly normal . . . at first glance anyway. But as he talked I inspected her again.

His voice went on: '. . . So I said to myself: action stations! And isn't she the dinky one now?'

I looked at her again. Now I realized. Her eyes had been dug out. In their place were two red jewels, wedged into the skin – buried there, winking.

'She's precious now, all right,' said the voice.

'But she can't see!'

'They're real rubies, those are.'

'But she's blind!'

'Oh yes, they'll all be wanting her now.' The voice, up in the mist, was getting vaguer.

The lift was still rising.

'Where are you taking her?' I shouted.

No answer. I needed to know, terribly.

'Where are you taking her?' I shouted, louder.

But the girl turned her back on me, I heard the taffeta rustle, and then I woke.

Chapter Nineteen

I 've had no dreams tonight, because I've stayed awake in this
chair. Outside it's lighter now; I can see the blanket that I've
wrapped around myself. It's the brown blanket from my bed.
Remember how I used to pull it over my head, so I couldn't hear
the noises that my parents made?

No sound from the next room. He'll sleep for hours yet, judging
by the amount he drank last night. Teddy's still asleep too. Mum's
on the night shift, so she won't be home for a while. The first planes
are already taking off; the walls shake when they fly overhead.

He's been drunk most of this week, my Dad. He says my face
upsets him, but I've told him it's not hurting nearly as much, now,
as when I arrived. He hasn't seen under the plasters, and I don't
dare look either. Tomorrow I'm going to Ashford General, to
have the stitches taken out, but I'll keep my eyes shut.

My eye, by the way, is going to be all right. I can open it now,
just a glimmer. Black eyes look worse than they feel; in fact, I've
been quite detached, watching its colour changes: plum to reddish-
green, like the lightening sky. Teddy's fascinated by it; he wants
one too. Now it's fading to an unhealthy yellow.

It hurts when I yawn, my face does, and when I sneeze. It would
probably hurt if I laughed, but I haven't yet. The cuts must be

healing now, because while I've been sitting here they've started to itch.

Ali's ring did them. I forgot to tell you that he wore a signet ring; his father had given it to him. He must have forgotten too, because after he'd been hitting me for a bit he saw what damage he'd done. I felt quite sorry for him then.

My Mum was upset too, of course. But you know how she hates anything sticky and emotional; she's always steered clear of that. She didn't ask me many questions about Ali. Soon she was moaning about men in general, how stupid they were, what beasts. *Brutes*, she said.

'You've learned the hard way,' she said. 'Oh yes, you've had a lesson and a half.'

It was almost as if she blamed me – as if I'd brought it upon myself. There was a note of satisfaction in her voice. And she's been so ashamed of me. On Tuesday a man was coming to look at the land and she told me to stay in my room, as if I had leprosy.

'Think this is my fault?' I asked, pointing to my bandages. But she just looked pursed.

In fact, neither of them asked many questions. When you haven't for years – when you've closed your eyes to what's going on you're not going to change that suddenly. You're not used to it. Teddy's the only one who goes on at me; when we're alone, and I'm more relaxed, I might tell him some of the gruesome details.

Dad, when he's had a few, he gets all worked up and tries to get me to tell him Ali's name so he can go and beat him up, but when he's sobered down he turns back into a coward.

Besides, I've no idea where Ali is now. When he ran downstairs to phone for an ambulance, I bolted myself into the flat and packed my suitcases. When the ambulance men arrived they behaved like my big brothers, they were so protective with me, and they wouldn't let him near. He was hysterical by then, so they probably thought he was still dangerous. I knew he wasn't, of course; he was wild with grief. But it looked the same to them, so I didn't say anything. At that point, anyway, I couldn't talk.

No, most of the questioning was in Casualty. The doctor was ever so young and earnest. You should have seen his reaction when he saw my face: him and the two nurses, bending over me. I heard the whispers, 'permanent scarring' and 'disfigurement'.

After they'd done the stitching and the dressings he came back for a little chat and that's when he said that in cases like mine, when the looks are affected, it was usual to refer the patient for counselling. I wouldn't go. He said I was still in shock, that's why I was behaving like this. In his gentle voice he asked several times how it had happened.

I didn't tell him the truth, of course. I could hardly say, 'I fed pork to my boyfriend.' I'd be carted straight to the shrink. So I just said it was a quarrel, I was trying to give my boyfriend the push and he got wild. Hurt pride, all that.

But he went on and on. He said that my attitude worried him. Did I realize (clearing his throat, his Adam's apple sliding up and down) — did I realize that I would be scarred for life, down my cheek and probably on my forehead too? He went on like that.

Another person joined him, an ugly girl wearing glasses. She went on about how many cases she'd seen; all women, she said.

'Knocked about,' she said. 'Knocked up.' She gazed at me with a little, pitying smile. 'Victims of men.'

The doctor replied, 'Let's just call it victims of circumstance.'

I'll tell you how it happened. It sounds so stupid, now.

I was going to cook us seekh kebabs for dinner. They're like little minced patties, highly spiced. I went to the butcher, along the Earl's Court Road. The butcher was a big, belligerent man with a line in heavily suggestive remarks. I didn't like him — in fact I was nervous of him, he was built as powerfully as my Dad and he had an uncertain temper — but we always had these flirtatious conversations as he slapped the meat about, preparing to chop.

That day I asked for mince, but it turned out that he hadn't any left. He just had some sausage meat. He started going on about 'my sausages not big enough for you?' so I cut him short by asking for a pound of the stuff.

Outside, blushing, I hesitated with my package. I didn't want to go back in there and ask for something else. I stood there in the sunshine. Then I thought: what the hell; Ali won't know it's pork. And I started back to the flat.

So you see it wasn't planned. I can promise you that. But as I walked home I wasn't simply feeling *what the hell*. Not if I'm going to be truthful. It was more a tingling, uneasy, queasy feeling of anticipation. I'd felt it often before – a sort of shameful, sexual feeling.

Ali came home from work. I cooked them, using a lot of chilli powder. I cooked rice as well, and popadums. After we'd taken a few bites we started snuffling with tears.

'Delicious,' he said. In the candlelight he looked foolish and young. He blew his nose. 'Honestly, you could've been cooking this sort of food all your life.'

'I haven't.' I wiped my eyes. 'I've spent my life frying sausages.' I said that to settle my conscience; I wasn't going to say any more.

He paused, munching. 'Do you know, you put on this flat voice when you talk about your home. A flat, complaining voice.'

'I don't.'

'Your face closes up. You should see yourself.' He paused. 'I wish I could meet your parents.' He went on quickly, 'Are you ashamed of me – is that it?'

'Of course not.'

'Then why can't we go? I won't let you down . . . I'll be terribly polite.' He looked at me, his eyes damp. 'Is there something you're keeping from me?'

'Of course not. They're just – very ordinary.'

'You despise them for that? *I* won't, I promise you. There're worse things than being ordinary.'

'Terribly ordinary and boring. I had a terribly ordinary child-hood . . . You know, friends round to play, lots of toys.' I took a breath. 'Want to know? Really? I'll tell you . . . Lots of pets, kittens, dogs . . . rabbits, guinea pigs.' I remembered Gwen's. 'My guinea pig was called Tosca.'

'Tosca? How highbrow!'

229

I hated him for making these words come pouring out of me.

'My Mum made me a lovely party dress. Know what it was made of?'

'What?'

'Pink taffeta,' I said, my voice rising. 'Oh yes, and long white socks. And a ballet dress – yes, she made me that too! In fact, we made it together.' I was shouting now. 'In fact Dad helped too!'

Ali tried to interrupt me, but I went on recklessly. 'And he used to drive me to ballet classes – he did! He took me. I went to them, and I'd meet all my friends there.'

'Darling – '

I stopped him. 'I had another little bed in my room, there was always somebody staying the night with us.' I blurted it out, my voice high and cracked. 'They did! And you know what?'

'What?'

'They put Smarties on our pillows, just for us! Little tubes of Smarties!' I tried to catch my breath, and hurried on. 'I had lovely birthday parties, you should've seen them! Oh, I was famous for that . . . Games in the lounge . . .' My voice shrieked it out. 'Jellies! Jellies and trifles! Then there'd be a knock at the door and it was my Dad, dressed up as Father Christmas – '

'On your *birthday*?'

I sat slumped in my chair. 'Oh, I don't know. What does it matter?'

'Stop it, Heather! Don't cry!'

'I'm not. It's these blasted chillies.'

'Heather . . . ' He leaned across the table.

'Shut up!'

'Here, have my handkerchief.'

Shuddering, I grabbed it and blew my nose.

'Please – stop crying,' he said.

'I told you, I'm not!' My voice was ugly and shrill. I hated him seeing me crying, I couldn't bear it. Why did he have to be here?

I looked at him across the table, his eyebrows raised, his hand out, ready to touch me.

'Don't touch me!'

230

'Darling . . . '

I longed for him to disappear, to snap into the empty air. I hated him looking at me.

'Heather . . . '

He'd made me say all that. Wasn't that hateful of him? He'd forced it out . . . all my words, pouring out.

'Darling . . . '

Suddenly I felt terribly tired – never, in my life, had I felt so exhausted. I felt as if I'd been vomiting for hours, and there was nothing left.

I looked at him. I felt entirely empty . . . Nothing left at all. After a moment I said flatly,

'Know what you've just eaten?'

'Pardon?'

'Know what those stupid kebab things are made of?'

'What?'

I paused. 'Pig meat. Pork.'

There was a long silence. I heard the drip of our bathroom tap. At last he whispered,

'What did you just say?'

'I told you. Pork.'

His mouth dropped open. Then the table banged against me as he got to his feet. He stood there a moment. Either he was swaying or I was dizzy. I focused on his shirt.

'Why?' His voice sounded weirdly conversational.

'Why not? It's all the same, really.'

He stayed standing. He said lightly, 'You went out and bought it?'

'Didn't have anything else in the shop.'

He moved to the side, around the table. I shut my eyes.

'Ouch!'

He grabbed my hair.

'*Why?*' His voice soared up like a soprano.

'Let go!'

'How could you?' his voice shrieked. 'How *could* you?'

'Does it matter?'

'Have you . . .' he paused. 'Done it before?'

I tried to shake my head, but my hair was pulled tight.

'Liar!'

'I haven't – '

'Liar! Little bitch!'

'I *haven't* – '

'Oh yes, and what about those men? You lied about them – '

'I didn't!' I was sweating.

He pulled me to my feet, dragging me upwards.

'Look at me!' he screeched. He jerked my head back. His skin had grown darker.

I was frightened now. I wished I hadn't spoken. His fingers dug into my arms.

'Stop it!' I shouted.

He shook me, like a dog 'How many has it been – since you met me?'

'None!'

'Liar!'

'Hardly any – you're hurting!'

'Come on – who's – got his end about?' He corrected himself. 'Got his end away?' He was crying now.

'That's a crude way of putting it.'

'Crude? Call *me* crude? Come on, Heather –' His grip tightened. 'Start counting.' His voice choked with his sobs.

'Oh, I don't know . . . one or two.'

'I want the numbers.'

'Give me a moment . . .'

'Got to tot them all up?'

If I yelled, perhaps someone would hear. But in that house, nobody would come. I'd better tell him, quietly . . . First I had to work it out. Scenes grinded and clanked around my brain.

'Come on!'

'Six – no, seven – '

It was then that he started hitting me.

Chapter Twenty

I feel exhausted, telling you that . . . Clammy . . . I'll just wait until my heart stops thudding . . .

Now I've told you, I won't tell anyone else. I shouldn't think Ali will, either. I expect he's gone back to Pakistan – after all, it was over a week ago and he hasn't turned up here, thank goodness.

I hope he's gone back. I hope he's all right. Believe me. I don't want any harm to come to him, now . . . After all, he was only trying to love me – the only person who's ever tried.

I just didn't seem to be able to love him back. Poor Ali . . . he didn't deserve any of it. But it was inevitable . . . Can you see that? Do you understand?

Poor, innocent Ali . . . the only person I've ever been able to hurt.

I'm not staying around here. When the stitches are removed I won't need the doctors any more. I've phoned Am-Air and told them I'm ill, but soon they'll want to know more. When I was talking about the butcher just now, I suddenly remembered: this morning I should be flying to Berlin.

I won't be flying again, that's for sure. You can see why they won't have me back. The passengers wouldn't find my face very reassuring.

I don't feel as sad about my job as I'd expected. It had never been the same as my dreams of it. In fact, in the future I'll probably remember my daydreams more vividly.

None of us will be staying, because the land's going to be sold. Dad's getting some big offers. Soon we'll be moving out, and I can tell myself that my childhood is over, at last. I tell myself that I'll be rid of it, when they move to their new house. They're looking at places in the Staines and Maidenhead area. They actually drive off side by side in the van; it looks companionable but they're already quarrelling about what they want . . . They've never agreed about what they're looking for, in life, and they won't change.

They haven't got on together, all these years, and a new house won't alter that; but I expect Mum will get her way, as usual. No pigs, for a start. When Teddy heard they were selling up he said he'd run away with the gypsies, but then Dad said he was thinking of starting up a garage business so Teddy changed his mind and said he'd stay. Dad says he's going into business with Archie from the pub, but Archie's a crook so we'll see what happens to Dad's investment. I've warned him, but you know he never listens.

'Only natural you'd be suspicious,' he said.

'Why?'

'After what you've been through. Only natural you don't trust 'em.'

'Trust who?'

'Folk . . . You know. I can see you've had a bit of a setback there.' He wagged his finger. 'But you'll see, Heth, I'm promising you.'

'See what?'

'In time, Heth, you'll see that there's some people to be trusted. Like our Archie, for instance.' He nodded, with his wise look. 'Archie's a good bloke . . . straight as me.' He paused. 'Straight as your own Dad.'

234

You've been with me so long that I ought to tell you how I feel about my face. But I've managed to put that off. So far I've kept myself swaddled and timeless, like an invalid. I'm still wearing my nightie; I haven't been out into the real world, and it's then that I'll be tested. I've got a lot of plans; yesterday my plan was to move back into London and work for a travel agent. It's all by phone so nobody need see my face.

Not that I'll look so bad – not disgusting, just scarred, as if I've had a calamity in my past. What did that doctor call me, when he gazed at me sorrowfully? A victim of circumstance.

When I repeat that, I have a prickling feeling, like blood seeping into a numbed limb. *Victim of circumstance . . .* I like that. It makes me feel better.

They haven't put a board by the road saying 'Prime Industrial Site' – nothing like that, because Dad's still not quite made up his mind. You know what he's like – hopeless at decisions. Only yesterday he thought he'd stay put after all. It's that twenty years' worth of junk out there. It looks impossible to move but then he says he'll be buggered if he's seeing it bulldozed into the earth.

'Break my heart,' he said. 'All that work.'

Mum said sharply, 'What work you talking about?'

I joined her. Whenever he's wavered I've had another go at persuading him. This place must be demolished; it's high time. I stop myself being sentimental; I've not been thinking of it as 'home', but 'development land'.

I bet you think he won't do it. That we'll stay stuck here, complaining as usual, unable to make the final break. You think I'll stay here in a resentful torpor, like my Mum's been living all these years . . . That they're hopeless sort of people and they'll always be, and that I'm as hopeless as them.

There's one way to find out. Next time you drive past the airport – past the Heathrow Hotel and the Sheraton – drive straight on until you reach the Mobil Self-Serve. I've described it often enough; you must be able to recognize it now.

Slow down and have a good look. See if there's a bungalow beyond it, set back from the road: a wooden bungalow with a pile of planks and plastic in front.

You just see if there is.